There Are Places

There Are Places

G. D. SPILSBURY

ERGAMOT

Bergamot Books
www.bergamotbooks.com
Please contact Bergamot Books for permission to copy or use material from the book.

Designed by Jeremy Eberts

Cover photograph by David Eberts

Frontispiece: Cape Cod, 1961

Phoenix image on page vi: Drawing by D. H. Lawrence for his privately printed 1928 edition of *Lady Chatterley's Lover*.

Quotation on page vii: Lao-tzu, *Tao Te Ching*, trans. Stephen Mitchell (NY: HarperCollins, 1991). For this book, the word "person" was substituted for the word "man."

ISBN 978-1-7354275-8-4

PRINTED IN THE UNITED STATES

To my teachers
and to theirs
through the ages

What is a good person but a bad person's teacher?
What is a bad person but a good person's job?
If you don't understand this, you will get lost,
however intelligent you are.
It is the great secret.

—Lao-tzu

Visits

I T WAS A CRISP APRIL MORNING in the Schuylkill Valley, the landscape marked by the long ridges of the Appalachian highlands, still a soft brown with winter's trees. Ellie Miller stood in her father's childhood bedroom in her grandparents' house where the front windows faced this peaceful view. The back windows, in contrast, came up against the town's tallest mountain, its steep incline fragrant with untouched woods. So much silence filled the room, for the stucco cottage perched on a terraced wedge above Egelman Road, whose macadam swath had also been carved from the mountainside. The Millers' house had been built in the early 1900s by previous owners. Fruit trees and tangled remnants of a kitchen garden grew in a patch of yard on one side of the house. On the other side was the kitchen door with sixty brick steps to the street and a grassy slope that stopped abruptly at the garage's rooftop—the garage itself a dugout in the hillside. Honeysuckle covered its roof, sending out an intoxicating fragrance as one passed by on the steps. Low boxwood bordered the pathway, exuding a strange pungency that Ellie never forgot and recognized ever after.

It was seven o'clock on Saturday morning. Ellie opened one of the windows that overlooked the front lawn that descended to a narrow plateau and goldfish pond, supported by a stone retaining wall from the street. Daffodils' spiky leaves shot up around the pond's rim, their tight yellow heads not yet open. Birds chirped merrily, for winter was over, despite early spring's capricious weather that included occasional snow, so wet it melted instantly, refreshing the earth and air. Ellie listened for a moment to the birds' spirited activity, their delight in being able to hop freely from tree to tree—winter's hunkering down in frozen bushes finally over. Their exuberance touched her heart, bringing a smile to her lips, despite the sadness and preoccupation of her grandfather Earl's impending death. He lay downstairs on a hospital bed in the dining room facing the sylvan mountain view from the picture window, but it was his last view, his last hours or days to see it, to see life, his life in the only town that had been his home.

For weeks now, the dining room had been a makeshift hospice where Ellie's red-headed grandmother, Lillian, also slept on a rollaway bed. The pastoral valley with its border of mountains had been desecrated in the 1960s with tract housing filling the flat basin. Luckily, it was possible to keep one's gaze above that ugly intrusion and see only Pennsylvania's serene beauty that never failed to transport the spirit to a higher realm.

Ellie quickly washed up and went downstairs. In the front hall, through the dining room's dark wood archway, she could see that her grandparents were still asleep. She tiptoed to the kitchen, with its old-fashioned wallpaper, linoleum floor, and permanent smell of toast and coffee. Everything was exactly the same as in her childhood when she came for summer vacations with her parents and older sister, Laurie. Many of Ellie's first memories and sensations lived in these walls and on the steep hillside outdoors—like sitting in a washtub on the grass, Laurie in a tub beside her, the two of them blowing bubbles from plastic pipes, Ellie less successful than her more capable sister. Each effort got closer to producing one of Laurie's big iridescent globes that soon popped, sending them into belly laughter. The men—Grandpa and their father, Dave—stood watching, faces intent on the little tots chortling in innocent fun and discovery. Two fathers who loved children. On each visit, Ellie and Laurie made a ritual roll down the front hill, their arms tight around each other to travel as one. Screaming with the thrill of danger, they flung themselves apart just before touching the fish pond's edge—Grandpa guarding them with a worried brow, at the ready to pull them from the water if they miscalculated. Best of all, as Ellie grew and gained more independence, she loved exploring her grandparents' home office—a narrow, dank room off the kitchen with metal file cabinets and desk drawers filled with curiosities. It was the world of business, of clients and records, of pens, pencils, receipt books, and a typewriter. Only now, at age twenty-three, did she realize that in that dark room—for it backed up against the mountain—she had come upon her destiny: the world of print. She liked desks, working at desks, she liked offices that produced printed results. Before she could write paragraphs, she made stapled books of drawings that told the stories in her mind. When she was twelve, her father gave her his Underwood typewriter when he bought an IBM Selectric. She put it to immediate use, loving the clack-clack of the keys as they produced professional-looking letters and words. She loved the sound of the carriage return's authorial conviction. After college, she got a low-paying job on a neighborhood rag, doing whatever the mom-and-pop owners needed—errands, calls, deliveries, research, but it didn't pay the bills and she had to waitress at night.

Ellie put the coffee on and a few minutes later, Lillian came into the kitchen through the dining room's swinging door. Her curly red hair and round, plump face looked sleepy. She wore a faded floral robe that zipped up the front of her short, soft body.

"Good morning, dear," she whispered lovingly, reaching up to give Ellie a kiss. "Did you sleep all right?"

Ellie nodded with a smile. She was familiar with Lillian's first hour of the day—when she padded around in a state of peaceful half-consciousness, her personality free from its childish traits that would surface later: resentment, grudges, and suspicion. Ellie had first sampled her narrower side around age four, when she played with Lillian's costume jewelry. The jewelry was another tradition the sisters had when they visited. Piles of it lay on Lillian's bureau top like an open treasure chest. Gleefully the girls decked themselves out with strands of necklaces, tinkling bracelets, and clip-on earrings, but always under Lillian's tense surveillance, for she didn't like sharing her possessions. On this occasion, Laurie was downstairs playing checkers with their grandfather in the cozy kitchen booth with its green vinyl seats and formica table. Ellie was suddenly on her own without her big sister directing their play. Her mother and grandmother stood by as her unschooled hands grabbed up necklaces.

"Put them down!" her mother said harshly.

Shame and fear instantly burned Ellie's cheeks—shame for being scolded in front of her grandmother and fear at the warning tone in her mother's voice. In reflex, she giggled with high-pitched silliness and grabbed a fake pearl necklace. She dangled it at the them as if to say, "Look at this one, let's play with this one!" It was her child's way of attempting to distract them from her misdemeanor and to win back her good-girl status.

But her mother grabbed her by the arm, and twisting it up lifted her away and banged her down roughly on the wooden chair by the door. Waves of panic cut off Ellie's breath— what would her mother do next? What worse punishment lay in store for her? Her hand still held the fake pearls, but unknowingly, for fear possessed every particle of her.

But her mother left the room abruptly. Instantly, Ellie's grandmother filled her place, her face bending close to Ellie's to give her the meanest look, while her hand snatched away the pearls. She stalked out of the room on her short legs, blowing out a huff of disgust.

Ellie had sat on the chair for quite a while, waiting to be excused. But her mother never returned, and eventually she got up and tiptoed back to the world of the living, not sure she was allowed to liberate herself and fearful she might be punished for it. She wanted nothing more than to find Laurie, hide behind her taller figure, feel her sisterly protection. Laurie, two years older, was her partner in self-preservation from their mother's unpredictable rages.

"How's Grandpa?" Ellie asked, returning her mind to the present and smiling at her grandmother. She generally accepted her grandmother's mercurial moods and behaviors and steered away from triggering them. Overall, she knew Lillian had a good heart, however mistrustful, miserly, and on occasion downright mean. Her dark sides were much the same as everyone else's.

"All right, things being what they are—he's sleeping now. He has so much phlegm and no more strength to cough it up."

"I heard him. I feel so bad for him."

"But he doesn't have pain, darling. When he cries out like that, it's not because of pain, it's his liver—his liver isn't right."

He had howled periodically throughout the night, a wounded animal in the wild left to die. And he was dying. Whenever Ellie stood next to his bed and met his large brown eyes, so alive in his gaunt face, her mind struggled to grasp that instead of being bedridden to get better, he was bedridden to die. And he knew it—he knew with those trapped brown eyes that he was waiting for life to shut down his consciousness.

"Did you find the coffee, dear?" Lillian asked absent-mindedly, moving around the room, opening drawers and shuffling their contents, then opening the basement door and bending over a tall tin can on the steps that housed pretzels and other happy-hour snacks. But she wasn't looking for anything in particular. She was just shuffling about while her internal motor warmed up for the day.

"Yes, it's just starting to percolate."

"Good."

Lillian pushed through the swinging door to the dining room, leaving it open. Ellie could hear her straightening up the table's surface, now littered with pills, lubricants, and other hospice-care items. Her job was nursing these days and she was good at it, having grown up in an era lacking modern medicines. She knew how to use herbs for common illnesses and pain. She had nursed her mother through death and was now ready to do the same for her husband. Ellie stole a glance into the dining room. Lillian was bent over the bed, stroking Earl's forehead and cooing soothing words in her high, musical voice. "I love you, darling, I'm right here, and I won't leave you, no sirree, you have my word!"

She returned to the kitchen. "He's resting comfortably. This could go on for weeks, you know." Her tongue clucked at the prospect.

"How?" Ellie whispered. "He's emaciated. He looks like he's been in a concentration camp." Tears came to her eyes—Grandpa living in that horrible dying state and conscious of it.

"Yes, dear, but look how he's lasted—this has been going on since November."

"But he wasn't this thin—even a few weeks ago he looked different. He's just a shell now." He was all bones with loose skin hanging from his arms and shoulders—the part of him that showed above his covers.

Lillian poured coffee into two cups and added a splash of milk to her own. "When your father was here in January, we looked for a home. The hospital said there was nothing more they could do for him. But in the end, I couldn't put him in a home. He needs to be here, with me, here in his own home."

"I'm so glad, Grandma. And so is he. Thank you."

"But your daddy, after all that work he had done! And the place he found—it was *bee-u-tiful*!" she said in her singing way. "They wanted fifteen hundred a week—can you believe it?—fifteen hundred!" Her bushy, red-and-gray eyebrows rose incredulously. "How's that possible? Why, it's highway robbery!"

"Thank God he's here, in his own home, with you."

"Yes, but if you only knew how hard your father worked to find that place."

They sat down at the booth in the cozy nook between the kitchen and the office. "Nope—I wasn't going to let that man die alone," Lillian said. "We've been together sixty years, and I'm strong, I can take this." She flexed her bicep under the robe, then dropped her arm and gave Ellie an angelic smile, eyes winking humorously. "But oh Lord, was that place your daddy found something to see!"

Ellie nodded, smiling, but her thoughts were still on her grandfather. She couldn't reconcile his death. He had meant so much to her in childhood, teaching her to roller skate and ride a bike in their spacious driveway in Philadelphia. And here at his house on the mountain, they had played checkers, chess, and gin rummy in the booth. She had listened with fascination to his bad English whenever he tossed down a card he didn't like: "That don't do me no good." She liked imitating his gruff speech when she rejected her own cards, and using his "ain't" back at him—it made them pals. He had been born out of wedlock but given his father's name on his birth certificate—Miller. His mother, Lizzie Kreitz, never married. Lillian said it was because of her lame foot, a birth defect that spurned suitors. Earl had gone to work as a boy, delivering newspapers, and after sixth grade, apprenticed with a printer. This led to becoming a journeyman and eventually a master craftsman owning his own printshop downtown. With no more than four or five employees at a given time, he produced invitations, flyers, programs, bulletins, yearbooks, and badges with ribbons that Lillian sewed on. Berks Printing Co. handled any sort of job work and prospered enough to survive the Depression and accumulate savings. Lillian was Earl's partner, endowed with her German ancestors' acumen for moneymaking. She also ran a side business, selling fine china, silver sets, and cookware to couples who published their engagements in the local newspaper. She called them and promoted her wares. She also made sure these customers went on to buy their wedding invitations from Berks Printing. Earl and Lillian had expected Ellie's father to join the company after college—a local college of course. But as Dave's high school years neared their finish, he announced he intended to become a doctor. They urged him to pursue pharmacy instead—they would help him open a drugstore downtown with a soda fountain. Bewildered, they watched their only beloved son apply to famous East Coast schools and leave them forever for that sophisticated world beyond their comprehension. Fortunately, after his many years of education and training, he settled the family in Philadelphia, close enough to visit. "But oh, what a home he bought!" Lillian often trilled when the subject came up. "And my God, did you ever see so many homes like it?—one after the other like a grand parade."

The impressive mansions, built nearly a century before by wealthy Philadelphians, were beyond the elder Millers' class and taste. Nevertheless, they came every Christmas and sat stiffly on the elegant sofas, feeling out of place and disconnected from the growing grandchildren who now spent all their time with their private school friends. The days of checkers and gin rummy were over.

"When your father was here last weekend and saw his dad, he broke down," Lillian said to Ellie as they drank coffee in the nook. "I never saw him so shook up—he cried, your daddy cried. It was something."

Ellie nodded—her father crying was hard to believe. He had been brought up traditionally—"men don't cry." But the 1970s were allowing him openings to the new freedoms and behaviors granted to men, like hugging his father at the start and finish of their vacations. Before that, a strong handshake had been the manly way of expressing love and loyalty. Even Grandpa was open to the new mode of hugging his son, however stiffly and quickly. And Dr. Miller, still handsome in a dashing way, wanted to be part of the new trends, the incrowd. He grew his dark hair and silver-sprinkled sideburns like the TV celebrities and bought casual clothes for social occasions that in the past had required a jacket and tie. He wore a navy-blue turtleneck for winter ski parties and a pink, short-sleeved shirt for summer barbecues. Of course, his teenage daughters egged him on, wanting hip parents, parents who accepted sexual freedom and women's lib. By this time, the Millers had also produced their longed-for son—Dave Jr. His arrival had transformed their unfulfilled family life to lively times that revolved around the adorable baby. Little Dave—nicknamed "Jay" for junior—grew up with a happy, carefree personality nurtured unconditionally by his elders.

"He rushed out of the room," Lillian continued, glad to air the thoughts that had been bottled up in her all week. "We heard this terrible noise, and Earl cried out, 'Is that my Davy? Is that my Davy crying?'" I ran after him—he was right here, all crushed up in that corner." She pointed to Ellie's corner of the booth. "He was sobbing like I've never seen. His whole body shook. I tell you, it was something."

Ellie tried to imagine the scene of her father all balled up and crying in the nook—the man who never winced, the man who never shirked an unpleasant duty, the man who handled any crisis that arose in their family, such as Ellie's expulsion from her girls' school when she was caught smoking. He had gone in and talked to the headmaster. He had come back out with the verdict: she could return to school. Everyone looked up to him because he was a doctor. It had happened more than once that in a public place an urgent voice called out, "Is there a doctor in the house?" Dave was the one to get up and attend to the victim until an ambulance arrived. Jean was proud to be his wife, appended to him, though her face generally was less open to showing affection and love. Ellie wondered if her cold, Presbyterian upbringing had shaped this trait in her. She did liven up for parties—her chance to dress up and be admired. She loved drinking gin and tonic and laughing with others, her gaiety charming and contagious. Her beauty, too, always shone above anyone else's in the room. She was the belle of any occasion and derived fulfillment from that role.

"I said, 'Don't cry, son, don't do this to yourself.' But oh, if only you could have seen him, Ellie, how bad he hurt. I thought I'd die." Lillian pressed her hand to her heart, eyes lifting to the ceiling. "No sirree, I'll never forget him saying, 'That's my father, that's my father!'"

With a sigh, Lillian wriggled her roundness out of the booth and shuffled back to the kitchen. "A little more coffee, dear? And how about some apie cake? Or shoofly pie? I know you like shoofly pie. Remember to take some home with you." She opened the fridge. "And lookee here, I have scrapple—Habbersett's—the real McCoy."

Ellie followed her. "No thanks, Grandma, I'll make some toast. What about you?"

"Nothing for me. I might have a piece of cake later. The toaster's on the table." She pointed toward the nook.

Ellie opened the bread bin near the open dining room door. She imagined her grandfather was lying awake in there, listening to them. It felt surreal that a wall separated the realm of the living from the realm of the dying, as if her grandfather had been set aside from life, no longer part of it.

"Our pastor's been so good to us," Lillian said, refilling

their coffee cups. "He came to the hospital every day and checked on Earl. I swear, that man has God in him—never misses a day visiting the sick. And let me tell you, he has a special feeling for your grandpa. Why, just the other day, when he came up all those steps just to see Earl, I saw tears in his eyes. He told me this death is real hard for him."

"He's not dead yet, and he can hear us," Ellie said quietly.

Lillian didn't answer. She turned away and padded around the room eyeing objects that might need straightening. "Yes, indeed, there isn't anyone who doesn't love Earl."

Ellie heard the resentment in her voice—his popularity being greater than hers—the usual lot of women who worked hard, who often made and upheld the foundation of a striving household.

"Sixty years we've been together, sixty, I tell you."

"It's a long time."

"You'd better believe it, kiddo." A sudden belly laugh rippled through her, and her eyes twinkled up at Ellie from behind her glasses. "And don't you go thinking it was always a bed of roses—it took a lot for us to stick together." She turned and swayed in her robe back to the nook. "Let's sit again, dearie, I'm just waking up. And it's so nice to have you here, someone to talk to."

They resettled themselves, and Ellie put her bread in the toaster. Lillian continued her morning musings. "I'm going to be honest—that's the way we are in this family—am I right?"

"Yes. We can talk."

She nodded. "It's like this, Ellie, if I could do it all over again, I wouldn't have gotten married—or not so young. I was only eighteen, and if I had waited, who knows who I might've married. But I married Earl."

Ellie smiled patiently. She had heard this story since childhood—how her beautiful grandmother from a small business family of several generations had been too good for the humbler roots of her grandfather, especially given his illegitimacy. In those days, fatherless children were stigmatized for their parents' sin.

"But oh, how he loved me!" her musical voice sang with eyes rising to the ceiling. "And mind you, I wouldn't have anything to do with him. And Earl was no plain Joe—he was something to look at! He had eyes to melt your heart. But, I said no, I refused him."

Ellie smiled teasingly at her grandmother and continued the next part of the story, for she knew it well. "But then one day, at a big picnic, he climbed a cherry tree to impress you."

Lillian let out a hearty laugh. "Don't you know it! That boy thought he could woo me with cherries, but he went out too far on the branch and it broke. I'll never forget the sound of it cracking. He landed flat on the ground and lay there like he was dead. I ran over to him and took his head in my lap. Finally, he opened those beautiful eyes of his and I felt my heart lurch. That's how it all began." She laughed. "I can't believe it's been sixty years now." She dabbed the corners of her eyes under her glasses—tears that were bittersweet. "But I tell you, honey, if I could do it all over again, I'd be free like you. Don't go and get married till you have what you want. Life's too short. I wanted a career but got married instead."

"But you had a career—you've been a successful businesswoman."

"That's true, but I wanted to be an actress!" Her shrewd blue eyes shot sparks at Ellie. "Mind you, I had talent—I could sing and dance, I played the piano. I wanted to be on the stage, but my father wouldn't hear of it. He was so strict with me."

"Why couldn't you be an actress?"

"It wasn't ladylike. They were considered loose women—you know, easy for men. Papa made me work in the family business. How I hated it—we made machine parts for the local companies. I had to sit in that horrible old warehouse and do the books, day after day, only free on Sundays. And let me tell you, Ellie, that was no place for a girl. There were only men there—greasy, dirty men. They liked to pester me. They touched me, pinched me. They made rude passes—such things were allowed back then. I thought I'd die." Her round cheeks shuddered with the memory. Ellie could relate. Only recently had such gross behaviors been made taboo.

"Well, maybe in the end business inspired you—I mean with Grandpa, the two of you building your own business."

She chortled. "Damn right about that. Your grandpa and me—we worked—every day, before the sun came up and into the night. We started at the bottom and did everything ourselves—we planned, talked things over, took one step at a time, and saved. We counted every penny."

Ellie smiled. She could imagine her grandmother counting every penny. She had seen several old-fashioned change purses bulging with pennies in the top desk drawer of the musty office.

"We wanted children, but I didn't get pregnant. It was ten years before your daddy came along, and we had already resigned ourselves to being childless. We weren't happy about it, un-uh, but I was willing to adopt. Your grandpa said no, he didn't want that, someone else's child. By the time Davy was born, we had already bought the plant and had enough savings to start investing. Later, we were able to help with his education and your first two homes. Don't forget, he was still in medical school when you and Laurie were born."

Ellie listened, understanding where her father's business sense came from—his hardworking, thrifty, American-dream parents. As soon as he had a hospital salary coming in, he, too, had begun to invest, mainly in real estate like his parents, but also in stocks, something Lillian and Earl wouldn't touch, having lived through the crash and Depression. They preferred certificates of deposit and government bonds. Lillian had shown Ellie a stack of envelopes waiting for their twenty-year maturity date. Lillian also cashed Earl's Social Security checks and hid the wads of bills in a paper bag behind the dining room's tall cupboard—emergency funds, she said. Thousands of dollars lay hidden there. And Lillian still sold china and silver sets to young couples. She also owned and managed summer rentals on the Jersey Shore. Work, money, saving fueled her life.

After their second cup of coffee, Ellie went into the dining room and leaned against the side rail of her grandfather's bed. Whenever he rested peacefully, she thought he might be dead. She stared down at his gaunt face, his mouth sunken without its dentures, his sharp nose distinguished. Even now—with only the rattly bones of what had once been a proud, virile man—he was handsome, strong featured, his face carved precisely with an artist's chisel. Tears rolled down her cheeks and into the crack of her lips. Earl's eyes opened and they stared at each other. She memorized his brown eyes that still shone with life—scared life—and she wondered if he was also memorizing her, before his unknown journey beyond the earthly conscious state that would physically separate them forever. What was that like, she wanted to know, to be him and aware of taking these last looks? She picked up his gnarled hand—the hand she had often studied for its capabilities despite its similarity to an ancient tree. She felt his old familiar grip—strength was still there in that wasted body that could no longer move. But the hand could still squeeze with intention. With her other hand, she smoothed back his silken white hair, rubbed his fleshless shoulders above the covers, and tried to smile. "I love you, Grandpa," she said, "you're my sweetheart." His face remained immobile but the gentle brown eyes with their shining pupils acknowledged her words. She wondered if she reminded him of her father, if her youth and the bounce to her step took him back in time, when his son would return from college, filling the house with his vibrancy—the house so silent and empty without him. The morning before, she had showered and combed her dark hair back from her face into a ponytail. Wearing pants and a flannel shirt, she had walked into the dining room with a bright smile for her grandfather. His eyes had popped in alarm, almost in fear—was it the fear of seeing a ghost? He thought I was Dave, young Dave, Ellie had thought. When he saw she wasn't Dave, his head had rolled listlessly on his pillow. What he wanted now, in his last living moments, was his son.

As Lillian moved through the kitchen and dining room, opening drawers and cabinets without an objective, Ellie went into the living room, its wood archway facing the dining room's identical one, with the front hall and stairs between. She looked around, breathing in the old empire-style furniture with faded brocade upholstery. Around the stone fireplace hung long-forgotten Christmas tree lights. They blinked when plugged in but had lost their luster to years of caked dust. The forgotten condition of the room gave it a hazy gloom, as if time had stopped there decades before.

At the far end of the room, next to her grandmother's piano, Ellie opened the closet whose shelves were chock-full of Miller memorabilia: photographs, letter packets, broken instruments, yearbooks, baby books, newspaper clippings lauding Dave's high school achievements, election badges her grandfather had printed, crochet needles and yarn, and a tiny, black leather boot with miniature buttons that had belonged to her father. For a while, Ellie sat on the couch and looked at the old photographs—her grandmother at eighteen when she was slim and comely in a soft period dress before the 1920s. A newer one showed Ellie's parents in their famous glamour, seated at a homecoming ball in the late 1940s. Her dad wore a black tuxedo that matched his black hair. He laughed confidently into the camera, his arm around his fiancée's bare shoulders. She wore a strapless satin gown that highlighted her smooth curves. She smiled, with less self-assurance than he, yet pleased to be forever captured as a good-looking couple at a fancy event. Last, Ellie looked at a photo of her grandfather in his fifties, posing outdoors in a fine suit, his posture upright and proud. His lack of an education didn't matter in his community. He was an exemplary citizen in every way.

Ellie went back to the kitchen and immediately saw a frosty brown beer bottle on the counter, her grandmother apparently not shy about starting so early. In the past, she often made a point of declaring that she never touched a drop before five o'clock, but maybe she did, or maybe the stress of Earl's decline had made her start earlier. The German Americans—the Pennsylvania Dutch—loved to make merry—it was part of their culture. Ellie's father had grown up in the community's century-old way of enjoying themselves at big meals on Sundays after church. They met at their community center high on the mountain and spent the long afternoon eating, drinking, laughing, flirting, and dancing. The children frolicked outside and came in rosy-cheeked when the mid-afternoon dinner bell rang. Everyone sat at long, communal tables and spoke their forefathers' dialect. When the band played, the kids danced too, with their friends, parents, and relatives, swinging their arms and legs to the music, their faces lit. This warm, cohesive tradition had died out after the Second World War, around the time Dave set off to make his own life, beginning with college in New England—a foreign region to his parents, whose farthest frontier was New York City. But Dave continued the merry-making of his heritage, so Ellie grew up never questioning drinking and laughing together as a positive part of life—or once the work day was done at five o'clock. At least Lillian was drinking the local brew's half-size bottles.

"Ellie, come help me with your grandfather," Lillian's chirpy voice called from the dining room. Ellie joined her at Earl's bedside. His eyes looked scared.

"He's all washed and fresh now," Lillian said. "I bathe him every day and then rub him down with nice cream. I shave and comb him, don't I, Earlie? I make you look real pretty." She bent over his face and kissed it several times in a circle. "I love you, darling, what will I ever do when you're gone?" Her croon wasn't entirely authentic, and Ellie braced herself for one of her grandmother's ploys. She didn't have to wait long.

"Isn't it wonderful to have Ellie here? She's going to help me take care of you."

With that, Lillian whipped the covers off Earl, exposing his naked, wretched body and limp penis. Ellie froze in horror at her grandmother's insensitivity and her grandfather's mortified face, his eyes instantly meeting hers. Her grandmother's mean streak had purposely taken advantage of his helplessness to violate his modesty, his personal rights to his body, his self-respect. She had acted heartlessly. Ellie didn't know how to extract herself from the situation and stood there in a state of unbreathing guilt and pain for her grandfather, and dislike for her grandmother's antics.

"Here, Ellie, take this cream and rub it into his back and

shoulders," Lillian said cheerfully, as she pushed Earl to his side revealing the bones of his buttocks.

Ellie took faltering steps to the bed while her grandmother cooed over the shriveled body on the sheet. "Ellie's going to make you all soft and smooth, my darling," she singsonged. "Do his back, honey. No one's ever going to say I didn't take wonderful care of this man. Why, just look at his skin—not a blemish on it! Even the nurses at the hospital couldn't get over it. 'This man has been kept,' they said. 'Yes, indeed, this man has been cared for.' Go on, Ellie, do his back." She pushed Ellie's arm and then stepped away. Ellie squirted a patch of cream into her palm and spread it across the sharp, protruding shoulders of her grandfather's back. The skin was indeed soft. His body was the size of a starved boy's, shivering in the nightmare of this ordeal Lillian had imposed on him. Ellie hoped her loving hands conveyed her oneness with him—the two of them separate from her. Meanwhile, Lillian moved to the kitchen door, reached inside for her beer on the counter, and took a satisfying draft. She put the bottle back and returned to the business of nursing, wiping her mouth with her hand.

"Ellie's making you look real pretty, sweetheart. She'll always have this moment to remember, helping Grandma take care of you. You'll always have this, Ellie—you'll be happy for it someday." She unceremoniously shoved Earl to his other side. "Not on your life could I put this man away," she crowed. "No home could care for him the way I do. In the hospital, they never bothered to turn him. He got terrible bedsores. I wouldn't let them touch him after that. I took three buses every day to get to the hospital, because that's how I am. No amount of trouble is going to stop me. And look at him now, look how beautiful he is." She leaned over the bed, beer on her breath, and spoke to the back of his head. "You're still beautiful, you hear me, Earlie, beautiful! And I love you, darling." She kissed his hair. Surely he despised her in that moment, Ellie thought.

Finally, the trauma of morning care ended. Lillian flapped a clean sheet over Earl's wasted body and left him on his side to stare out the picture window at the abiding mountain range under a blue sky. "I'll feed him in a little bit," she said, returning to her beer in the kitchen. "But it's hardly worth it—he doesn't eat. That's what's going to get him."

"He can hear you, Grandma."

She ignored the comment but used her foot to kick the swinging door closed. Then she cut a slice of apie cake and took a bite while standing at the counter with her beer. New memories came to her. "Marie was here on Thursday. Marie was your grandpa's secretary. He took her out of the orphanage and helped her through school. They were devoted to each other. He can't talk anymore, but when Marie came in and he saw her, he cried out, 'Marie!'—just like that, 'Marie!'" Lillian's blue eyes shot darts at Ellie. "Did you hear me? He loved her. I saw it—the way he looked at her." Her plump hand lifted the beer bottle for a sip. "But I'm not jealous. I'm not that type. I'm happy Earl and Marie were so close."

Ellie nodded, feeling glad her grandfather had had Marie in his life, however intimate or platonic, and she imagined the latter, knowing Earl's values. But this was the first time Grandma had ever mentioned her. She wondered if her father remembered Marie, and if he knew anything about this bond.

"Oh, yes, it was something when he cried out 'Marie!'" Lillian repeated. "I'll never forget it, as long as I live. Won't you have a beer, Ellie? It's made right here. This is the only place you can get the little bottles. They aren't distributed."

"No thanks, Grandma."

"I always have my beer, but I'm careful. And these times are hard on me."

Ellie understood her subtext—for now the five o'clock rule was suspended.

"I guess I'll go up and get dressed now," Lillian said, and her rotund figure moved off to mount the stairs in the front hall.

Ellie sat down on a dining room chair next to Earl's bed and tried to read the book she had brought, but her sight was glazed. How could she concentrate on anything but what was happening in this house full of memories and her dying grandfather two feet away? She felt as hollow and unreal as she imagined he felt.

Lillian soon returned. She hadn't taken long washing up and putting on clothes that should have gone to the laundry pile—a brown jersey with an old spill on the front and loose polyester pants whose hemline was inches above her ankles. Her old black shoes from the five-and-dime were worn on the sides, for she walked on the outsides of her feet, with slight bowleggedness.

"I can run errands for you, Grandma," Ellie offered, following her grandmother into the kitchen. "Do you need anything?"

Lillian opened the fridge for another beer and answered from behind the door, "Once all of this is over, I'm going to look better after myself. I don't have time now. Since the fall, I haven't been to the hairdresser. I haven't left the house since Earl came home. A boy from down below comes up for the garbage and Peggy Mullen brings me my groceries. I give her a few dollars for gas. What I put up with for your grandpa! But I know it's right, what I'm doing is right."

She popped off the beer cap with a bottle opener fastened to the counter's side. "Have one, darling, won't you have a beer with me?"

"It's too early for me, Grandma, I'll have one later."

"Beer was the drink in our house growing up—it was like water or soda for us. But mind you, I watch myself, and I never drink too much." She poured some of the beer into a small glass and shuffled toward the nook. "Let's sit again, I want to talk. I'm alone most of the time." She put down the glass and bottle and reached way up to hold Ellie's face between her palms. She pursed her lips for a kiss, and Ellie bent to receive it. "I'm so glad you're here, darling, it's such a comfort. We're family, we can talk."

Ellie felt glad to please her grandmother, even though she didn't know how she would make it through the day keeping her company. There was nothing in her own life—her dreams or troubles—she could share with her grandmother. And she didn't have a boyfriend to gossip about. Only family topics connected them, and Lillian repeated her pet subjects nonstop. With an inner sigh, Ellie dutifully slid into the booth.

"I tell you, if I could do it all over, I wouldn't have married Earl. It was instinct that made me do it. He was the kindest, sweetest boy I had ever met, and let's face it, that's saying a lot. But if I could live my life over again, I'd experiment like all you girls today. I only knew one man in my life, and I think people should know before they marry if they can live together. But I won't complain. Dad was good to me, we were good to each other, and we made it through. We never went to sleep on a fight. I want you to remember that, Ellie, if you ever marry, don't go to bed on a fight, always make up first. I only hope it's that way for your father. You don't know how I worry about his marriage to that woman!" Her lips twisted.

"His marriage is fine, Grandma, you needn't worry about it," Ellie said, though it was common knowledge that her grandmother had no love for "that woman," and the feeling was reciprocal.

"Really? Can I really believe you? I worry all the time. I tell your dad, 'Dave, you never laugh anymore. Why don't you laugh anymore?'" She gave Ellie a piercing look through her glasses. "You can tell me, we're family, we're close—does your mother ever give him a hug or a kiss? I never saw it." Her hand banged the table. "And look how he does everything for her! She's like a queen who thinks she deserves it! Does she ever do anything for him?"

"Of course she does—a lot!—and she loves him."

"Really? Can I believe you? I want to believe you, I want to believe there's love between them."

"I promise there is."

She shook her head. She lifted her glass and drained the sips left in it.

Lillian's words about Ellie's mother hung in the air. Ellie imagined her parents. It was partly true that her father took the initiative with her mother. When he came home from work, he opened the front door with his usual happy whistle that beckoned her. With slight reluctance, she would let herself be folded into his arms and accept his rocking, loving, sweet talk against her hair. Sometimes she would join him in his armchair to curl up in his lap, all cuddly. So she did reach out first on occasion.

Lillian poured more beer into her glass, always a few sips at a time. "We were so unhappy when your father called and told us he was getting married."

"But he was bringing you his good news."

She shook her head. "It wasn't the right time, and we told him so. We said, 'Davy, you still have medical school and all those years of training. What're you going to do if Jean gets pregnant?'"

"Which she did."

"He wouldn't listen. He knew what he wanted—her. And your other grandmother was against it too. We talked on the phone—we agreed they were too young, what with Davy having that long education in front of him. But in the end, we went along with the plan, because that's what they wanted."

She sniffed her beer as if it were brandy. "Help yourself to a beer, Ellie. Don't you like the kind I buy?"

Before Ellie could reply, a loud knocking on the kitchen door startled them. Lillian quickly hid her beer bottle and glass behind the toaster and worked her way out of the booth. "Now who could that be at this hour? It isn't even nine o'clock."

She let out a delighted cry when she saw who stood on the other side of the door's windowpane. A cluster of bells tinkled as she opened the door. "Well, lookee here, look who's come up all those steps to see us. Come in, Pastor. Ellie, come meet our pastor!"

Ellie smiled and shook hands with the pastor while Lillian bubbled on. "This is my granddaughter, Pastor, Davy's second daughter, Ellie. She's come all the way from Philly to help me with Dad. Oh, the work I have when I'm by myself! The two of us washed him down and rubbed him with cream. I'm going to feed him next, but he can hardly swallow. He had a terrible night with the phlegm. It's getting too hard to bring up."

"Well, it sure is nice of you to come and help your grand-mum," the pastor said. He presided over the stone-and-timber Lutheran church at the end of the street. He was in midlife, tall, a little bent, with nervous but friendly eyes. His tight brown curls threaded with silver coated his head evenly, and his permanent smile creased his thin face like a mask.

"This is *von*-derful that you're here, Pastor," Lillian sang out, using her Pennsylvania Dutch *V* on *W* words like *wonderful*. "It means so much to Earl. Can I give you some coffee?"

"Oh, no, nothing for me, but thank you, Lillian. I just wanted to stop by and see how Earl was doing."

She led him to the dining room. "Tell me, Pastor, did

you and Diane go out for dinner last night?" She shot Ellie a glance. "Friday's his night to take his wife to dinner."

"Indeed we did—we ate prime ribs at the Ben Franklin. By golly, were they good!"

"And what a bargain! Your father went there last week, Ellie. The pastor told him about it. The prime ribs are only five dollars—big, gorgeous pieces of meat!"

"I'm afraid it won't last, once everyone finds out about it," the pastor said. "But, of course, that's what we want—prosperity for our businesses." He leaned slightly over the hospital bed. "Morning, Earl, how're you doing today?"

Earl struggled to say something but only choking sounds emitted.

"Don't worry, Pastor, he's glad you're here."

The pastor put his hand on Earl's ragged shoulder. "And, I bet my bottom dollar just being home these few weeks has made you feel like a new man. You've got Lillian's home cooking and the best nursing care in the county."

"He's not eating, Pastor. It sets off his coughing. He can't catch his breath. Why, only three weeks ago, when Ellie was here, he could still get out of bed with the two of us helping. We could walk him to the table, and he could eat dinner sitting up. He wouldn't let me feed him, not in front of Ellie. He wanted her to see he was still a man and could do it himself. Oh, Lordy, I thought there was hope."

A few more exchanges took place around the bedside until their small talk ran out. Then, the pastor straightened his shoulders, indicating it was time to take his leave.

"Well, I'd better get myself over to the hospital now, but

it's sure been good to see you, Earl, and I'm glad to know these ladies are taking such good care of you. And your view—the best in town, I'd wager." He gave Earl's shoulder a farewell squeeze and then turned to Ellie with his friendly smile. "It's been a great pleasure to meet Lillian and Earl's granddaughter, and I know they appreciate your being here."

Ellie smiled back and shook hands politely. Her grandparents' way of life was so different from her family's in Philadelphia. Here the lifestyle was homey and old-fashioned, based on community friendship and values, a connecting tissue helped by the church, something missing in the younger Millers' sophisticated city life—nor did they seek it.

"Thank you for your visit, Pastor," Lillian said, accompanying him to the kitchen door. As soon as it closed, she went to the nook for her beer and sat down. Ellie joined her, resigning herself to more of Lillian's repetitive conversation.

"Our pastor's a good man, a real friend to us. Before Earl got sick, he and his wife would come over to play pinochle with us. We'd sit right here, have a beer together, play cards. What good times! And how he loves your grandpa—this death really hurts him."

She sipped her beer and wiped her mouth. Soft peach fuzz covered her upper lip like a faint mustache. Her habit of twitching her nose and upper lip like a rabbit called Ellie's attention to it.

"Don't you know," she went on, her mind drifting to her favorite topic—Dave, her son—"your daddy's a brilliant man. Am I right? Just look at all he's done, and still in his forties. I never saw anyone work the way he does. And it's going to kill him. I don't want to be here for that, oh no, I'd rather be dead."

"He's fine, Grandma, you don't have to worry about him."

"Oh yes I do!" she sang out. "Your grandpa and I worked hard too, but we knew when to stop. Your daddy never stops. He's on the go every minute. A person's heart can't take that. And maybe that's why he never laughs anymore. He has to worry all the time, keep up with all the paperwork he's made for himself. Your grandpa and me, we worked for a comfortable life. I never wanted more than that. But your dad, he's never satisfied. I tell him, 'Davy, stop buying, don't you have enough now? What do you want more for? Pay off the homes, pay off your debts, enjoy life while you still can.'"

"He does enjoy life, and he laughs. He loves to laugh, and we love hearing him laugh."

"No, I tell you, he's not the same. He's pushing himself. Is it your mother? Does she want more, always more?" She shook her head as if the verdict were already in.

Ellie blinked with relief when the phone rang. She didn't want to have to take sides in the war between her mother and Lillian. "It's probably Mae," she said, knowing Lillian's younger sister called every morning to ask how things were going with Earl.

Lillian scraped out of the booth to answer the phone fastened to the wall by the dining room door.

Mae lived across town with her husband, Leo, in affordable senior housing. Both of them were obese with multiple health problems, but always eager to see their only nephew, Dave, and any of his children when they visited. They had no children of their own, and the Millers were their closest relatives. Usually, Ellie drove over to their immaculate apartment for an hour's visit, which always made her grandmother resentful. Lillian disliked sharing her family with her younger sister—her lifelong rival. At one time, they had stopped speaking to each other for five years because Lillian had accused Leo of making a pass at her. Ultimately, Ellie's father had managed to negotiate a truce, but only for a relationship of restrained politeness on Lillian's part. Mae was more softhearted, gregarious, and flexible than Lillian.

Lillian came back to the nook. "You were right—it was Mae. She hopes you'll stop by."

"I can go over tomorrow on my way home," Ellie said.

"Good. That'll please her." She took the last sip in her glass and licked the taste on her lips. "Mae and me, we never got along. Mae always got what she wanted—she was Papa's pet. She was cute and affectionate. He fell for that. I could never be that way. I was smart and argued with him. I wanted to finish high school, I wanted to be my own boss, and that made him angry. He made me go into the family business, while he let Mae go to beauty school and open her own shop. I was closer to my mother and took care of her when she died. I held her in my arms her last hours—oh, I'll never forget!" Her plump arms cradled the memory of her mother close to her body. "I told her, 'Mother, it's all right. Don't be afraid, I'm right here with you.' I watched her take her last breaths." She paused for a moment, lost in the memory.

Ellie studied her face—round, with a redhead's flawless, creamy skin, not a serious wrinkle showing in her late seventies. That's what made her smile look so angelic. She had a dainty nose, turned slightly down at the tip and flaring back at the nostrils. Her keen blue eyes—so like Dave's—showed intelligence, but her mind lacked worldly education. She loved good times with others, livening up, even getting boisterous. She welcomed the visits of her granddaughters, who told her all about the current lifestyles and trends in Philadelphia—nothing she wanted for herself but liked hearing about. She didn't trust other people when it came to financial transactions, even simple ones at the grocery store. She clutched her black change purse suspiciously before feeling forced to open it. But merrymaking with family and friends was a part of her heritage that offered warmth and the feeling of love and togetherness. And she loved her son. She listened to his advice, and financially they had become partners, though she let him take the lead, as he had learned more about estate planning. When the grandkids were younger, she and Earl came to Philadelphia for Christmas, but she couldn't handle the commotion of so many people—seven of them in that big house. It was too many personalities for Lillian to cope with, and on Jean's turf, not hers. She couldn't have sole access to Dave. She hardly had thirty seconds alone with him, and usually by the kitchen bar when he mixed drinks at five o'clock, for otherwise he was off doing things, always in motion. The holiday commotion also made him uptight, short on patience. Ellie knew her grandmother's sulks and insults during those holidays would have resulted in permanent estrangement, if it hadn't been for her father cajoling her out of them. She would manage goodbye thank yous and kisses, then return home to hibernate for a while, abstaining from corresponding with the granddaughters, but still answering Dave's faithful Sunday calls, when they talked about money and investments. Money was their common ground, what they always did together by phone or in person. Eventually, when the bad blood had subsided, Ellie would call to propose a weekend visit, and Lillian's voice would stammer in relief, "Oh, Ellie, I was just getting ready to call you."

That afternoon, Hen and Myrtle stopped by. Hen was a distant cousin of Lillian's, a few years younger. Lillian led them straight to Earl's bedside. Hen bent his jovial, pockmarked face over the safety rail and said, "Why, howdy there, Earl, how're you doing today?"

Myrtle also leaned in and stroked Earl's white hair. "You're sure lookin' good, Earlie, as handsome as always. We want to see you get well again—back on your feet, you hear?"

Earl's head moved, and his throat croaked in an effort to speak. A choking episode followed that left him panicked to catch his breath. When it finally ended, his head lay limp on the pillow—it was no use, life, free will, was over—forever. The group around his bed stared in awkward understanding, which made their false cheer, their brightness of hope, impossible to maintain. It was a relief to leave him alone and follow Lillian to the kitchen, the realm of the living. Once more Ellie was aware of how the dining room's wall was a border between the two realms.

"We can only stay a minute," Myrtle said. "We know you have lots to do, Lilly."

"Oh no, not at all—I'm so glad you're here, and Ellie's helping me. I say we celebrate with a highball! How about it? These times are hard—let's remember the good." Her hopeful smile, with bobbing brows and twinkling eyes, forced them to linger in her time of need. If they left, it would be a rejection, cause disappointment, even resentment or a grudge, given Lillian's personality.

"Oh, all right, if you're sure," Myrtle said, after exchanging a helpless look with her husband.

"*Von*-derful!" Lillian said, clapping her hands. "Ellie, could you make us some highballs?"

"Sure, tell me how."

Lillian chortled. "Why that's easy, darling—whiskey and soda over ice—and no skimping on the whiskey, and just a splash of soda. Use the taller glasses. Now come sit down, yous all, just like old times. I'm so glad you came to see Earl—it cheers him up. If only he could be with us now."

The visit soon became lively with the highballs going down. Ellie had one too and appreciated the immediate high—the escape from the tedium of being alone with Lillian. And yet, she came for these visits voluntarily, for Lillian was family for her own loneliness.

Lillian was now bubbling away with exaggerated praise for Ellie. "I couldn't do any of this without her help, she's been a godsend! And Hen, she's interested in our family's history. She takes notes when we talk. You have to help her. You know much more about our family than me. Ask Hen all your questions, Ellie." She winked at her cousin. "Ellie's a writer like me."

Ellie smiled and nodded, despite wondering about the comparison. It was true, though, that her grandmother liked to write letters, and now and then they contained a verse—the rhyming, sentimental kind on greeting cards. Maybe it was true that a strain of her grandmother's ear for music had come down to Ellie in the way of words, their sound in her ears.

Dutifully, she asked Hen a few questions about the family tree, but his knowledge quickly turned out to be as limited as Lillian's, and the subject petered out. However, it led the elders to happy recollections of their youth—their times and culture so different from Ellie's, with the '60s and '70s social and sexual revolutions.

"We had to hide everything we did with our boyfriends," Lillian said, "like finding a way to meet without a chaperone. We had to sneak."

"Not like today," Hen laughed. "I would've had me a ball if I was a boy today!"

Lillian burst out laughing. "Don't you know it—we had rules for everything!"

"But we sure managed to find ways to break 'em!" Hen said.

"Remember Carl and Ruby? Don't tell me you forget what happened to them!"

"Hmm, better remind me," Hen said.

"Canoe rides, does that ring a bell?"

"Oh, yeah, those two were always setting off on canoe rides!" Hen laughed.

Lillian jumped from the booth and slapped her thigh

in hilarity. "And that's why they had to hurry up and get married! Think of it—the two of them in the canoe managing that." She chortled—this was racy! The others half-laughed along with her. Then, she slid back into her seat. "It was easier for you boys. But girls like me were watched by their fathers. I had a hard time of it. What about you, Myrtle? Could you sneak out for a good time with Hen?" Lillian's eyes glittered in the hopes of another juicy story, one that might finally be revealed, given the liberal times.

But her prompting was a conversation stopper. Myrtle's lips sealed tight, and Hen's laughter died out with a sigh, eyes going down.

Ellie quickly changed the subject. "Do you live near here? Do you have kids and grandkids in town?"

Myrtle was happy to tell Ellie about their daughter, now grown and living in Chicago. The grandkids were in college, so it wasn't often they all got together. "We aren't as lucky as Lillian with all you grandkids visiting," Myrtle said. "But lookee here, I always carry a few pictures in my purse." She got them out to share.

The hour wore on, the peak effect of the highball wore off, and the get-together came to a pleasant close, everyone ready to hug and say goodbye, with repeated well wishes and intentions to meet again soon. Standing on the threshold of the swinging dining room door, Hen and Myrtle bid a cheerful goodbye to Earl, everyone aware it might be the last time they saw him alive.

A few days later, Earl died. Lillian told Ellie the details over the phone. "He choked on his phlegm—oh my God, it was horrible. I'm glad you weren't here to see it. I called 911, and a nurse came. She had that thing that sucks the mucus out. But he was too frail. After she got him breathing again, I went with her to the door, and that's when he died. Oh, Lordy! He was gone when I came back." Her voice sailed away with the memory.

The following weekend, Ellie's family gathered at the hillside home for Earl's funeral. They arrived in separate cars, for the girls lived independently and Jay was still at home with their parents. He was fifteen now, good-looking, and as carefree as always. He had been born before the feminist movement, before Laurie and Ellie challenged their father's sexism. They had laughed along whenever Dave's eyes twinkled at them that now, finally, the family had "family jewels" to pass on. Ellie had never asked Laurie if Jay's birth had filled her with relief from the shame of being born a girl and a disappointment to their parents. Or, perhaps, Ellie—being the second girl—had been the greater disappointment. And Laurie was different. She was naturally headstrong, bold. In college, she had become a vocal feminist and was now halfway through medical school, determined to outdistance their father. She and Ellie were still sisterly, but their lives had taken different paths—Laurie the achiever and Ellie the shy and insecure writer.

After Jay's birth, Ellie's mother had blossomed into a happier person—no more rages. She loved social life, dressing up and fulfilling the role she had been raised to achieve—the wife and envied beauty of a successful man. This was also what her husband wanted—an enviable ornament on his arm. Unconsciously, Jean leaned on Laurie with her Main

Line education and friends to dictate the latest lifestyle trends essential for the family's outward appearance. Ellie's cohort wasn't Main Line but more the fringe. Now, with Jay soon to leave the nest, Jean was thinking about her future, how to fill her days. Laurie told her to get a job—she could teach, she had already taught first grade briefly before getting married—she could go back to it. At a recent family dinner, with her daughters home for the meal, Jean had playfully broached the topic of taking courses for a teaching certificate. Dave had vehemently opposed it—their friends would think he couldn't support his wife! Laurie had argued back like a defense attorney, and Ellie had agreed with her. Jay, when asked his opinion, had shrugged benignly—"Mom should do what she wants." Jean—now supported unanimously by her children—had sat back with a pleased smile. She knew in a day or two Dave would grudgingly concede.

The dining room had been cleared of the hospital equipment and restored to its formal mid-century decor. The family hung out there because of the table and chairs and the picture window's view. The room's high perch overlooking nature lessened the claustrophobia of dealing with death and a funeral. Despite the somber occasion and Dr. Dave's pale, strained face, the family's usual excitement of being together enlivened the atmosphere. Jay was their pivotal point, generating fun and laughter, despite his left arm being in a plaster cast, the result of a daredevil skateboard trick.

On the day of the funeral, Mrs. Miller's dress pumps could be heard tapping on the old wood staircase as she came down. Ellie and her siblings waited for her in the dining room, annoyed at her lateness. Their father and grandmother were already at the funeral parlor greeting guests without the rest of the family there for support. But Mrs. Miller was always late, always dawdling over her appearance in order to delay the moment of presenting herself to others and seeing their stares and judgment. Even now, with her own kids, she was all nerves, and chattered in a fluttery voice on the stairs just to let them know she was about to enter—but the warning was more for herself than for them. At last, she stepped into the archway, a proscenium framing her hourglass figure in a dark purple suit. She had been to the hairdresser the day before and her blond sheen cupped her pretty face. Her tasteful jewelry, the gift of her husband, marked her social status. Although she always nearly panicked to face other people's stares, she also dressed for that very effect—the effect of her beauty. It had been the browbeaten cornerstone of her upbringing.

"Grandma must be getting pissed we're late," she said lightly.

"You mean *you're* late," Laurie said.

The phone rang, and Jay leaped to the kitchen wall to answer it.

"I dread this," Ellie said. "Who wants to see Grandpa all madeup and looking fake?"

"We're doing it for Grandma," Mrs. Miller said. "We might not want open caskets ourselves, but this is what she wants. And it's probably what everyone expects around here."

"Hey, Ma," Jay called from the swinging door, holding the

phone's receiver in his good hand. "Grandma wants to know where we are."

"Oh, dear, tell her we're leaving right now. Come on, kids, let's go. Who's driving?"

"Me, but I need directions," Laurie said.

Blank faces stared at her.

"Wait, Jay! Don't hang up! We need directions!" Ellie said.

"I hung up."

"Shit!" Mrs. Miller said. *Shit* was her new, favorite word, now that the liberal times allowed women of her ilk to say it, as well as other once-forbidden words.

Laurie pursed her lips and turned to Ellie. "Did Daddy tell you the name of the funeral home?"

"No."

She glared at her mother—the last person on earth to know. "Ma?"

"Well … he might have mentioned … no, I didn't hear what he said."

"You mean you didn't listen," Laurie said.

"Let's go," Ellie said. "Maybe her church knows—it's down the street."

Eventually, they made it to the funeral parlor, passing through streets of a vernacular architecture—row houses with little pointed towers running entire blocks. Stone churches anchored heavily to many corners. All had become shabby, the town's golden century in the past.

Greeters in black suits ushered them into a dark, window-less room smelling of candles and disinfectants. Large vases of flowers added another, almost sour odor to the room, as if death and the underworld dwelled there. A few rows of chairs had been set up in one half of the room, and a handful of white-haired people from Lillian's church and circle of friends sat there. They stared at the newcomers—obviously city folk by the way they dressed. Mae and Leo sat in the front row next to Hen and Myrtle, the only relatives left in Lillian's line. Earl had no line that they knew of. The Millers hugged the relatives and smiled with nods at the other guests, but didn't linger by the chairs. They moved to the other half of the room with the open casket, where Lillian, Dr. Miller, and the pastor stood greeting an older couple who had just arrived. Ellie noticed how the couple shook hands courteously with the family but warmed up with Dr. Miller, whom they called Doc. He was a member of their clan, most of them having known him in his youth, through his Boy Scout and high school years. They were proud of him, proud that their hometown boy had risen so high in the world beyond their borders.

Lillian was hardly recognizable. She had dressed up in a navy-blue suit and low black heels, her posture straight and proud. She wore makeup that brightened her visage, and Mae had cut and curled her hair early that morning. She looked poised and self-assured of her place in this community. She didn't need Dave to preside over the occasion—this was her event, and he was her supporting son.

Laurie and Mrs. Miller stayed close to Dave, while Ellie and Jay hesitantly approached the casket.

"Jeez," Jay said, "this is weird—he looks fake … but maybe alive."

Ellie stared with the same unease at what the undertaker had created. Earl's chiseled cheekbones, forthright nose, and sealed eyes faced the ceiling under layers of undetectable makeup that resulted in a wax museum face. The white hair—the only natural thing about him besides his black eyelashes—was brushed back beautifully from the unreal face. One look was enough for her. "Come on," she said, nudging Jay's shoulder toward Laurie and their parents. The pastor and Lillian had moved away to talk to the seated guests.

"Hi Daddy," Ellie said, giving her father a hug. "How are you doing?"

"I'm okay. I've had a lot of time to get ready for this, so don't worry about me."

But his face was drawn and ashen. His heavy drinking the night before had left him with droopy jowls and puffy eyelids. Nevertheless, his dark hair and distinguished carriage lent him stature.

"I want to thank you for being with Grandma last weekend—and other weekends—she's mentioned it several times—how supportive you've been," he said.

"I wanted to be here—I loved Grandpa, I still do."

"I know, but thank you, and also for your poem." He patted his suit coat's breast pocket. "I read it, and I want you to know it means a lot to me."

Her heart leaped hearing that her poem had pleased him. It gave a lasting life to Earl—to his soul—for both of them.

Dr. Miller turned to Jay and patted his shoulder. "How's the arm, big guy?" he said quietly.

"Fucking broken, Dad—whadda ya think?" Jay said.

"Listen, try to watch your language around here—these people are older and more conservative, but they care, that's why they're here, and they deserve our respect."

"Okay, but they didn't hear me."

"Just watch it, that's all."

Laurie and Mrs. Miller moved closer.

"Dad, did you know Grandma bought three cemetery plots—one for you too?" Laurie said.

"Yes, she mentioned it once, but I told her I don't plan to use it, and she should sell it."

"But Dad, she bought them *after* you got married. She left Mom out."

"Okay, let's not talk about that now. The plots aren't of interest to me. Grandma's Grandma, just accept how she is. She means well."

"Oh, ho ho," Mrs. Miller said.

Dr. Miller put a comforting arm around her back to show whose side he was on.

Jay looked up from the printed program he had been skimming. "It says here Grandpa was a Mason. What's that, Dad?"

"I don't know much about them, or Dad's involvement, but I believe he joined because he was a master printer. They're a secret society—like a brotherhood with meetings and rituals," Dr. Miller said.

"You mean a cult?"

"No, just a club of men committed to good values. Hey, listen, I want to reiterate, these are good people here— neighbors, friends—please show respect."

"Yah," Jay said, and moved away. Ellie followed him. At family gatherings, they often stuck together.

"Want to check the outdoors?" Jay said.

"Yeah, air."

"Got any cigs?"

"No, I quit."

"Again?"

"Hey kids," Dr. Miller called quietly after them. "Don't stray too far, we go to the cemetery next."

Several hours later, they said goodbye to the last sprinkling of friends and relatives who had come back to the house for sandwiches and drinks. Life was now ready to go on, the funeral over. Lillian and Dave settled in the nook to read Earl's will. Mrs. Miller and Jay sat together on the living room couch to pore over old photos and memorabilia from the stuffed closet. Laurie went upstairs to study her medical texts, and Ellie went out for a walk on Egelman Road. The street was quiet, few cars used it, though she had grown up knowing how dangerous it could be—a toddler had once wandered out and been killed. The neighborhood was one of working folk, with young men tinkering under their car hoods on weekends. Laundry flapped from clotheslines and the sound of TVs came through the closed windows of nondescript houses. Ellie tried to imagine her father growing up here, and what it was like to have a vision that went beyond it, and to take, independently, all the steps that led out of it. And how she, as a result, had grown up in a completely different culture, one of privilege.

That evening the family gathered for dinner in the dining room—a last supper before everyone went their separate ways in the morning. Ellie knew it would be hard for her grandmother to be all alone, and yet, she would be all right. Even if she padded around in a daze for a while—even if she sipped beer before five o'clock until her self-discipline returned, she would still have purpose living inside her, financial purpose. She would start thinking about the summer ahead, when she could resume her stimulating rental activities on the Jersey Shore, where she took satisfaction in earning her entire year's living expenses in three short months. She loved taking in money, especially cash, and counting it, licking her thumb every so often to separate the bills.

Ellie and Laurie made dinner—Laurie in charge. In the fridge, they found chicken, green beans, and a big jar of Lillian's pepper hash—a sweet-and-sour slaw. When they sat down to eat and Jay helped himself to the vegetables, his eyes twinkled at his grandmother—"Well, whadda ya know kiddos, we're having *wedge-tables* for dinner."

Lillian roared with laughter, the kind that couldn't stop but just fed more. The others joined in. "Don't you know it!" Lillian finally gasped, wiping tears from her face. "That's how we talk in these parts. Davy, pour me some more wine, would you please?" she said, holding up her glass to Dave at the other end of the table.

The wine and beer had been flowing all evening—French wine Dave had brought from his own cellar, knowing his mother only offered purple stuff from an open gallon jug that had sat on the cellar stairs for years. Soon, Grandma was howling with enjoyment, purging her weeks and months of stress, turning them into hilarity with the family, even with her nemesis—Jean—who was also laughing and joking with abandon.

Raising her voice to be heard above the din, Lillian said, "I have a story for yous all."

The table quieted, flushed and shining faces turning to her.

"You'd think I deserved just one day of peace after Earl passed, but no sirree, that wasn't in the cards. Those boys from Schneiders no sooner came for Earl's body, than another boy knocked on my door. I opened it just a crack to let him know I was in mourning. 'Mr. Miller died this morning, you'll have to come back another time.' He apologized for disturbing me. 'I'm Frankie Getz, I think you know my mother,' he said. 'I'm getting married next month and want to buy a silver set.' 'Wait,' I told him, 'come on in, I'll show you the patterns.' You see, his mama's been real good to me—she works on the *Gazette* and sends me customers."

"Always ready to make a deal, Grandma!" Jay teased.

Lillian chortled and wagged a finger at him. "Darn right, sonny boy! And your daddy learned it from me. Am I right, Davy?"

From the other end of the table, Dave nodded but with a detached smile. Ellie thought he was the only one who couldn't forget their recent loss.

"Is it true, Grandma, what Laurie said, that you bought Daddy a house here when he graduated from medical school?" Jay asked.

Her face lit up. "Indeed we did! We thought he'd take a job at one of our hospitals, but oh no, your daddy had much bigger plans for yous all!" Her red brows bobbed as her eyes circled the table. "And we had found the perfect place—it had four bedrooms right on Doctors' Row."

Ellie hadn't heard that story before. And it was the first time she'd heard of Doctor's Row. She would have to follow up on her next visit—do a drive by.

"*Vell*," Lillian said, taking a deep breath. "Isn't this just *von*-derful! Earl's gone, but here we are—we're still a family. And Grandpa's not really gone, he's with us, he'll always be with us. Why, I can feel him right now—he's here in this room. Can you feel it?"

The others weren't sure how to answer.

But Lillian was oblivious to them, her eyes rising to the ceiling. "Why hello there, Earlie, we're so happy you're with us tonight—oh my darling, we're all together, forever!" Her eyes came back down and circled the table with her angelic smile. "Let's all hold hands," she said. "We might not be all that religious in this family, but we're just as thankful for what we've got."

They granted her wish and hesitantly joined hands, for holding hands at the table was something the younger Millers associated with prayer, which wasn't part of their household. But this wasn't about prayer or religion, Ellie thought, it was about family and being together. And maybe that was like religion, or pure religion without a church— just the individual's soul connected to something intangible beyond the body and mind.

"Yes, indeed," Lillian sang in her soprano voice, "I'm so thankful for all of you. We're family, we have our differences, but we always manage to get through our ups and downs. We forgive and stick together. We know how to love each other, and that's what matters." A sneaky smile then twinkled in her eyes. "And don't any of you ever forget, I'm still the head of this family!" She released the hands she held and blew happy kisses at all of them. Then, she raised her glass in salute to her descendants. Automatically they lifted theirs to her.

Martin Dubin

IT'S AN OCTOBER DAY in a rural Boston suburb. Woods along the potholed road rustle softly, their red, yellow, and orange leaves filling the air with a cool, earthy fragrance. Old stone walls crusted with lichen and moss exude a romantic, picturesque past, one that elicits nostalgia. The mottled gray sky cracks open in places, revealing a patch of blue or a jagged bolt of sunlight. Given the region's capricious weather, it's still possible for a golden afternoon to materialize and close the day with sunset's embers.

I see Martin Dubin coming up the road toward me. His eyes fix on his white sneakers but I know he's seen me. He's a hands-off kind of person, antisocial, with topaz eyes that refuse to let you in. Hey Martin! I call out, inside my head. He looks up as if hearing me and jerks his chin in acknowledgment. We've been together on and off since August, and the only thing I know about him is that he looks good, especially in our woodsy, autumnal setting. His coloring goes with it, all auburns and browns, crisp hazels, and dark cherries. The sight of him in sporty attire sends electricity through my veins. We're young, living in our parents' homes, and horny.

When Martin comes close enough, we both stop. He's not a talker and gratuitously flashes his trademark smile, the one he sees in the mirror every day, the one he knows is irresistible. Then he turns it off and his handsome face becomes detached, unreadable.

We live in isolation and take long walks for diversion. That's how we connected with each other in late summer, though we've been neighbors since childhood. Our families never interacted except to shake hands at other neighbors' holiday parties. I hadn't laid eyes on Martin since junior high when his features were unformed, his hair too red, and his handsome young manhood impossible to predict. I'm not antisocial like him. I want to be part of the stimulating world I've lost since college graduation. But I love studying Martin. He's such a puzzle.

I do an about-face on the road and head back toward the private drive that serves several houses, including my family's. We don't need to agree on our destination, it's always my place. So far, since August, our relationship has been about sex. We both want it, and being neighbors and physically attracted to each other has made it easy. I glance at Martin. He's taller than me with a beautiful head and crispy auburn hair cut to its shape. He's a tennis pro at a suburban country club, with a body carved by a sculptor who idolized male limbs born to lunge, sweep with power and grace, smash balls with a killer's instinct—all with growly grunts—and then walk away on taut, cocksure legs. His brow, though, is always knitted as if in deep, perplexing thought. He only smiles to watch his smile's effect on others—the way a woman's face instantly melts as she looks at him. Or a man's double take and immediate dislike. Otherwise his inscrutable indifference marks him. And of course, that's what challenges me. I want to break through his armor without giving myself away. I refuse to melt for him, even though I do.

Our family homes dot a rolling swath of land developed by Boston's blue blood families—the so-called Brahmins—during the Gilded Age. Two winding, private lanes lead to a dozen eclectic mansions with carriage houses. In Martin's lane, which is older, a few original colonial homes intersperse the grand domiciles. They are Mayflower families' original dwellings until shipping, trade, and banking brought wealth and influence requiring grander appearances. Boston's identity never deviated from its colonial motivation—money—the power and challenge of amassing money through savvy enterprise and ingenious innovation. On his walks, Martin occasionally stops by old Hugh Cushing's place. Hugh is a bent and shabby Brahmin descendant in his nineties, glad in his lonely existence to have a visitor, even a taciturn one like Martin. Hugh inhabits a three-hundred-year-old house, its clapboards painted in humorless, Puritan red. Martin likes to tour the downstairs, hear his footsteps on the wide plank floors that tilt. He likes to feel himself passing through the tight hallways that connect doll-size rooms painted in dark colors or faded wallpaper. All of the ceilings press down in a claustrophobic way. He likes to stand in the doorway of Hugh's bedroom, the former parlor, and stare at its barren frigidity. He tries to imagine being a farmer or a tradesman back then in the 1600s. To have been an olden-days man who somehow managed that truncated rope bed with a woman.

Martin comes to see me when he feels like it. I never go and look for him, though I always hope our walks will intersect. His whole aura exudes "No Trespassing." Even so, something inside him still needs closeness, body to body, that fleeting moment of blending and ersatz love. He returns to me when he feels like it because I'm easy, receptive. I'm safe for his fear of revealing his feelings, his desire and vulnerability to anyone, especially a woman.

Because of Martin's oddity in relating, he plays games when he comes to see me. I play along because I want sex as much as he. But my desire is different. It involves genuine interest. I want to get to know him. And I like watching his deliberately odd behavior—like wandering the front hall of my family's home with a fake loony shuffle, bumping his shoulders against the walls. He wants to provoke me in order to initiate sex. He can't do it a normal way, with banter and affection. He can't let down his defenses that way. By inciting a tussle, our body contact can lead to making out, which leads to sex. And with our bodies peeled from clothes and sealed in naked passion, we are, for just those transitory seconds, sublimely close.

"So, you decided to stop by today," I say, as we head up the private lane toward my house. My tone's ironic, a bit needling.

"Ugh," he answers.

"Ugh" is Martin's first response to anything said to him. It helps repel strangers or ruffle me.

"I see you got new sneakers," I say.

"Ugh," he repeats, his green-sprinkled topaz eyes trying to psych me out. But I won't budge. I'm always determined to get him to move first, but so far unsuccessfully.

"How's tennis?" I say.

He straightens, rolls his lips to their most desirable rose-bud position. They would be his best feature if it weren't for his nose with its Roman bridge. He holds this pose for a few seconds as if for a photojournalist after one of his tournaments. Click, click, click—quintessential male specimen, auburn all over—shadowed cheeks, manly chin, stiff macho hair. Tennis player. Regional star. Just out of the shower and wearing sexy jeans and his league's jacket. I'm ready to take on his ego—I know that the more it's inflated, the lonelier and unhappier he is.

"What?" he asks, releasing his pose and resuming our walk, the lane peppered with acorns.

"How's tennis? You've been gone two weeks." I don't mention California and his claim to be going there the last time he came over.

"Oh, I had some tournaments. I'm getting a special credential."

"What kind?" I ask, knowing he dropped out of college and may feel a need to make up for it—in spite of his contempt for all college graduates. "Is it one of those certificates with a gold-embossed seal?" I sound a bit snarky.

"I don't know, just some sort of recognition the league's giving me. That says I'm good, so I can teach more places."

I back off, suddenly feeling guilty, suddenly relating to his need for an outside identity. I'm in the same boat. We're both twenty-three and in the dark about how to find or create the expected adult life—the outward achievement of a career, spouse, children, home, and personal fulfillment. But I have the advantage of a college degree, even though I'm nowhere in my life.

It is two weeks before, and we want sex but don't have it. Something goes wrong with our games. We're on the third floor of my house, in one of the maids' rooms from bygone days. My parents work and my older siblings have grown up and started flourishing careers. I've set up a makeshift office in the maid's room with a desk, typewriter, and telephone. Two creaky iron beds that came with the house when my parents bought it are behind my desk, the farther one pressed up against two cloudy windows. The sun has set and the room lies in dusk. My desk lamp makes my shadow large on the opposite wall. The house with its strange noises—pipes, groans, unseen presences—makes being alone in the growing dark scary, full of suspense, like a stranger might suddenly appear in the doorway with a leering grin.

Most of the rooms in the house have old-fashioned call boxes that allowed masters and mistresses to ring for their servants. The servants' rooms line the third-floor hallway that ends in a spacious games room with a fireplace, sunporch, and bathroom—now my bedroom. The mansion's original kitchen is in the basement, four stories down. It still has its original cast-iron stove and an adjacent wash room with three deep granite sinks. A dumbwaiter is in the pantry, a little room with stained-wood shelves, drawers, and glass-paned cabinets. Food once traveled upstairs to another pantry with a swinging door to the dining room, painted pastel pink, almost a gray-pink. Sometime between the two World Wars, the mansion's owners abandoned the basement kitchen and converted the upstairs pantry into a kitchenette with a new refrigerator covering the dumbwaiter and the built-in ice boxes.

It's Friday, the end of the work week, and Martin has just come over after a six-day absence. I had no idea he was coming, and in our short liaison he's only phoned me twice. My parents are out. It's their regular Friday night letting loose at a fine restaurant. Martin has let himself in. I hear him trudging up the backstairs' hollow column, each landing with its own call box. He exaggerates his steps as if demonstrating either the drudgery and boredom that awaits him (me) or something more sinister. I sit frozen at my desk, fingers poised over the typewriter keys, thoughts fixated on how I'm dressed in ugly old shorts and a baggy T-shirt, long hair uncombed. I'm on my last sentence of a story for a Japanese tabloid whose editor calls me irregularly for sensational American news. This week's topic is the government's abortion shut-down. I have to call people and pump them for information. I hate this job, especially when the story's deeply personal like Elvis Presley's death back in August. Trying to reach people close to him and pressure them for quotes when they were entitled to privacy for their grief was a horrible experience. Besides this job, I hate living with my parents in rural isolation. I'm young, I need people, action, adventure, excitement. Before Martin's unexpected arrival and footsteps on the stairs, I had been planning to get out of the house, go to Cambridge, walk the streets, and maybe check out Passim or the Orson Welles for vicarious social life.

Martin barely looks at me when he comes through the door. He goes straight to the twin bed against the windows and flops face down on it. I get up and sit on the bed across from him, my legs dangling to the floor between us.

"Hey, the work week's over," I say. "Want to go to Cambridge?"

He makes muffled sounds in the pillow like he's dead to the world. Maybe sex is all he wants. We've never gone anywhere together. He rises on his elbows as if planning to say something, but then collapses back down. He does this a few more times, adding in grunts when he lands in the pillow. I guess he's trying to annoy me so I'll jump on top of him and initiate the tussle that kicks off our sex. But I don't do it. I want to resist this stupid pattern. And I want to go out, walk off all my cooped-upness from the work week of phone calls and writing. Of course, he's been running around on tennis courts all week and probably wants the opposite. One of us will win. He flings out his arm as if to land it on my knee but it only hovers between the beds for a few seconds before dropping down. Too late, Agnes, the dead hand tells me—you lost your chance to grab me so I could growl and pull you onto the bed with me.

One reptilian topaz eye swivels out of the pillow to gauge my intention—am I going to jump on him or not? I decide to let him win. But as soon as I make a move, he lurches from the bed, thrusts through our tangle of legs, and says, "Goodbye."

I'm stunned. I stare up at him from the bed. I see his looming shadow on the wall behind him—a menacing predator, a King Kong. He sees what I'm seeing and likes it. He grins and starts hulking toward me, arms out. I yelp in delight and roll off the other side of the bed to start a chase through the house, one that will end in kissing and sex. But I'm barely out the door when his arms go limp and he says in a bored voice, "I'm going to California tomorrow."

"What?"

"Yup. I'm going to cruise straight through."

"That's crazy. You'll fall asleep at the wheel. And why're you going?"

"For the hell of it. To listen to music without interruption."

"No stops at all—Big Sur, Yosemite?"

"Nope, just there and back."

We're both playing for time with this stupid conversation. We haven't made love yet, so there's still a chance we can make it happen.

"I'm leaving at eight in the morning."

"Well, say hello to California for me."

"I will."

"I wish I could go too."

"I told you, you could."

Oh yeah, you just dreamed up California thirty seconds ago. "Yeah, I know you invited me, and I really wish I could go. Sex on Route 66, that would be historic, at least for us. But I have to read my story to Hiroto tomorrow night and it's not finished yet." Hiroto's the Japanese tabloid's editor who records my stories.

I flop backwards onto the twin bed nearest to the door, my legs a V in shorts. Martin stares at me for a moment and then steps to the door. He didn't like my move. And oh, how I want him.

"Be sure to drive carefully," I say coquettishly. But it feels like pleading.

He snatches the pillow from under my head and stuffs it in my face. "Agnes is buried."

"Just as well," I say in a muffled voice. "She's vulnerable." All yours.

He lets go. I don't move. I don't breathe. Is he going to take my cue and drop down on me? Or do I have to grab his leg and pull him down? But something inside me won't let me do that. I've been the one to initiate sex every time since August, just to save his pride, and suddenly my arms have gone on strike. My inner voice is rebelling: This guy has to show he desires you for once!

The silence, my paralysis, my face still under the pillow, lasts too long. Then I hear it—Martin's swift departure out the door, down the flights of old wooden stairs to the front hall and double doors with a vestibule between. I sit up, totally deflated, burning with anger and disappointment. I hear the sound of his car engine igniting, revving. I hear the wheels crunching, spinning over the front circle's gravel. Slowly the sound of him fades, becomes obsolete. I think of all I have missed. Martin Dubin and his strong arms around me, his soft sigh, his breath of near love on my cheek when he comes.

Now Martin is back from his supposed jaunt to California. We're ambling up the private drive that winds through the Gilded Age mansions. Woodsy paths connect the houses. Some of the houses—like Martin's—face soft, whispering meadows offering pastoral views with purplish hills in the distance. In the olden days, neighbors visited one another for social life, the women for tea, gossip, and book talk and the men for tennis on a neighbor's court, or bowling in the former Russells' basement, the lanes now a decayed wreck. Most of the homes had games rooms for leisure-class entertainment that included the growing children. Learning manners and social etiquette of the elite class was of supreme importance. When speaking, a certain British inflection had to be acquired to distinguish the Brahmin-Mayflower class from the rest of the city's humbler inhabitants, mainly the Irish.

Martin and I fork left to my driveway. It curves gently upward between ancient pines rising from continuous beds of golden-brown needles. After two weeks apart, Martin must be as horny as I am. Why else was he on his way here? But he gives no sign of being glad to see me, though he listens to my prattle about how suffocating my life is, and how I need to find another job, move the hell out of my parents' house. He doesn't ask questions, he just listens, so I shift the focus to him.

"So, what's new with you, Martin?"

"Nuttin'," he says and flashes me a sideways grin. It's the smile that makes me automatically smile back. I see in his topaz eyes that he's inviting me to come onto him—give him an affectionate or combative push. I take the bait but with mischievous intent. I let my body in its soft fleece jacket rest against him while I lift my lips to his ears and murmur as if swooning with desire, "Oh, Martin…"

He waits, poised for magic words like: You're so beautiful!

Instead I sigh, "When can we play tennis?"

It works. He instantly reacts, whipping me up and turning me effortlessly in a flip that lands me back on my feet while I protest with screaming delight. Back on the ground, I'm tingling all over, thrilled beyond endurance. His arms, his closeness, are all over me, obliterating everything else. But in our game, I have to conceal my feelings or he won't find me attractive. His sex drive depends on having an opponent. I take a deep breath of autumn's fragrant air to compose myself. I close my eyes and imagine the maple trees in all their shades of red, some the color of Martin's hair, a mix of ginger, copper, and fiery red. I love his hair. I want to rub my face in it.

When I open my eyes, I find him smiling at me, victorious for catching me in a state of blissful adulation.

We head on and the world rights itself. He answers the

question I asked before he spun me through the air, "I never play tennis with girls."

"But you'll beat me. That'll be fun for you."

"Too easy, boring."

"You can give me lessons. I'll pay you."

"You couldn't afford me."

I wonder if I'll ever see Martin on the court, his body doing its art while crushing an opponent. When we were young, I glimpsed him from the distance during one of my teenage walks. He was standing on the improvised basketball court next to his carriage house. He just stood there holding the ball, lost in the same perplexing thought that still furrows his brow. And he wasn't beautiful then, which made him humbler. He hadn't yet gained the freedom and arrogance that came with physical blessings. He didn't yet know his power over women.

I breathe the air again. Its clear, chill note is so divine. "I love fall," I say from a deep place inside.

"Me too," he answers.

Spontaneously, I take his hand and kiss it. I drop it.

He says nothing, but I feel a reciprocal warmth emanating from his body to mine, like a caress. And all because of the weather, the season. Momentarily we united because of that. We share mid-October's crisp air, its mix, its brew of leaves, earth, sky, pumpkins, and apples. October's pervasive earthiness, its slanting angle of the sun that changes shadows, fills me with exuberance and inspiration—but I have no outlet for it. It would take flying, human flight like a hawk, to satisfy what's zinging in me because of autumn, and because of love. Or, if not love, at least sex with Martin. And we're on our way to it. I was afraid his two-week absence, ostensibly to California, might be permanent, but he's back and we're going to make love this time. I'm going to see his legs out of his sexy jeans. My knees soften just imagining losing myself in the marvel of his body, the soft auburn fuzz on his legs. I look at him and wonder if his knitted brow is busy undressing me, imagining me. I will never know.

We take the last bend in the drive, and the landscape suddenly opens up to a dramatic view of my family's Gothic mansion on its slight elevation allowing plush lawns to cascade away from it. A magnificent, fiery red maple tree lights the scene with godly presence. Pine, yew, hemlock, cypress, holly, laurel, and myrtle surround the stucco house and carriage house—lush horticulture from a long-ago gardener's imagination. Ivy grows up the house's main chimney and forms an arbor over the pointed arch door. Loose tendrils hang down from the frame as if setting the scene for a haunted fairy tale. Martin likes the strange feeling inside the house, its eerie silence and invisible vapors that suggest lurking ghosts—ghosts who scurry off as soon as the front door creaks open. It's easy to imagine that long ago, terrible things happened in this house—violence, insanity— and that those involved are still present, unable to rest in their graves. When all alone at night in the four stories' drafty spaces, its haunted sounds can be terrifying—weird clangs, pattering feet, and suddenly slamming doors. Martin has heard all of this and likes it, as if it's part of a dim past life he himself knows.

We enter through the first wood-carved, monastic door that swings back on aged hinges. Ivy pokes Martin's face, as if warning him not to trespass. We pass through the second door into the cold vapors of the long marble hallway.

"So, you're back from California," I say casually.

He doesn't answer because he didn't go.

"You must have stayed in your car the whole time to make it there and back so fast."

He rolls his eyes at me and walks away down the hall, glancing into the cozy den as he passes it—the family's hangout.

"Where's Mummy?"

"At work."

"And Daddy?"

"In Egypt. Inspecting tombs for the secret of life." My father's an anthropologist with a tenured position, but his true passion is importing ancient Egyptian and African reproductions to sell to his fellow bourgeoisie with whom he networks while playing tennis.

Martin walks in front of me toward the closed double doors of the living room at the end of the hall.

"Come on, Martin, let's play tennis, the weather's good—not too cold," I say.

"I told you, I never play with girls."

"I run for everything."

"That's what they all say, Agnes."

"Yeah, but did they all go to tennis camp? I won the award for most improved."

He suppresses a grin. "That tells me everything."

"Whaddo you mean?"

"How bad you were to begin with."

I laugh. "Ah, but you don't know how good I was to end with."

"I know I'd walk all over you."

"I'd love that. And so would you."

He thrusts open the double-paneled doors painted a pale laurel green and enters the living room, an entire wing of the house that's never used unless we have a party. At the back end, a set of French doors, shimmering like jewels, open onto a substantial grass terrace with an Italianate balustrade. The terrace, fifteen feet above the ground, overlooks a bucolic backyard—a long, velvet-green corridor with a vanishing point in the woods. Towering pines border the receding stretch with a small goldfish pond ornamenting the middle ground. At the vanishing point, concealed by sweeping pine fronds, lies the old path to Martin's group of houses.

Our eyes take in the living room's filmy dusk. Little light enters the room, for the tall greenery outside shades its windows. The austere furniture sits as if in a graveyard, the room's opaque air shrouding it. Facing the French doors is the grand fireplace—big enough to walk into. Bookcases rise to the ceiling on either side of it. Faded green and blue volumes fill the shelves—world classics that came with the house when the last Brahmin widow sold it to my parents. Perhaps this is the very room where the ghosts congregate. It's sealed off from our own earthly lives and has the advantage of the mildewing books—the last vestige of the ghosts' former lives. Perhaps my parents sense this uncanny presence and keep the doors shut tight until they throw a party.

Martin bends over the length of an antique xylophone my father brought back from one of his African expeditions. No one in the family ever played it, partly because it was intended for decoration—an *objet d'art*. Martin has a go of it whenever he comes over. I wait while he taps the wooden bars with the rubber mallet, a newer purchase. He's not trying for a melody. He likes dissonance, going against convention, even though he doesn't tolerate such deviance in his appearance. His clothes are always impeccable. Sporty. He doesn't drink, smoke, or do drugs.

I come alongside him and he stops playing immediately, grits his teeth—I've interrupted him in a moment of creativity. "I want to know one thing—did you see *anything* in California?"

I hear a mumble in his throat.

"Was that uh-huh yes, or un-unh no?" I say.

"The latter."

We break into smiles, though Martin tries to suppress his. He looks down and bongs the mallet on a resonant note. He frowns. When he thinks he's got his face under control, he looks up again. Big mistake. My grin is insane. He laughs and quickly walks away. I laugh too, for we both know his laugh cost him several points in our game. I wonder if I'll ever see him smile freely, without shame, blame, or ego. I want to see that.

I follow him out of the room. At the stairs he says, "Wait here."

I obey—he has a plan.

He hikes the old oak steps to the second floor and walks down the carpeted hallway to the opposite wing of the house. I hear his footsteps descend the back stairwell. I hear him pass the kitchen's landing and continue on to the pit of the house. The old kitchen and laundry room are down there, but there's much more—dark, scary storage chambers and the old, gigantic oil tank. Insects and mice live down there.

I go to the kitchen stairwell and call down, "Hey, bring up some wood—we can build a fire—first of the season."

I think his machismo will like building a fire, but when he arrives in the den with an armload of wood, he drops it at my feet. I'm already sprawled across the love seat, legs dangling to the floor.

"Go ahead, Agnes, build your fire."

"Why don't you?"

"I never did Boy Scouts."

"Me neither."

He pulls back the fireplace screen. "Then let's do it together."

I make a face. "If I weren't so comfortable."

"You're a lush. Come on, get up."

He kneels down to start the work. I sigh and go to the fireplace. I take a sheet of newspaper and begin rolling it into a long, narrow tube. Martin watches, frowning. "What're you doing?"

"Making paper logs."

"Are you for real?"

"Yes, Martin, I am. Touch me. Go ahead, touch me. I want you to feel that I'm real." But what I really want is for him to touch me first to inaugurate our sex.

He scoffs. "Crumpling the paper is better."

"Then do it yourself," I gripe, flinging my paper log at him.

"Calm down, Agnes."

He abandons the fire project and stands up facing me. He sees I'm cross, my head going back and forth in frustration with him. He always manages to make me feel deficient, guilty, worthless, and self-conscious. I want to know what he'd be like if he weren't so handsome. Would I see anything in him? And now, after not getting in touch with me for two weeks—when he lives practically next door—what am I to him? Am I just a lay when he feels like it? So far, yeah.

But he's more than that to me. It's his whole combination of looks, manner, and the suggestion of something deeper brooding inside him that attracts me. I want to break through his resistance to exhibiting tenderness toward me—god forbid, love. But, why am I doing this to myself, when I already know his kind of love—love that's indifferent, love that's handy, love that fleetingly fills the human loneliness gap—will never work for me in the long run.

"Okay, we'll play tennis," Martin says.

Wow, I wasn't expecting that—a concession. Was he reading my thoughts? Did he worry about losing me as an easy sex outlet? Did he sense I might kick him out before he got laid after a two-week hiatus? Or maybe he was screwing one of his cute blonde tennis students—until she set off alarms by wanting more of him. All of his cute blonde tennis students in short white skirts are young, leisure-class wives.

I don't waste a minute. I go straight to the hall closet under the front stairs and get out my dad's racket and mine, plus two cans of brand new, optic yellow balls. My dad will bitch about that as there are already open cans.

We head downstairs and out the cellar door, the fastest way to the path that connects to Martin's group of houses. The sun is coming out, the sky shedding its clouds and gloom. The air is still chilly but decent for tennis. We pass the goldfish pond mid-yard and soon after duck under low branches of soaring pines to enter the path. It's peaceful inside the woods, a fragrant and magical universe, with wildlife rustling for concealment in the tangly underbrush. We walk single file along the path until it ends, opening onto a grassy embankment facing Hugh Cushing's Puritan red house. From there we take the private road toward John Trumbull's court, where Martin has privileges in exchange for giving John a good game once a week. We pass a few magnificent homes well separated by stands of trees or pastures with New England walls. I love this place—Martin's older side of our housing enclave, with its own private lane from the street. The more rustic setting, with its mix of colonial and later homes and their ghostly lives, fills my imagination. At the turn of the twentieth century, only a few people owned cars, and shopping malls didn't exist. Nature and friendships formed an important part of the neighbors' lives. They shared music, books, and personal pursuits and talents that created stimulating social life and entertainment between trips to the city's Athenaeum, music hall, bookstores, and lectures. I wonder if being here with Martin one hundred years later is my way of experiencing a taste of that past—going from my house to his on an ancient path.

"Martin, do you think—"

"No."

"Just what I thought," I say.

He swipes his racket at me and hides a smile.

We pass his driveway, and at the top of its slope, I can see one wing of the crumbling, stucco mansion. Martin's house has always been my favorite among the interlocking properties. Its faded peach shutters and tiled roof enchant me. I know from visiting it once with my mother that nothing inside was ever updated. The kitchen still has a wall of empty ice cabinets. The front hall's grand curving staircase and wood floors have lost their luster. Martin's father bought the house from the last Brahmin descendant, whose surname appears all over the city but is no longer recognized by my generation—Boston has grown too distant from those first Brahmin families. The world's immigrants have inhabited it for decades, with their names blazoned on every business and in city politics. But the Brahmins still dominate the brokerage firms. Martin's father is as old as my grandfather and now lives in Florida with Martin's mother, his second wife. Martin's father is the son of late nineteenth-century Jewish immigrants from Berlin. He built a clothing empire in the 1960s with outlets in all the proliferating shopping malls across the country—Dubin's. Martin's half-brother, Seth, much older, lives in Seattle and teaches psychology. Martin lives alone in the mansion.

We take sides on the Trumbulls' red clay court that gives off an earthy odor that mixes with the pine, birch, oak, ash, and maple nestling and breathing around it. And now, with the sun glancing off the trees so that autumn sparkles, I feel the two of us ensconced in a timeless hidden treasure—a tennis court in the middle of nowhere. I'm full of nerves and anticipation. I can play well when nothing's at stake, but given Martin on the other side of the net, I'm sure to blow everything. We don't talk. He behaves considerately, pitching me a first soft ball as if I'm one of his country club students. I stroke it back, long and clean. It made a good sound. Soon enough, all I hear is that rhythmic pop of the ball as our forehands and backhands stroke it with casual ease—the warm up. Martin has exquisite form, despite holding back on his power stroke. My thoughts wander to him at the club with his adoring female students. I see them—the young women—trying so hard to carry out his instructions in order to win his favor. At the same time I know their minds are on their bodies, hoping he'll notice their feminine figures, even though his brow looks so concentrated on the lesson, as he sends them one soft ball after another. I can see them running on tiptoes, their little white skirts flashing and calling attention to their cute derrières and naked legs. I smash a ball back at Martin feeling jealous. He starts in surprise but bangs it right back so that I miss it. I feel angry envisioning Martin being nice to the twittering women when their lessons are over. He has to smile and give them positive reinforcement. He has to accept their invitations for iced tea in the clubhouse. Or maybe, just maybe—being Martin—he apologizes for having to leave, softening the blow with his inimitable smile that only tortures the women more, for they can't help imagining the taste of his kisses from those very lips. In this scenario—Martin escaping them—I'm thrilled he's relieved to be heading home alone in his car with music playing. Yes, returning home to our country refuge, and knowing I'm there for comfort and sex—me, his woman. I laugh and Martin gives me a quizzical look—what's so funny, Agnes? I return the look, thinking: Do you ever have fantasies of me, Martin?

We play on, striking the balls with an easy, synchronized rhythm. But after a while, Martin ups the ante with an official, two-set match. My right arm has to hit harder, stressing my elbow. He's clearly ready to show me his goods, and destroy me. Our volleys are shorter, my misses regular. And my heart's pumping harder. He has me running all over the court—right, left, up to the net, back to the baseline. I can never get his killer lobs that drop on that final white line. Then, I fall running to get one of those lobs. As I tumble down I swipe at it, losing my racket. Vanquished, I lie on the court watching the ball sail feebly up to the net, where it bumps the headband and drops dead on Martin's side. He's standing midcourt, sure of the point he just lost. He goes to the net, flicks the ball up with the edge of his sneaker and racket, and says, "Nice, Agnes. Even if sheer luck."

I get up and brush clay from my jeans and fleece. That's the first point I've earned in what ends up our first 6–0 set.

As we near the end of our second set, I win one more point. It's 5–0 and 40–love. Most of his shots go skidding to the baseline corners faster than my eye can see them, let alone my legs and racket reach them. But then, by a stroke of luck, I get one of the balls and send it right back to him, the same corner side-line shot while he's on the opposite side of the court. I watch him scramble to get it, sneakers digging into clay. His arm stretches way out so that he looks like a levitated body—horizontal. But his hoped-for catch misses, cracks off the rim of his racket, and shoots crazily off the court. With a crash, his heroic leap lands him in the chicken-wire fence, leaving a permanent Martin Dubin dent. He hobbles back onto the court. "Wicked shot, Agnes," he says.

I feel so fine, I heard a note of appreciation in his voice, and this time he didn't say "sheer luck."

The match quickly concludes with the last point he needed. We sweep the court, brush the lines, and head to Martin's house where he wants to shower. The afternoon is waning, the sun now low in the sky and hidden by the trees, though we can see its glow through the branches. Martin twirls his racket like an accomplished entertainer as we walk along, his mood lighter than usual. I wonder if I can invite myself to shower with him. Then we can make love in his bedroom for the first time.

We reach the slight slope to Martin's house. The rectangular lawn is bumpy and weedy. It faces a long-abandoned meadow that ends on a horizon of purplish hills. We cross a long terrace of broken flagstones that face this pastoral view. I have always loved the rusticity of his home. It's so in need of tender loving care—not renovation. Just the original vision and fixtures restored, the age left intact.

Martin's parents pay a cleaning woman to do housework for Martin. I know this from my mother who's active in the neighborhood grapevine. She's also heard that his parents want to sell the house and move Martin into what used to be the Vendome Hotel. It's now luxury condos following its tragic fire that took the lives of nine firefighers. But Martin refuses to move.

"Wait here," he says as we enter the empty front hall. Most of his parents' furniture got moved to Florida or sold. He points to the curving staircase that has a circular railing on the second floor. "If you move, I'll tie you to this post," he says, touching the bannister's top.

"I'd like that." I smile at him.

He smiles back. "Then I'll do something you won't like."

"What's so secret up there?" I say. "I want to shower with you."

He hesitates. "No, you can't come up. Mary quit."

Oh, Mary his cleaning lady quit. "*D'accord*," I say, sitting down on the bottom step to wait. It baffles me that he cares more about his messy bedroom than sudsing up with me in the shower. It's a lost opportunity, a great new sensation for lovers. We could get closer. Why are his fantasies so different from mine? And when will I wake up to the reality of him and move on with my life—enact goals?

I look up when I hear him returning, his agile step on the stairs. I'm instantly back in the dream. He looks so dazzlingly fresh. I realize he always looks as if he just came out of the shower. Does that mean he showers all the time—not just after tennis, but compulsively? I'm suddenly aware of my own gritty, ungroomed look—definitely not his equal.

We pick up our rackets and head back to the path. I have no idea how our lovemaking will come about, but I'm so ready for it, and it has to happen before my parents get home from work. I lied earlier when I told Martin my dad was in Egypt. I said it as part of our facetious games.

Soon, we're quenching our thirst in my kitchen. We stand side by side at the sink eating quartered oranges that squirt juice. They smell so good. Martin spits his seeds right into the garbage disposal's hole. I spit mine into my palm. Suddenly Martin turns to me, flashing a hideous, orange-peel grin. I startle and laugh but then freeze. I get it—he's going to stalk me with that leering orange mouth and gorilla arms lifting at his sides. He's going to corner me and rub that orange rind all over me while I scream in protest.

"Gross! Get away from me!"

A menacing laugh rumbles in his throat as he steps forward and takes my arms. I wrench free but he gets me again. His foot swipes my ankles. He easily catches me before I hit the ground and lands us both on the floor, all in a graceful movement. I laugh while I wrestle to get that ugly orange mouth away from my face. I drag myself under him the short distance to the dining room, where for some reason I think salvation lies. He's loving my struggle and allowing it. I hear his demonic laugh down there in his throat. It is only a matter of seconds before he pins me down for a kiss with those orange lips.

I gasp and surrender. We're under my mother's end of the gargantuan dining room table, my shoulders pressed against one of its massive claw-foot legs. An overturned

Sheraton chair lies by our side attesting to my effort before giving up. Martin has me, his face right over mine, his eyes burning with laughter. He turns and spits out the peel. His breath comes onto my face, erotically pleasant with citrus. I breathe it in, its sensual aroma flowing into my veins. He hovers there another second above my face, his topaz gaze glued to me. "Pretty," he says involuntarily and quickly tries to cover up this admission with lovemaking, conquest style. I purr inside, my arms around him—he really did say "pretty."

I'm in a state of love-elation the next day. Reality barely exists, even though I'm going through the classifieds for any job that sounds remotely like me—something in an office related to cultural or sociopolitical topics. I have no connections, nor do my parents whose workplaces are niche subjects unrelated to my degree in journalism. I got the gig with Hiroto in Tokyo through a former college professor, but the assignments are sporadic, and because of the work I've done so far, I no longer want to be a reporter. I'll do any other job that involves thinking. And those kinds of jobs take connections, introductions, so I should be thinking about grad school where I can start building a professional network. Meanwhile, I need an interim job for money, for independence.

None of this urgency about my situation daunts me because I'm so high on Martin and how he muttered "pretty" yesterday, acknowledging he notices me, that something on my outside, at least, appeals to him. I'm zinging on this scrap of validation so much that I feel sure it'll be easy to get another job—I can conquer the world because Martin desires me.

I'm reading the classifieds in the den when the phone rings, and being the only one home I answer it, not expecting to hear from Martin, given his past record of long absences and general indifference. So, his voice totally surprises me and a big smile spreads over my face. My heart leaps in happiness.

"Hello Agnes, do you know who this is?"

"Hmm, I'm not sure."

He breathes heavily into the phone like the bogeyman.

"Oh. Hi Martin."

"Good guess."

"It wasn't hard."

"I tried to make it easy."

I can feel his rare smile on the other end of the line. I can't believe he's called me the day after seeing me. Maybe our amazing sex under the dining room table in the tanginess of orange peel elated him as much as me. Or was it the tennis?

"What are you doing right now?" he says.

I rustle the newspaper in my lap. "Reading the classifieds. Did you teach today?"

"I teach every day, till one o'clock."

"Want to come over?" I try to sound casual.

He pauses, probably preparing himself to sound barely interested. "Maybe." But before I can think of a clever come-back he adds, "You know, it's super nice out—Indian summer. Want to bat some balls?"

"Tennis or yours?"

"Gross, Agnes." He pauses. "Both if you like."

"Good. Can I see your room?"

"Only if you win the match."

I hold back on my tendency to be ribald when dealing with men. It's a result of my lifelong rebellion against them and their condescending, insulting attitude toward women. In no way do I want to repel Martin while we're having the nearest thing to a normal conversation.

"When should I come over?" I say.

"Now, or soon, while it's still sunny."

Done. We say goodbye. I'm all a flurry. My brain's in chaos. "He just called me, he wants to see me," plays like a refrain in my head.

I rush upstairs, stripping off my clothes as I go and plunge into my parents' stall shower. All the other bathrooms in the house have claw-foot tubs that fill to the neck. I wash, shampoo, and sing for Martin, my eyes closed the entire time. Maybe today I'll shower again in his bathroom with his wet body. I plan my outfit. I see myself in it—cut-off jeans, the really short ones, my psychedelic, tie-dye T-shirt, and my college sweatshirt that zips up the front. Sneakers with invisible socks so my legs look their longest. I want to ooze with desirability when I knock on his door and he opens it and sees me. I want to see his eyes when he sees me. I'm a girl—do guys prepare like this?

That afternoon we begin a new phase in our relationship. We start seeing each other nearly every day, playing tennis in the afternoon, followed by sex at my house. But one day, he lets me see his room and it's not so bad. It's typical of a guy—clothes flung over a couple of chairs, gym bags, rackets, and tennis magazines on the floor, empty glasses and dishes on the bureau top, where there's also a TV and *TV Guide*. I open one of his dresser drawers and see his tennis shirts in all colors, neatly folded—the impeccable side of him.

Martin grants a shower together. It's in his bathtub, not a stall but a modern renovation with a curtain. We lather each other up, sampling the feel of our bodies in a new environment. Under the spray, slithery with soap, and flesh bumping in the limited space, our intimacy grows. We're primordial, amphibian—man and woman—naked, slimy, instinctive, sensual. Our bodies communicate so differently from our minds. Our bodies in the shower solidify our relationship.

As October rolls to an end, leaves litter the court, but Martin and I play on top of them and sweep them up afterward. A few times, we finish our match by driving down the pot-holed road to eat pizza at the Greek sub shop that serves the quaint commuter rail station. One night we go to the mall for a movie. Then, our ten-day togetherness ends because Martin has to go to Connecticut for his last tournament of the season. Luckily, Hiroto calls me with a new assignment— the story of "Son of Sam," the serial killer sentenced to life in August. Hiroto wants the entire chronology of Sam's gruesome story—his childhood traumas that contributed to total derangement, crime, capture, and the trial. I'm in the library researching newspapers and periodicals all week and on the phone for direct quotes. As the days go by, I don't have time to pine for Martin. That is, until I go to bed at night and, lying there, feel my body stir with longing to hold him close, feel our blended desire.

Finally Martin returns home, never calling with advance notice. In the back of my mind, I had been worrying that his silence might mean he had stepped back from our recent intimacy to his former hands-off self, or given me up altogether without letting me know. Luckily that's not the case. He calls while I'm at my desk in the maid's room, typing up the last paragraphs of the longest story I've had to write for Hiroto. It's due tonight at eight, which is ten in the morning Tokyo time. I read while Hiroto records. Someone else types the transcript, and yet another person translates it and probably gets the byline.

"You're back!" I say eagerly when I hear Martin's voice. "Did you win?"

"Nah. A hotshot from Florida creamed me in the final round."

"Oh! I'm so sorry. You can cream me if it makes you feel better."

"Thanks, Agnes." He pauses a beat and adds, "I guess you mean in tennis."

"Well, now that you mention it…"

"What're you doing?"

"Finishing a story. The editor's calling me tonight."

"What are you doing after that?"

"I was planning on seeing you."

"That's what I thought. You're hard to get rid of. Can I come by when you're done?"

"Yes! After eight. And I'm dying to get out of here! I've slaved all week. But my parents are home, so let's go to town."

"Fine," he says.

We hang up. Now I really have to hurry to finish my story with enough time to shower and dress for Martin. I feel unsure of myself. I feel ugly in my slovenly work clothes. I've hardly exercised because of work. My appearance needs a lot of attention if I'm going to face him.

By dinnertime my "Son of Sam" story is neatly typed and waiting by the phone in my makeshift office. I'm showered and looking my best in black slacks and a dark fuchsia sweater. My hair's washed, dried, and glossy. I'm wearing gold earrings that sparkle near my cheeks, brightening my complexion. I go down the winding backstairs, breathing in the aroma of chicken simmering in olives, capers, and prunes—a Roman dish that arouses erotic urges. I would love to eat an enormous plate of those sensual ingredients, but can't as I have to be thin for Martin when we tear off our clothes later on.

My mother's at the stove when I enter the kitchen. She looks at me. "Why hello, dear, how nice you look—all fixed up. Did you make your deadline?"

"Hiroto's calling at eight. I'm so glad it's done."

"I don't blame you—who wants to spend hours thinking about Son of Sam?"

"Not me. Your dinner smells so good, Mom."

She nods in agreement and sniffs the pot. "It's your father's favorite, now that he doesn't eat red meat anymore."

I look at my mother. She's perfect—prim, blond, nothing out of place, as if her whole being has been hair sprayed. She wears an April Cornell apron, what all the bourgeois women in her circle are wearing, but she doesn't need an apron. She works spotlessly. She herself is spotless and so is the kitchen. I always worry about disturbing her arrangement of food on my plate. She herself doesn't eat, she just moves her fork around as if she's eating. But she never misses dessert.

"Martin Dubin called," I say nonchalantly. "We ran into each other while walking." My parents don't know anything about my affair with Martin.

"Oh? How nice—someone your own age still living around here."

"He's coming over later. We're going out. I wanted to warn you."

She smiles. "You don't have to warn me, dear. I'm glad Martin's around and the two of you ran into each other. I always worry there's not enough social life for you here in the boonies. But I know you'll find a real job soon and an apartment of your own in town."

"Well, I just wanted to warn you about Martin."

Her china blue eyes widen at me. "Why? Is something wrong with him? Did he gain a lot of weight? I haven't seen him since he was a boy."

Right then, the doorbell rings, startling us. It's only seven o'clock, so it can't be Martin.

My mother scurries to the front door, me trailing after her.

She swings open the inner and outer doors to the vestibule and welcomes Martin, her voice tinkling with sociability. "Why Martin Dubin, I hardly recognize you. You're all grown up now, and my goodness, you've become so handsome. How are your parents? It's been an age since I've seen them." As she talks, she hastily unties her apron, touches her starched hair, and gives Martin her famous Princess Grace smile, her eyes glued on him.

He stares at her through his antisocial half lids. "Ugh," he says.

I laugh. My mother twitters, presses her hands demurely under her chin, and replies, "Why, how nice! I wondered what would happen to the house when they moved to Florida, but I guess you enjoy living there all alone."

"It sucks."

"Oh." My mother laughs again, as if pleased with the conversation. But she also backs off toward the kitchen, eyes confused but smile undeterred. "Well, I'll leave you two alone to get reacquainted."

Our eyes meet in reacquaintance and secret amusement. My mother has no idea we've tested out most of the bedrooms in her big nest.

Martin waits for me to say something, but I can't. I'm too diverted by my mother and how, even in her fifties, she can't resist Martin's male mystique. He's put her in a tizzy. I'm sure she's now in the kitchen thinking of all the extra things she can pull out of the fridge for dinner, now that Martin will be seated on her right.

"What?" Martin says to me, but with a look of conceit as if reading my thoughts.

I graze against him, inhale his freshly laundered shirt. My breath on his neck hopefully conveying my waves of sensuality. Yes—his right hand comes to my hip, his fingers press into me.

"Glad you're here," I say, then add in jest, "You sure look good for being a loser."

His lips press at my double entendre, but he doesn't answer, so I answer for him—I want to be sure he knows I actually care. "You're gonna kill that guy next time. Have you had dinner?"

He shakes his head.

"Then you can eat with us. You're here early."

"You said seven."

"I said after eight. I have to read my story at eight." I smile lovingly at him. "Come on, you can stand us for ten minutes at the table. Mom's made a Roman dish—chicken stewed in olives, prunes, and wine. It's guaranteed to put you in the mood."

"I'll need that, given the prospects."

I laugh. He's evened the score.

We go into the den that my father calls the library. We settle ourselves on the love seat, thighs touching. The scent of him has me so intoxicated that I just have to nestle closer. My right arm slides around his front and his left arm comes around my back. We instantly make out. We never have much to talk about—he's taciturn—but making out works really well for us.

I put my hand on his pubis, move it down and feel the hardness in his jeans. His hand feels the reciprocating excitement in my breast. We are so hot for each other. It's been a week. We might have time to run upstairs for a quickie. I whisper it, and the idea of it excites us more. We start to get up, holding hands, but my mother calls us right then.

"Dinner! Dinner's ready!" She's calling from the end of the hall by the kitchen. Then she starts ringing her vintage school bell for my father. He's too far away in his study to hear her voice.

A few minutes later we're all seated around the mahogany table. It's so polished, so gleaming, that we can see blurry images of ourselves on its surface. My father sits at one end of the table facing my mother ten feet away. A large vase of purple freesia obstructs their view of each other. Martin and I sit in the middle, also partitioned by the freesia. The table is too wide for our feet to communicate subterraneously. Martin declines a plate from my mother and an offer of wine from my father. He accepts a glass of water from me. My mother smiles at everyone and lifts her fork, signaling we may now begin. My dad's head bends over his food, tuning out the world while he eats the aromatic concoction fit for the gods—himself.

"You remember Martin, dear, he's the son of Joe and Susan Dubin," my mother says, forcing my father to look up and join the conversation.

"Oh, and how are your parents?" my dad asks, glancing up at Martin with obligatory interest. Dad's got the kind of conceit that makes him dislike Martin right away.

Martin doesn't answer him.

My mother quickly fills in. "And it's been what, Martin?— two years since they moved to Florida?"

"One." Martin says, dropping his forehead into his right hand as if it aches.

"I've heard from Judy Hallowell that they love Sarasota but miss the Boston Ballet."

My father gives Martin a puzzled look. "Who's living in that house with you?"

"I am."

"You mean alone? Just you? Why that's…" he stops himself from saying something rude like *crazy* or *preposterous*. After all he knows it costs at least $15,000 a year to heat a house like Martin's—for just one person. "Then…well…you never find it lonely?"

"Un-unh."

"He likes it, Dad," I say. Then, knowing my dad's passion for tennis, I add, "Martin teaches tennis."

"No kidding." My dad's eyes perk up and take in Martin's upper body and right forearm resting on the table. "I see."

"Daddy plays tennis too. He's the one who sent me to tennis camp."

"You had potential," Dad says, clucking his tongue because I failed to live up to it.

"Dad was a linesman at the Davis Cup," I say.

"That's right, but just a linesman—I didn't play," Dad says with modest pride.

"You two should play sometime. Dad can give you a good game, Martin."

My dad looks interested, but Martin pretends not to hear.

"And where do you teach, Martin?" Dad says.

"Around."

"At Longwood?"

"Un-unh."

"That means no," I say.

"No to us," Martin says under his breath. But my mother and I hear him. We know he means his Jewish father who, despite making a fortune, doesn't meet Longwood's "social criteria." Martin's mother is a gentile. I know this detail from my mother, who's the queen bee of town gossip.

"Freddie, Agnes finished her Son of Sam story today, and she's reading it to that man in Tokyo tonight," my mother says, quickly steering the conversation to a new topic.

Dad gives me a sharp, annoyed look. "Did he ever pay you for Elvis?"

"Don't worry, Dad, he will. He cuts checks once a month, and then it takes weeks to get here."

"Well, I hope you find something better soon. Something with regular hours and a paycheck," Dad says, while trying to sprinkle salt on his salad. The summer's humidity clogged all the salt shakers in the house and no one has cleaned them. "Marilyn, why is it we never have a salt shaker that works?" Dad gripes. "Could you please do something about it?"

My mother scurries off to the kitchen.

"Why don't you do something about it yourself, Dad, if you're the one who wants the salt?" I say.

He hisses, but because Martin is there he refrains from telling me I'm fresh.

My mother returns with the Morton salt box and plants it on the table by my dad. He grimaces at the solution—pouring salt from a spout.

"How was your trip to Egypt," Martin says to my dad.

"What?"

"Egypt, your trip to the pyramids a few weeks ago."

I laugh and look down. Daddy looks at me in bewilderment. Martin stares at me through the freesia, the corners of his lips tipping up in a smile. "Liar," he breathes.

"Who's talking?" I grin at him. "California or bust."

He represses a smile. I love our secret world that time is turning into a history, a history with inside jokes. It's been a week since we've seen each other, and I feel our excited vibrations.

We excuse ourselves from the table and go upstairs for my phone call with Hiroto. Martin lies on the bed by the windows and listens to my recitation of "Son of Sam," received by a Dictaphone. I feel his eyes on my back the whole time. I read standing up, unaware of my words because I'm so focused on what Martin is thinking as he stares at my body. Is he criticizing or admiring it? Probably criticizing. That's the way everyone is—faultfinding. No, I tell myself, he's liking you, desiring you, have faith in yourself.

As soon as my call ends, we have a quickie and get out of the house. It's cold under the night sky and I wear my fleece-lined jean jacket. Martin wears his white padded sports jacket, with his league's emblem over the left breast. His khakis are pressed. His white sneakers gleam. He definitely exudes a professional athlete's stature, and I feel like the lucky groupie tagging along with him for the night.

In the driveway we briefly argue over whose car to take for the twenty-minute drive to town.

"Yours'll be hard to park," I say with a dismissive wave at his big blue Buick.

"Yours doesn't play music," he says.

"Yes it does."

"Not like mine."

We take his car. Our suburban roads are empty and we reach the expressway in no time. Martin plays Elton John's "Tiny Dancer" on his car stereo. He plays it every time we're in his car. I never comment because his liking the song makes me ponder his deeper, hidden, inside self. The lyrics are about a man's love for a free-spirited, dancing-in-the-sand seamstress for the band who's marrying the music man, who's "in his hand." I know for sure I'm not the tiny dancer in Martin's hand. Did he, at some point in his life, worship such a light and feminine spirit? Or is Tiny Dancer his dream, yet awaiting him out there? I think how everyone has hope like that, but no one ever finds their dream love because real relationships aren't a dream.

We get to Boston. As usual, downtown is windy, blustery. The John Hancock building's eight-hundred feet of original windows had to be replaced because the wind kept knocking them out. The city core is shaped like a knob or a big fist, and water surrounds it. Wind travels fast over the water, whipping the city from all directions, especially in its famous wind tunnels. Seagulls, even at night, are part of its waterfront persona, their white wingspans arcing between buildings while they send out their lone and piercing cries.

After we walk Beacon Hill's charming brick streets, we head to the river, crossing Storrow Drive on a footbridge. We get to the embankment and stare down at the dark, murky, lapping water. Martin starts singing the '60s song "Dirty Water," mimicking the singer's sneer: "That's where you'll find me, along with lovers, muggers, and thieves." He grabs me and pretends he's going to dunk me in the slimy soup, but then lets go. We turn back—the river's no romantic hangout.

We make our way through the Common to Tremont Street in the shadow of Bullfinch's gold-domed State House. Here, near the subway stop, in the heart of Old Boston, the city is littered and seedy. I'm amazed that in this place of Revolutionary history and early architecture, no one running the city cares about the debris and homelessness. It's here, and along all the surrounding, unnavigable serpentine streets, that America's traditions and culture began. It's here that shipping and commerce on the wharves created opportunities to make fortunes and where the ensuing collective wealth never stopped growing. These streets still form the city's banking and investment hub. From the State House's height, the financial district fans out all the way to the old wharves, now in the process of long-term commercialization.

Martin takes interest in the Granary Burying Ground behind its spiked iron fence. "My mother might have an ancestor here," he says, "an English Pilgrim. I'm going to check."

"You can't," I say, pointing at the locked gate.

Martin stares at the padlock as if weighing his chances of jumping the fence.

I feel alarm. I imagine the police suddenly materializing and arresting us. I grip his arm. "Don't even think of it."

That's all he needs to prompt the opposite. He steps up on the fence's cement base, which gives him leverage to clear the line of black bayonets. With a deep "umph," he heaves himself up and over, landing in a deep knee bend on the other ghostly side. I gape in amazement at his feat of athletic ability. He stares at me from the other side, chest proud in his gleaming white jacket—easily spotted by police if they appear. He brushes grit from his hands and says, "I wouldn't try it, Agnes. You'd get stuck on a spike."

"Ugh."

"Ugh pain or ugh ecstasy."

"Ugh both."

He laughs and takes off, skimming through the old thin and crooked stones of all heights. I'm alone on the deserted street, doing nothing, looking suspicious, especially as I keep glancing up and down Tremont Street for cops or homeless men who might come along and talk to me. I swear under my breath and try to keep track of Martin's white sweatshirt between the haphazard graves. His head twists as he bends to read the corroded inscriptions.

"Martin! Hurry up! We have to go!"

He joins me on the other side of the fence and rubs his hands in preparation for his return vault. He lands next to me and I feel such relief.

"Did you find your relative?"

"No. Just the usual suspects—Spirit of '76."

Our last stop is Quincy Market next to Faneuil Hall. Since the area's renewal in preparation for the bicentennial, it has become the city's liveliest nightspot. Part of its mystique is the colonial and revolutionary history steeped in the old cobblestone streets and quaint storefronts. The Revolutionaries met at Faneuil Hall to debate the Stamp Act and tea crisis. They formed their views for independence, for democracy. They cohered to fight a war. Now their efforts and successes are commemorated in trendy shops, eateries, and bars. An Irish pub is the current favorite hangout to drink and sing-along to Irish songs. I point the bar out to Martin. "Come on, let's go in for minute—I want you to see this place. Everyone loves it, they love the music. My mother's a regular. It's given her permission to come out of the closet with her Irish roots."

"Well, good for her," he says.

We go inside. It's awful—crowded, noisy, smoky. People are inebriated and singing along to the band's ballad. They sway, moved to tears by the music. It's a kind of communal soul-raising experience and reminds me of the spiritual revivals in Black churches. These locals from all around Boston purge their current and ancestral sorrows through the music. The night's release—that they'll pay for in the morning—connects them to real or surrogate kinsmen who share the same deep soul pain. It's the sharing, drenched in music about love, loss, and life, that feels so good, so universal.

I get close to Martin's ear and raise my voice above the din. "People come here for hugs and comfort. The booze and music fill them with gratitude for having soulmates. They're feeling collective grief."

Martin stares at me with his big cat eyes. "Go back to college, Agnes."

"I plan to."

He blinks as if weighing the truth of my words, then says, "What are we doing here?"

I put my arms around his waist and smile at him. "We're here so I can hug you. Free love."

He smirks and gives me a perfunctory squeeze. "So, are we staying or going?"

"Going."

It's midnight when we pull around the gravel circle in front of my house. Martin turns off the car. The headlights go out. We get out of the car and stand for a moment, appreciating the deep country dark. Wind stirs in the pines. They surround the property like towering sentries, blacker than the night sky. In the round opening above us stars twinkle like living entities connecting to us. It's quite chilly and the wind's rustle in the trees foretells what's soon to come—white frigidity, brittle bark, biting or howling wind, frost on the breath.

We stir, taking a reluctant step toward the front door—the night is so free, so full of mystery and potential in its depths of black sky. It's hard to leave it and go inside. The house is silent, its only sign of life the lamp above the front door peeping through ivy. The place feels dark, abandoned, and a little scary with its Gothic windows and steep slate roof with chimneys. Unseen presences lurk around it, perch on its high-up trim. My parents are inside, sound asleep in the wing above the living room.

I lead the way to the door. I hear the gravel crunching under our shoes, Martin's crunch echoing mine. I wait on the stoop. This moment feels so pregnant. It's about us and tingles in the night air. It's something serious about us, what we are to each other. Martin comes onto the stoop, and for the first time in our months of being together, of making love, he wraps his arms around me, holds me close. I feel his heart beating against my chest. I feel it beating for me. I press as close to him as I can. I feel his warmth and our fusion—it's divine and might never happen again, not like this. Humans, I think, rarely fuse, souls blended to one. I breathe out, grateful, elated, my soul expressing what I will never say: I love you, Martin Dubin, I love you forever!

He inhales me, an inhale of the same pure contentment, as if he took in my unspoken words. I look at his dark-red whiskers sprouting over his chin and jaw—testosterone for me. I see the ruby of his mouth, the elegance of his nose. I smile at him.

"Do you want to live together?" I ask spontaneously, surprising myself.

"What?"

I repeat it, loving the wildness of it—the risk.

"Where?"

"Here. Anywhere."

"How?"

"Like housemates. You can have your own room on the third floor with me."

His lips try to smile. He's struggling. He wants to say something, but can't get it out. Being personal is hard for him. Finally he says, "No, I'd drive you crazy."

I unlock the monastery door. Martin's hand takes my arm. I turn back. He wants to kiss. He wants to feel the shape of my ribs under my jean jacket. And I want to feel his touch. I love his touch. I don't breathe at all when I'm feeling his touch.

We go inside after the kiss, the kiss like a pledge to each other. The long hallway is dark and we walk hesitantly to the front stairs. Martin drops down on the little square landing above the first two steps. I sit on the step just below him and put my hand on his knee. I look up at him in the shadows cast from the windows on the landing above the staircase. His face is at rest, all curves, beautiful like a woman's.

"What do you think?" he whispers.

I tense. He's leaving it up to me—an answer for us. I squeeze his thigh. Why am I surprised to find it's like a brick, wider than the spread of my hand? It shifts my attention away from serious matters. All I want now is to lose myself in lovemaking—with him.

"This is what I think," I murmur, letting my fingers crawl up his leg. I lift to move over him and press him down on the square landing, his legs stretching over the bottom steps where I was just sitting. With closed eyes, I feel the rise and fall of his lungs, the pumping of his heart. He's young, healthy, male. I hear the weather vane on the roof twist on its rusted hinge. It's the ghosts. They're up there changing the direction of the wind and of our lives. They're warning us about winter, the frozen earth until March. They're sending us a message that we can't stagnate all those months the way we are now in our parents' homes. Does Martin know this or is it just me?

We lie there on the landing making out until a bed is needed. Martin pulls us up. "Come on, let's go."

He starts climbing the stairs, his shoulders looking weary. Does putting our love on the table for decisions kill the life in him? I crawl up on all fours behind him.

"How could we live together?" he asks. "I like TV, I can't stand pretension, and I haven't read a book since eighth grade."

I grab his right ankle. He tries to kick it off and keeps climbing, half dragging me, but we're only playing our old game because the serious idea of living together is like an electric shock in our safe, going-nowhere relationship. At the landing, he reaches down and pulls me up. The dim lamp above the front door filters through the landing's diamond-paned windows, casting shadows on Martin's face. His eyes pierce me. "I'm a bastard and I'd drive you crazy," he says. "I've driven everybody I know crazy, including myself. So it won't work."

I nod. I accept his decision. At least we've achieved some-thing—we've talked about us, the subtext "attachment."

Upstairs on my bed, a few minutes later, he lies on his back, chest bare, brow furrowed in thought—maybe still stuck on the idea of living together. I sit next to him, engraving in my memory the sight of his chest with its fiery V, like superman's emblem. I drop down and rub my face over the soft curling wisps. They exude the faint fragrance of Martin's skin. It's enough to make me lose my mind. His hands come onto my shoulders, the fingers ever so light. Martin's touch—the feeling of his fingertips—is to die for.

Weeks have passed. It's now early December, the air cold and clean, not yet frigid, still perfect for long walks in parkas.

Martin and I are just returning to my house after an hour's amble through our peaceful, invigorating countryside. We stop at the goldfish pond. Martin finds a pebble to toss at the fish.

"Don't even think of it," I say.

He tosses it at me instead, a fake throw accompanied by his devilish look. The pebble plops off my down jacket. We've been living together in my house most of the past month. He goes off to teach tennis in various club bubbles every morning and returns in the afternoons. My parents accept the situation, though with unspoken discomfort. Social mores have changed—it's the late '70s and unmarried young people are living together. Parents have lost their former authority.

This past week, I've applied to graduate schools without telling Martin. Why am I so afraid of sharing my goals with him? If I get in, we can still be lovers—the schools are in New York, only four hours away. But whenever I think of us lasting, a thud lands in the pit of my stomach. If I get in, something will change in our relationship. I have to tell him about the applications—now, today—it's pressing, it's as if I've lied to him. And it's hard because I know that in his own way Martin loves me.

My parents are in the den reading when we come in the front door, bringing the brisk fresh air with us. We pause in the den doorway to say hello. My mother's reading the *New Yorker* on the love seat, and my father's dozing over the *Globe* in his brown leather chair, his feet on the matching hassock. Brahms trickles from a speaker set in the tall bookcase next to the fireplace. Comfort imbues their atmosphere, and I think they've achieved the life they wanted—success in the established world. Yet for me, it feels empty of something, something I want for my own life—something beyond convention's approved mold. I must get away, go to grad school, and make my own life.

"Well, hello, how was your walk?" my mother says brightly.

"Hi Martin, hi Agnes," my dad echoes, shaking himself awake.

"How," Martin answers, raising his hand, Native American style, as grade school and American Westerns taught us. He knows this gesture is now offensive, taboo, but he likes to be contrary.

"What do you two have planned for the rest of the afternoon?" My mother asks conversationally.

"A nap," Martin says, pressing his pelvis in anticipation.

My mother twitters. "Well, certainly, with all the walking the two of you do."

My father rustles his paper, annoyed with the conversation's drift. "So, will we see you at dinner tonight?"

"If you want to eat—it's our night to cook," I say.

Dad grimaces at my cheekiness and Mom smiles. Her graciousness never wavers.

Martin and I hang our parkas in the hall closet and go up the front stairs. At the end of the second floor hallway, we mount the wood-carved, spiral staircase to my room—the Gilded Age games room—with its marble bathroom, pull-chain toilet, and porcelain tub. Martin dives onto the four-poster bed making the frame groan in protest. I sit down on its edge and look at his back. I imagine the winter ahead, the coming snow that'll blanket our quiet meadows. I see us throwing snowballs at each other—me shrieking happily at his greater skill to hit his target. I see us rolling around like little kids in the fresh powder, making angel wings with our arms or stuffing icy particles down each other's sweaters. There's only one ending to our games—kisses, wet and tingling with snow—delicious tasting. It's time now to tell Martin, especially while his face is half buried in the pillow, only the left eye visible and fortunately closed. I lay my hand on his back.

"Hey," I say, "I applied to graduate schools in New York this week."

I feel him stiffen under my hand, but he says nothing. He waits like a cat poised to run.

"I've saved enough to get started there—even if I don't get in. A friend from college says I can stay with her till I get settled."

He raises his head, twists to shoot me a look. "God, Agnes, why can't you ever make up your mind?"

"But I have. And I do."

He snorts into the pillow.

I slowly mount his gorgeous, tapering back and massage his muscle-padded shoulders, afraid he'll thrust me off. "What about you?" I ask softly, hopefully.

"What about me?" he grumbles.

"What're you going to do?"

"Teach tennis. Same as always."

"Could you teach it anywhere?"

"No. I like it here. I won't leave Boston."

He rolls onto his back, so I'm sitting on his pelvis, his hands on my hips. He stares up at me, eyes with that inward, unresolved look of his. I smile, a little sadly, full of heart for him. It's true, I can't picture him in New York City.

"You're just yourself, Martin, that's what I like about you."

"I know."

And I know he'll never say he likes me, especially now that I've dropped this bomb on our easy rhythm. But I know he's comfortable with me, loves me in his self-protective, aloof way. I know he'll miss me. Just not enough to leave his fixed environment.

I lie down on him so that our bodies are like boards nailed together. I kiss him. I hear the wind in the chimney. I hear the weathervane crank around in a new direction. The ghosts up there will finally be rid of us and have their games room back. I close my eyes and feel the house, its echoing chambers of the past—of humans with their anguish to capture their life's memories into one tangible container— memories of youth, of love and loss, of human creativity and the mysteries of the universe. I think how it's all too transient for any of us to ever finish processing our lives, to ever make our earthly existence feel complete, done, like a book—a life between two covers that sits "everlasting" on the shelf. We can only make the most of what we have, what we are in the moments and the years that tick away. But that's not enough for any of us. We're never ready to say goodbye. We're never finished with our lives.

I sigh and kiss Martin until his lips unfreeze and he's

mine again. I run my hands lovingly through his auburn hair. I feel the contours of his beautiful head. I imagine us folded like this in each other's arms through all the winter nights. A dream, one I'll always remember. I think this, but I don't tell Martin.

There Are Places

I N 1969 THE UNITED STATES was in throes of revolution, protest, and change. A new society led by defiant youth was taking control, transforming America's outdated values and institutions. The Vietnam War had to end. Blacks were entitled to equal rights, and feminism was on the warpath. Music, the younger generation's own folk and rock music, exploded and made history at Woodstock. Carol Edmund was caught up in the movements, their collective tidal wave, though hardly knowledgeable of their finer points. She was sixteen and more focused on boys and dreams of love. Her parents' stunned state at the upheaval going on—long hair, hippie attire, free love and sex, outspoken children, marijuana—benefited Carol, for their blind acquiescence to the times allowed her to change schools, from all-girls to progressive coed. On her first day, under a bright blue September sky, she wore bell-bottoms, an embroidered Mexican blouse, work boots, and a black corduroy cap. Her light brown hair waved down past her shoulders in the popular style, and black eyeliner gave her blue eyes allure.

The sight of so many boys crossing the courtyard between the school's brick buildings that had once been a seminary set her heart beating with excitement—boys!—boys with hair to their shoulders and a few with beards. Boys in jeans, boys free to be themselves. She found in her first classes that the teachers were open-minded, supportive, and encouraging—whether young or old—and could be addressed by their first names: Jeanne, Sue, Lou, Jon. Students could smoke on the steps of their own student center, housed on the first floor of one of the buildings. The aura of freedom and acceptance had its intended effect of motivating the rebellious teens to develop their interests and talents, to produce creative projects whether in science or the arts. Carol knew she wanted to be a writer, a poet, but on her first day at a school with boys, all she cared about was starting afresh where no one knew anything about her, and she could present a new image, a new identity, one modeled on older girls she had admired at her old school, like Becca Katz, who had been a radical counterculturist. Becca's free verse appeared in the school magazine she had created for her small cohort of revolutionaries. She defied the authorities and wore miniskirts and high-heeled boots to school. It was said she and her best friend led a risque nightlife as go-go dancers downtown. Right after her graduation, Becca joined a hippie commune in an abandoned building in Boston. The group published a profane opposition newspaper demanding a violent revolution. Carol tried to write poems like Becca's, letting words flow freely in a stream of consciousness, even if they didn't make a lot of sense. They could be felt. She wanted to share her poems and be admired the way she had admired Becca.

Right away Noah Hoffman noticed Carol, and she felt flattered. He was a senior and the editor of the school newspaper, most of which he wrote himself. He had dark, curly hair to his shoulders, parted in the middle, Jesus style. He was good looking, with a grown man's beard and body. But as soon as they got together, she clammed up, unable to form a single sentence. She was afraid, convinced of her foolishness. He was above her—a man-boy, a senior heading to college, the editor of the student paper.

Noah didn't waste time getting to know her. He took her hand and led her to his room in the boys' dorm—one of the school's few prohibitions. They made out on his bed, just the confirmation Carol had wanted about her appeal, but now that she had it, she didn't want it. She didn't feel desire. He was too fast. After less than a minute of kissing, he pushed her hand down his pants to feel his erection—a first experience for her—and it grossed her out. The "thing" was leaky, slimy. She lost all attraction and felt panic to get away. They never spoke to each other again—just looked afraid whenever they crossed paths on the campus.

Carol's poetic ambitions led to meeting Lola Cohen. Lola was a senior and the editor of the literary magazine. Carol kept dropping poems into the big submissions box in the creative writing classroom. If it hadn't been for the literary magazine, Carol and Lola would not have met, for their social grooves were entirely different. Lola wasn't a hippie. She looked like a mature professional, dressed neatly in expensive skirts, dresses, fashionable shoes, and accessories. Her long, blond hair was always brushed and tucked behind one ear. She looked and spoke with the sternness of an older authority, voicing sharp opinions that ended conversations. Her blue eyes scrutinized with judgment. She rarely smiled. She was serious, driven in an angry way, and did not talk about herself.

Carol and Lola's social lives never intersected. Lola was a day student who went home to her family after school. Carol was a boarder, and boarders often snuck out of their dorms after "lights out" and partied along the river, carefully concealed to avoid patrolling cops. Doing forbidden things— drinking, and for some, smoking pot or tripping—satisfied the need for a thrill among this wilder group. For Carol, drinking freed her from ingrained inhibitions and brought out her natural personality. She had good looks but didn't trust them, mainly because her mother had drilled into her that looks were all that mattered for a woman. Looks alone would determine who she captured for a husband, for looks were all men cared about. Carol grew up believing that her physical shortcomings were her own fault. It never occurred to her, or to her mother, that her looks came from her parents' DNA, not from something she had created. Thus it was, she sought fun times with boys for validation, for only those superficial, exterior experiences mattered to one's self-worth.

Often, after cavorting with friends, she stayed up till the wee hours of the morning listening to Judy Collins or Leonard Cohen in her candle-lit dorm room, letting her soul and spirit embody their melancholic, wistful songs of love. That's when her poetry flowed—her body relaxed on the floor next to the flickering candle. Other nights when she slept and woke at dawn with liminal dreams floating up, she reached for her pen and pad and with eyes still closed scribbled the words that seemed to drop from her lips. But during the school day, her mind returned to its trained groove on superficial things—boys, love, sex, her future as a wife, mother, and poet, but especially as the wife of an important man.

Carol knew about Lola before they met, for their fathers were colleagues and played tennis together. In their academic circle, John Edmund was known as an unbeatable player, but Sol Cohen gave him a hard game and occasionally won a set. Because of the tennis connection, the Cohens and Edmunds occasionally met at dinner parties. But when it was the Cohens' turn to reciprocate, everyone was invited to an upscale restaurant. Carol would hear about it the next day—how Sol's brilliant conversation had entertained them all, and how his chain-smoking wife, Lisa, was even wittier. She was the scion of a New York publishing family, and before marrying Sol had published a few poems in leading magazines. After such dinners, Carol's parents joked about the Cohens, probably to bolster their own egos, for the Edmunds lacked the Cohens' elite background and the arrogance that came with it. John Edmund was a self-made university professor, and Lee Edmund had gone to a college that was more like a finishing school. Dr. Edmund could be counted on to gripe, "When it's the Cohens' turn to entertain, they invite us to the most expensive restaurant in town and then ask everyone to split the bill. And Lisa always orders lobster or filet mignon and then sits back and smokes her way through the whole meal. She's going to die of lung cancer!"

Mrs. Edmund loved such gossip and added her own dig with an airy laugh. "Did you notice how she left her asparagus tips, just the tips, all lined up on her plate? I think she did it on purpose, just to mock us!"

"I don't deny Lisa's a brilliant woman," Dr. Edmund said, "but if she's so damn smart, why the hell doesn't she see how she looks in that bikini she wears at their pool—her stomach's like a deflated beach ball!"

Carol had listened with keen interest to her parents' ridicule before meeting the Cohens' three children at her new school. They were Lola, Duke, and Will, named for *Twelfth Night*'s Viola and Duke Orsino and for the bard who had written the play. The Cohens had met their junior year of college, when Harvard and Radcliffe staged the play together. Sol had played the Duke and Lisa had been the stage manager. When a son arrived three years after Lola, they named him Solomon Jr. with the nickname Duke.

At school, Carol paid no attention to Duke or Will, they were too young. Will was prepubescent with silky brown hair and bright, eager eyes, and Duke was fourteen, gangly, with curly blond hair and features that hadn't yet matured. Carol's indoctrination had been to take interest only in men with movie-star looks, and Mrs. Edmund was as critical of her three daughters' boyfriends as she was of the girls themselves.

The school's literary magazine took shape over the year under Lola's competent stewardship. Lola liked Carol's poems and quickly enlisted her help sorting the submissions, typing the accepted pieces, and proofreading the final galleys. Her manner was always brusque, efficient, and never personal the way Carol was used to being with her friends.

One day, Lola handed her a present, the shape and feel of a book. "Here, this is for you. I think you'll like it."

Carol was so surprised. It wasn't her birthday or any other special occasion, and yet, the book was beautifully wrapped with a shiny gold ribbon—the curly ends prepared with exacting care. "For me?" she asked incredulously. What had she done to deserve it? After all, most of her thoughts about Lola were on her appearance—her roundish figure and mature look. She wondered what kind of boy would fall in love with her, for it wouldn't be the ones in her own circle. She had been amazed to see the photograph Lola chose for her yearbook picture—it showed a beautiful, smiling face that Carol had never seen in person.

The gift was a book of poems by Pablo Neruda.

"Please read it and let me know what you think," Lola said briskly.

Carol read the poems that night and loved the music of the words, loved absorbing the entire collection in one sweep. But she didn't know what she would say about Neruda if Lola grilled her. She was so afraid of that, but luckily, Lola never asked.

Over the weeks and months of that school year, more gifts followed: poems by Garcia Lorca, *Labyrinths* by Borges, and *The Bell Jar* by Sylvia Plath. Carol dipped into them but continued to feel anxious about responding to Lola's judgment of her intellect. She abandoned Borges—over her head—and didn't relate to Plath's disdainful voice, even though she felt awe at the writer's descriptions of depression.

Carol loved reading plays most, and she wrote a few skits for the school's morning assemblies. When Lola heard about this, she got them tickets to Samuel Beckett's *Endgame*, playing in Harvard Square. The performance blew Carol away. The actors, the stage, the theatrical realm transfixed her. What it all meant in its absurdity was beyond her, but its essence and impeccable art enthralled her.

Afterward, leaving the theater, Carol noticed Lola's calm demeanor, her usual tense severity gone. They walked along Brattle Street in the lamplit night, the actors' magic still enveloping them, uniting them in a sisterly warmth that was new to their relationship.

"What did you think?" Lola asked, looking slightly up at Carol who was a couple of inches taller.

"I loved it! I totally loved it! Thank you so much for inviting me!"

"I liked it too. Beckett's amazing. Have you read *Waiting for Godot*?"

"Not yet, but I will—tomorrow."

"And read Tom Stoppard—*Rosenkranz and Guildenstern Are Dead*—it's playing here next month. We can go. I can lend you both plays."

Every week offered something new with Lola—a poetry reading in a bohemian café, a visit to her acting class in a church basement, another visit to her yoga class, and a film at the already iconic Orson Welles cinema. To Carol, Lola led a busy life outside of school. She was in the vanguard of anything new going on, from books and events to lifestyle and health trends. On campus, a Canon camera often hung around her neck, and she spent time in the darkroom.

In May, when the literary magazine came back from the printer, it was a campus sensation—large format with a bright, jazzy cover. The pages were filled with artwork, stories, and poetry copied in calligraphy.

"Why don't you have anything in here?" Carol asked Lola, as she flipped through the magazine on the day they distributed it outside the student center. Carol knew the pages by heart, she had seen them through every stage of production, but she hadn't noticed Lola's lack of a contribution.

"I don't have anything ready," Lola snapped in her tight-lipped way that was almost a reprimand.

"Why not? You write, or you've said you do."

"I do, but it's not ready yet."

"Is it stories or poems?"

"Just stories."

"What about?"

She paused. "Family. You have to write what you know."

"You could at least have included one of your photographs."

"Aaron's are better."

"Who says? We women need equal recognition. We have to stop sacrificing to men."

"Then, you should have brought it up earlier."

Lola closed her lips to anything more on the topic. Her inner life was private. She never talked about her parents, her ancestral roots, her hurts or longings, her romantic interests, or her dreams. And Carol never felt she could ask Lola about her love life—the topic girlfriends talked about most.

One day, as the school year came to a close, Lola came into the student center carrying the submissions box. She plunked it down on the table where Carol sat drinking coffee while doing homework. Some boys who had a band were warming up in the far corner—the drummer making a horrible commotion. Lola tossed him an exasperated grimace, then turned back to Carol.

"This is for you."

"What?"

"Leftovers from the magazine. I'm bequeathing it to you—you're the editor next year."

"What? Just like that? What about Jon?" He was the faculty adviser and might have a say in how the torch got passed.

Lola snorted. "Jon doesn't matter. This is my baby, and I choose you. Just be sure you do a good job. That's all I ask. I'm counting on you."

Carol felt her blood tingle with excitement—the literary magazine—editor of it—a prestigious identity.

"Wow, Lola, far out!"

"You already know the ropes. You're the only choice." She reached into the box and pulled out the printer's brochure. "This is the printer—his phone number. I'm trusting you, Carol."

"I promise I'll do a good job. Man, Lola, I can't wait!"

The school year ended, and Carol didn't see Lola again before she headed off to Antioch College. In the fall, Mrs.

Edmund drove Carol back to campus for her senior year. As they passed the Cohen's house, Mrs. Edmund said, "I ran into Sol the other day. He's heartbroken that Lola chose Antioch and refused to consider Radcliffe—his choice, of course. He said she's shortchanged her career potential."

Carol thought it was just like Lola to choose Antioch— she had a defiant streak about asserting her own opinions, differentiating herself from her parents and family, their establishment goals. Besides, almost everyone at their school wanted to go to Antioch or another progressive or experimental school. Hampshire College had just opened, and Berkeley was a destination.

Carol began her senior year looking forward to boys and the resumption of their party life. Immediately, though, her ultracool boyfriend who wore leather pants and to whom she had lost her virginity the previous spring—dropped her. "Why?" she asked him, totally shocked—what could possibly have changed?

"You cut your hair, and I don't want to be seen with a girl who looks like she sold out," he answered with disgust.

What a blow! Even more so as he hooked up the next day with a classmate who had the classic hippie-girl look— long blond hair, gypsy skirt, macramé accessories. She was a permanent fixture on the campus lawn, playing her guitar and singing sorrowful songs that awed her peers. Yeah, Carol mourned, a much better catch.

Slowly, Carol's broken heart healed, helped by making friends with a new student, Daniela—who happened to be Becca Katz's younger sister—Becca who had been Carol's idol at her old girls school. Daniela was a junior with a low, sexy voice and exotic eyes. She called herself a witch and made astrology charts at a table in the student center. She introduced Carol to the *I Ching*, and every day they tossed ancient-looking coins to read the book's wisdom—their daily horoscope. Carol envied Daniela's beauty and stick legs in miniskirts. She wished she could lose herself in geometry and draw its shapes, axioms, and notations the way Daniela did, but most of all she loved talking to her friend about everything—from love, family, and sex to books and writing. They became best friends and spent weekends at Daniela's home in Cambridge.

That fall, Carol applied to colleges and collected materials for the literary magazine. When she talked to the printer about costs, it turned out she had nowhere near the funds needed to produce a magazine like Lola's. How had Lola afforded the deluxe size and the glossy color cover? The printer just shrugged—the bill had been paid. So, the trim size got smaller, the cover became black and white on cheaper card stock, and a couple of stories had to be cut to lower the page count. It had a spiral binding instead of Lola's smooth binding. Everyone noticed that Carol's edition was less striking than Lola's, but the content—the stories, poems, music, and artwork by fellow students—was enjoyed. Carol was proud of her own poem in the collection, and on her next visit home presented the booklet to her parents. But their reaction came as a surprise and ultimate embarrassment.

"How could you do this to us?" Mrs. Edmund said, unnerved and glaring at Carol. "Now everyone's going to think we're terrible parents. Your father's upstairs—miserable."

Carol was stunned. She hadn't thought of the poem that way. She had thought only of herself and her deepest feelings. But now, hearing her parents' distress, she felt sorry for making her sadness public. All Carol had heard from the day she was born was her father's lament for his lack of a son and her mother's guilt for producing daughter after daughter, four in all. Fortunately, the Edmunds' whining about having no son eased when Dr. Edmund's career advanced, giving the couple a comfortable lifestyle with nonstop distractions.

That night, following her mother's admonishment, Carol lit a candle in her room and slowly turned the pages of the literary magazine, pretending to be her parents. She stopped on the page with her poem—stared at her name under it. Then, she read the lines as if with her mother's and father's eyes and instantly felt her cheeks grow hot with chagrin, whereas when she read it from her own point of view, tears filled her eyes. But now, with the new awareness of her parents' humiliation, she shut the booklet and put it out of sight. She never wanted to see her poem again, especially the incriminating lines about being unloved for being a girl.

Carol's graduation day was a product of the preceding years of student rebellion throughout the country and on college campuses. The poor headmaster, Mr. Blake, had taken a beating, lost control of the school, spent its last cent, and accumulated debt. The trustees told him to resign. Many of the seniors refused to shake his hand as they received their diplomas. It had become customary to laugh contemptuously at any adult authority. He was a scapegoat and hadn't done anything wrong—he was a victim of his times. Carol felt sorry for him and shook his hand, overjoyed to be graduating and heading on to the promised land of college—college in California!

As soon as the graduation ceremony ended, Lola came striding over the courtyard to Carol. She looked elegant in a soft yellow dress and heeled sandals, but her face wore a scowl. It was a day of loving hugs, laughter, and joy, so Carol ignored the look and held out her arms. "Lola!"

But Lola only hugged stiffly and drew back fast. Angrily she snapped, "I can't believe the magazine, it's awful! And I trusted you."

"I'm sorry…"

"That spiral binding! And your cheap cover!"

"But Jen's drawing's amazing."

"But the stock you chose, the binding!"

"Well, how did you pay for yours? The printer said your kind of cover and binding would cost one thousand dollars. We had nowhere near that kind of money."

Lola didn't answer. She looked away, tight-lipped, angry. Only then did it occur to Carol that Lola's parents might have guided and subsidized her exquisite edition of the literary magazine.

One college summer when the young women were back home and working—Lola as a research assistant to a colleague of her father's and Carol as a waitress on the Cape—Lola phoned out of the blue to invite Carol to Nantucket for the weekend. The rest of Lola's family was already there for the month.

"I'd love to come!" Carol said, thrilled at the prospect of finally discovering Nantucket.

"We need to take your car," Lola said.

"Fine, I'll pick you up." It occurred to Carol that Lola had invited her only because she needed a ride.

"It's been a while, we'll have a chance to catch up," Lola said, as if reading Carol's thoughts.

Carol switched her weekend shift and on Friday set out for Cambridge. She had no problem driving seventy-five miles to pick up Lola in Cambridge, and then drive back down to the Cape for the ferry. She was always up for adventure, and Nantucket was a coveted place, an island with an elite mystique. The coolest boys and young men sailed there.

Lola had not changed much during the two years since Carol had seen her. She still had a stern face and clipped speech. She was majoring in social justice and intended to go to law school for a career helping victimized women.

"Why are you wasting your summer waitressing?" Lola asked as they sped south on the two-lane highway.

"I need money."

"Restaurants are derelict places, a waste of your time."

"Definitely derelict. Barhopping after work every night."

Lola tsk-tsked. "You should be doing something toward your future. Are you planning on graduate school?"

"I don't know yet."

"There aren't any jobs for English majors. You'll need a master's or a PhD to get a job. You'd better be planning for that."

"I can teach. That'll give me summers off for writing."

"You'll still need extra summer income, but yes, teaching's a good career for writers. So start finding out now which schools are known for education, so you get a degree from the best one. And you need to decide what kind of school you want to teach at. They have different requirements. You'll need a PhD if you want to teach at a university. But no matter what, Carol, you need to start volunteering right now, while you're still in college, so you have credentials when you apply to graduate school."

"Okay, I'll start volunteering in the fall."

It was so like Lola, Carol thought, to act more like her parent than her peer. And always pushing her to achieve. Carol's parents rarely gave such advice. They left her alone to find her own way—yeah, waitressing and bar hopping, Carol smirked to herself. She was aware that Lola had been brought up to strive for an important career in the world, compete and achieve both personal and "establishment" perfection, while she herself had been brought up to become someone's perfect wife, and whatever she pursued beyond that was fine, for she'd be supported by her husband, whom she would serve.

The ferry ride to Nantucket was inspiring. The young women appreciated being out on the deck, surrounded by a bright blue sky with stark white clouds and sunshine. Gusty wind pummeled their faces and the ocean's surface. As their boat approached the island's harbor, Carol had her first glimpse of Nantucket's quaint setting—a small bay with wooden piers, little boats, and shingled shacks. Seagulls arced over the picturesque scene, their languid cries like the long notes of a song. The summer wind felt divinely fresh and tossed her hair that had grown long again. She drew a deep breath of the salty air that mixed with the briny water. It felt so good to dock at such a fairy book place, a peaceful island retreat, where gentle waves lapped the shore.

What Carol hadn't considered in her anticipation of finally discovering Nantucket was meeting Dr. and Mrs. Cohen. They had rented an apartment a few miles from town—an initial disappointment for Carol, as the harbor's cobbled streets, colonial houses, and little shops drew her curiosity. She wanted to wander about immediately. This was Nantucket, the whaling capital of the world, Melville's milieu—though she hadn't read *Moby-Dick*—it was too fat and about seamen, but she'd need to read it one day as an English major.

They drove up to a set of new shingled buildings hastily plunked down on sand and scrub for the rental market. Dr. Cohen swung open the door to the family's unit as soon as he heard the car arrive on the driveway's crushed seashells. He was tall and bulky, clad in baggy shorts and a T-shirt, his feet bare, his legs hairy blond. He exuded energy and virility. His exuberant voice blasted them before they were fully out of the car. "Ladies! Or I should say, Women! Welcome to our dump! I sincerely apologize for it—I don't know how the developers sneaked it past the zoning commission. If I lived here, it would never have been built. It violates the island's integrity." His blue eyes gleamed and drilled into Carol as she approached the door, which his large frame blocked—he had played football in college. His big grin dug jovial grooves in the sides of his face. He was quite attractive, secure in himself, and warmly communicative. "Carol, I want you to know that normally I take our family to the French Riviera for vacation, but this year, unforeseeable things happened at work, and by the time I got around to calling our realtor, nothing was left. So, I signed up for this *pissoir* sight unseen."

He hugged Lola, smacking a big, demonstrative kiss on her cheek. He gave Carol a short, inquiring look before giving her the same hug and kiss. "Welcome, welcome."

They went in. "You can put your bags in the girls' room— the boys are next door. Lisa and I are up that ladder in a sweltering space they call the master bedroom, better known as an 'attic.'" He laughed. "At least I'm getting a ton of reading done. Did I tell you, Lola, I'm giving a new course on Lawrence—inspired by Kate Millet's massacre of him. I'm in the midst of writing a rebuttal for the *New York Review*. Unfortunately it's due by the end of the month, so no vacation for me." He turned to Carol. "What do you think of *Sexual Politics*, Carol? I assume you've read it, since all of Lola's friends are hard-core feminists." He grinned, with a quick, twinkling glance at Lola. She huffed at him. His eyes came back to Carol, boring into her. "Well … what do you think?"

Fear possessed Carol. What did she think? She couldn't speak, she could barely breathe when confronted like that. Dr. Cohen's competitive nature, hidden behind his cuteness and winsome smile, crushed her. She felt like a female effigy or piñata dangling from a tree branch, facing a man with a swinging bat. She didn't have time—or enough practice as an awakened feminist—to acknowledge the chauvinistic dynamic affecting her. Instead she reacted the way she had been raised by family and society to react, by feeling inferior—even stupid—in a man's eyes, and blaming herself for her failure. She didn't have the hindsight to understand that he, too, was behaving with inherited conditioning, and it wasn't entirely intentional. He had learned by example and centuries of tradition how to control everything and everyone while simultaneously exhibiting outward affability. He didn't care or expect a reply from her, for his role was to stand ready with a one-upmanship rejoinder that would snuff her out.

"Leave her alone, Dad, we just got here," Lola said with another huff as she moved to the girls' room with her bag and tennis racket.

"Girls on the left, boys on the right," he said, drifting after them.

Carol's eyes glued to the floor with its thin, gray carpet covering concrete. Her mind was on Kate Millet's book, which she hadn't read but knew was required reading for any serious feminist, along with Betty Friedan's *The Feminine Mystique*. She regretted that her feminist advocacy was instinctive rather than academic, though she had managed to read Simone de Beauvoir's *The Second Sex* and Doris Lessing's *The Golden Notebook,* neither of which had been a page-turner for her. She wholeheartedly and militantly believed in female equality and pointed out every instance of chauvinism to the boys and men she knew, including her father, tarnishing their liking for her. Nevertheless, she knew she lacked true belief in her own equality to men. Her indoctrination to women's inferiority had been too strong. She was afraid of men, of their power, violence, and snuffing-out ability. Or was it her own power she feared—the fear of throwing off the female stereotype and being who she was and disliked for it, by both men and women.

"The boys are out playing tennis," Dr. Cohen said, breaking Carol's musings. He stood in their door frame, arms pressing into each side of it, his body filling the cavity. "I reserved a court for our tournament tomorrow—girls against boys." He laughed gleefully. Then he stared at Carol, eyes going up and down her body. "You look like a tennis player, Carol, and if you play anything like your father, I'm going to need Hermes' winged sandals if I want to win."

Fresh waves of fear rolled over Carol. A tournament with Dr. Cohen? "I don't want to play doubles," she blurted. "I'll play singles with Lola."

He laughed. "But I want to play doubles against the two of you. I want to see if your dad's talent has rubbed off on you. Don't worry, it's going to be fun, just a game, and Lola's counting on you to beat us." He chuckled at his daughter, suggesting enjoyment of teasing her about her feminism.

He turned and ambled back to his armchair in front of salt-clouded windows. Books scattered messily on the floor around his chair, and more books lay open on the coffee table, along with pads, pens, and empty coffee cups. Carol could feel his self-confidence, his gigantic ego pulsing from his heft. A fiery core drove his innate talents, fed his exuberance.

And what appeal he had with his curly blond hair, joviality, and curiosity. He was just the kind of man Carol had been raised to admire, men with effortless arrogance that made them stand apart as the most competent, the most exceptional, the most desirable for women to put their lives behind. She thought, if only Lola laughed all the time like her father she would be his female counterpart. But her tight acerbity made their resemblance hardly noticeable.

Suddenly Dr. Cohen remembered something and came back to their door. "Unfortunately, m'ladies, we've been warned that our nearest beach has a dangerous undertow. You'll have to drive to a safer one if you want to swim."

"We're going to bike to town," Lola said crisply.

"Good idea. The bikes are in the shed. Gee whiz, I wish I could come with you. It'd be much more fun biking and hanging out with the two of you than fighting Kate Millet." He sighed with mock regret and padded back to his chair.

Around dinner time, when Carol and Lola came back to the apartment, everyone was home, Dr. Cohen and the boys in the living room and Mrs. Cohen upstairs in the attic bedroom. Sixteen-year-old Will lounged in an armchair, his nose in a novel, and Duke, now a sophomore at Stanford, sat on a hassock by his father's chair, like an acolyte at his master's knee.

"The young women are home!" Dr. Cohen exclaimed, beaming with pleasure at their arrival. "Every household needs women to spice things up. We men are so dull."

"What're we doing for dinner, Dad?" Lola asked efficiently, as if to say: Why are you just sitting there?

"I got groceries this morning—fish and pasta."

"Then, let's get started."

"Where's your mother?" Carol asked Lola.

The room fell silent for a beat, then Dr. Cohen replied, "She's upstairs, reading. Lisa's a *rampageous* reader. I just learned that word from Lawrence."

"Reading's just an excuse to hideout with her cigarettes," Lola said with disgust.

"I was just telling Duke—who so far has proven himself to be a rising star in mathematics—that his next goal should be a Rhodes Scholarship. Follow in his father's footsteps," Dr. Cohen said, changing the subject with bright alacrity. "All it takes is unswerving dedication to one's studies and goals. And by the way, kids, learning never ends—it goes on till the day we die. Look at me." He waved at all his books and pads. "Never forsake it. These student years of yours are gifts. You're planting the seeds for how you'll continue to grow in the future, how you'll succeed in your chosen fields. So, read all you can, learn, plant deep roots, and work, strive for perfection—never let your goals flag." He gave a big fatherly grin, filling his armchair with his bulk.

Lola headed briskly into the galley kitchen. "Come on, Dad, we have to make dinner."

"Okay," Dr. Cohen said, heaving himself up, but then dropping back down and scrutinizing Carol, who was still standing in the room absorbing his last words.

"I understand you're a literature major, Carol." He didn't give her time to answer but went right on. "May I ask what you're reading this summer?"

"Um…" Her mind blanked and her limbs froze. The boys turned their eyes on her in anticipation of a dramatic scene about to unfold.

"Well?"

"Uh … *Slaughterhouse Five*," she said hurriedly. It was the first book that came to her mind but wasn't one she had read recently. She hadn't finished anything recently.

"Well, that's good, Vonnegut's popular these days. I'm reading Thomas Mann's *Magic Mountain*." He picked it up from the floor and brandished the cover at her. "That is, when I have pleasure-reading time, which is practically nil. Have you read it, Carol?"

"No."

"Well, please do—it's a must. And what about D. H. Lawrence, my current subject? What've you read by him?"

"Um … *Sons and Lovers* … *Lady Chatterley's Lover*," Carol said, hearing the quaver in her voice.

"Not *Women in Love*? What about *The Rainbow*? They're a trilogy, you know—*Sons and Lovers*, *The Rainbow*, and *Women in Love*. They have a lot to do with Lawrence's own life, not to mention his fantasies."

"I saw the movie *Women in Love*," Carol said.

"Oh, so did I—great film. Tell me what you thought."

That I wouldn't want to be your student, Carol thought, facing him and her overall male inquisition, for all three sets of male Cohen eyes trained on her, assessing her. She heard Lola making noise with pots and pans in the kitchen, but it felt too late to follow her there, too awkward to turn and leave in the middle of a conversation focused on her. Feeling desperate, words tumbled from her lips of their own accord, mortifying her more. "I loved Gerald," she said.

Dr. Cohen's eyes lit up and he laughed. "I see," he said. "And what about Gudrun. What about their affair? Who was right? What did you think of them as a couple—their relationship, their antagonism? Were you disturbed by it?"

"She tormented him."

"Aha! But Gerald actually used the word *torture*. He begged Gudrun to stop *torturing* him! But was he innocent?"

"No, he was a cruel chauvinist pig!" Lola barked, marching into the living room, waving a pan top like a cymbal. "A pig capable of murder—he almost killed her."

Dr. Cohen looked delighted. "Tell me why, my darling."

Lola's pan lid swept the air for each point she made. "He treated her like a thing—physically and psychologically. He was a brute. He lacked her intelligence and fought it with inaccessible, unyielding airs that would force her to fight back, so that he—being inferior intellectually—would have to crush her physically."

"Bravo! But, I also contend he loved her and that she was too cruel with her quick tongue."

"He deserved it!"

"He was defenseless and she knew it. She used her weapon relentlessly, she savored her cruelty and its effect."

"Words were her only power against his fists and his misogynist indifference," Lola said. "Love can't exist in a state like that—what kind of love is that? Not love. Men—which Gerald represents—don't need to develop intelligence to fight back when they can annihilate instantly with their hands. Women have only their brains for self-defense!"

"I don't deny it. I grant his social conditioning created relationship barriers in him—"

"Fuck that—it goes way beyond that," Lola hotly cut him off. "His male ego was too all-consuming to ever admit love for a woman."

"But what I wanted to say was how ironic it was that his relationship barriers actually imprisoned him."

"And caused his madness."

"But if only she had been a little more loving, a little kinder, he might have changed and she might have gotten the love she wanted."

"Total fallacy. You know as well as I do that women can't change men. First of all, men will never give up their power. Second, Gerald was never going to come down from his colossal ego that included his superior social class. To love with the soul would mean weakness. But in Gerald's case, the bottom line is, he was violent to women."

"And I accept that, but perhaps because I'm a man, I still feel she drove him to violence, she kept at him until he lost reason. Her unrelenting, cruel spite right in his face drove him to his end. She killed him."

Lola stepped forward, raising her pan lid like a shield or a weapon. "For God's sake, Dad, a man's behavior is his own responsibility, not women's. Gerald's character existed long before he met Gudrun and was the foundation for his suicide."

Carol watched and listened, riveted. The exchange between father and daughter was something that had never happened in her own house. It was communication that went beyond small talk, gossip, and the daily news, and it enthralled her. She longed to join in. She liked such discussions and wanted to read *Women in Love* as soon as she got home.

Dr. Cohen put his hands on the arms of his chair and rose heavily. "Touché, honey. But tell me, those last scenes in the Tyrol—her invective, his brutality—weren't they some of Lawrence's finest writing?"

"Yeah, they're good. I just don't like the men in his books. They're laughably self-centered."

Dr. Cohen stretched fully, and when his arms dropped again, he said happily to Carol, "You're right to love Gerald, Carol, so do I."

Lola huffed with exasperation. "You just don't get it, Dad. Carol loved him only because she felt sorry in the way women are brainwashed and browbeaten to feel by our male-dominated society. Men want us to coddle their remote souls and be 100 percent self-sacrificing, while they retain their right to dominate us with rage and violence." With a last wave of her pan top, she stomped back to the kitchen.

Dr. Cohen's adoring eyes followed her. Carol wondered if his worship was for a daughter made in his own mold—the female version of himself—or for something else, something innate to egocentric men: an ultimate submission to, and relief for, a woman's greater strength, wisdom, and mental acuity—a woman's safe cocoon for a man.

Dr. Cohen stepped around his books and papers on the floor. "We can at least applaud Lawrence for his ceaseless effort to examine love and relationships—their constant and infinite conflicts and contradictions."

"I hope you're coming to help me before I've done everything myself!" Lola yelled from the other room.

"Indeed I am, my darling," he said genially. "The kitchen is not solely women's domain. A man must do his part. I truly believe that."

Carol and the boys set the table while Lola and her father made the dinner—pasta with a broccoli sauce and fresh halibut from one of the local seafood stores. Dr. Cohen wore a lady's apron around his waist, its hemline ruffled. It transformed him, stripped him of his authority and made him more like a teddy bear. And he didn't seem to mind. He fascinated Carol—his lively, talkative, and flamboyant personality that hid his cunning side. How he loved the game of triumphing and was an uncontested pro. And how he loved having his own daughter as his understudy.

When all was ready, Lisa was called to dinner, and her scratchy smoker's voice rasped down at them through the hole at the top of ladder. "All right already, stop your yakking. You'll have to call the fire department if you want me down any sooner."

The smell of smoke descended with her, enveloped her. Her round, wizened face was like an ancient bronze coin, the neck below it unnaturally thick with lines ringing it. Her eyes squinted unhealthily, perhaps from cigarette smoke wafting into them for so many years as she pored over books.

There was no wine, just sodas, and Carol would have liked some wine to feel socially at ease, particularly as Dr. Cohen directed most of the conversation at her, asking questions about her family and herself. He was like a clever detective impartially collecting information but with the ulterior motive of determining her innocence or guilt. At one point, Mrs. Cohen's voice crackled into the midst of the interrogation to say to Carol on her right, "Your father's a very handsome man, and I see your resemblance." Carol felt relief for the compliment—the only thing she had been raised to offer the world.

After that comment, Mrs. Cohen kept her graying head bowed over her plate. She nibbled her food, turning aside frequently to cough painfully into her hand with thick congestion rattling deep in her chest. Throughout the meal, her left hand squeezed and scrunched her nearly empty cigarette pack. When she was done eating, she growled, "Where's my ashtray?"

"It's prohibited to smoke at the table," Lola snapped, getting up to clear the plates.

"Imagine trying to sleep in the room where she's been flicking ashes all day," Dr. Cohen joked with his affable grin.

"Sleep outside in a hammock if it bothers you," Mrs. Cohen retorted.

"Unfortunately, they don't grow trees for a hammock in dumps like this," Dr. Cohen said.

"The real issue is: Why should Daddy have to move for your bad habit?" Lola said, snatching her mother's plate.

"I can't quit, honey, you know that. I'd do it for you in a

heartbeat, if only I could." Her mother's voice was suddenly loving, pleading, as she gazed up at Lola.

"You know perfectly well you're damaging all of our lungs—not just yours. It's selfish not to think of us."

"Thank God your generation's a huge improvement over ours," Mrs. Cohen said, wriggling out of her chair, her back prematurely bent.

Lola flung back hot words as she carried dishes to the kitchen. "Everyone in this family is so self-centered, and I'm sick of it! Daddy's totally wrapped up in feeling supreme, and Mummy's said, 'To hell with all of you, I'm going to smoke myself to death if I want to.'"

"Oh, Lolly! I love it when you take the floor, and I promise I'll quit again as soon as we get home. I just can't do it now, not here," Mrs. Cohen said, and then clambered clumsily up the ladder to her smoker's den.

Carol felt the drama of the Cohen household and wondered if her own home seemed so intense when friends came over. Probably not. Her parents were too self-consciously formal in front of others, and to each other unusually united. As young lovers, they had collaborated on life dreams that they went on to achieve together. That they lacked the main cornerstone of those dreams—a son—didn't stop them from carrying on with "just daughters." It didn't occur to them that they had wounded their girls' souls with their preference for boys and sons—it was just the way the world was, preferring men. Carol's thoughts continued to compare the Cohen's household to her own. Mrs. Cohen's smoking, irascible temperament, and removal from the others for her addiction seemed an unhappy focal point in the family's life, and Lola seemed to be her surrogate—mother, wife.

At bedtime, Dr. Cohen said good night to the boys in their bunks and then came to the girls' room to tuck them in. It was dark, but the hallway cast faint light into the room so that Carol, on the top bunk, could see Dr. Cohen's face and pale, gossamer curls. His mood was tender. He treated them like children. "Are you all snug and comfy?" He adjusted their light covers and continued to linger. Carol felt his reluctance to leave, for where would he go? Back to his lonely chair and diatribe against Kate Millet? No, he wanted to be with people, enjoy intimacy. Upstairs—his final destination—stank of smoke and relative estrangement, probably resentments and hostility. His next words put Carol on the alert, the way so many men, of all ages, had put her on alert during her short lifetime.

"So tell me, young women, do the men at college have good manners? Do you have boyfriends? I hope you don't let boys pressure you into unwanted situations."

"We're fine, Dad, we know how to take care of ourselves."

His face then came close to Carol's upper bunk. He peered at her. She stiffened, afraid. "Does that go for you too?" he asked.

"Yup," she said.

"Good, that's good."

She braced herself as his head tipped closer, as if to kiss her good night. But then he checked himself and said, "Well, good night, my dear ones, get your beauty sleep, tomorrow's our big tournament, ha-ha, girls against the boys." Glee had returned to his voice, and he rubbed his hands in relish, anticipating the match. Carol relaxed, safe again. She thought how for just a moment—when he checked himself—she had seen and felt his vulnerability and deep loneliness.

Carol and Lola went on to whisper for a few more minutes from their respective bunks. Carol told Lola about her summer love interest—the head chef at the restaurant where she was waitressing.

"He's older, thirty, and more experienced. I don't know him that well—we don't talk when we're alone."

"But you're having sex?"

"Well, it's only been once, and he ignores me now."

"Are you sure he's not married?"

"I never thought of that."

"Did you have an orgasm with him?"

"No."

"You know, you should scream when you have an orgasm, let all your feelings out, otherwise you're repressing them."

"Really? I don't think I could scream, it would be too embarrassing."

"It's natural to scream, and it increases your pleasure."

"Who says?"

"My dad, or Masters and Johnson."

"You talk about orgasms with your dad?"

"No, we talk about Masters and Johnson, their research."

"Have you ever screamed?"

The room went quiet, and Carol changed the subject, figuring Lola was still a virgin and didn't want to admit it.

"Why does your mother hole herself up all day?"

"She reads. She says everything else bores her."

"Even her family?"

Lola didn't answer.

"Does she still write?"

"I don't know."

"You don't know if your mother writes?"

"She probably does, but I don't live at home anymore, and even if I did, she's never liked talking about her writing. She feels she sacrificed it for us."

"Yikes."

Another pause followed. Carol hoped Lola would say more about her mother, but she didn't.

"I guess if she's alone all day, she can smoke in peace," Carol said.

"Right. She's an addict, and addicts are in the power of their substance."

Carol didn't know what to say to this, but luckily Lola went on, revealing a family secret in a brusque, clinical tone. "I never told you before, but my grandmother committed suicide when my mom was thirteen."

"Oh," Carol breathed in shock. "That's terrible, I'm so sorry."

"Yeah. It's probably why she's such a recluse. She was different when we were little—more involved. But pain and grief grow on you if you don't deal with your traumas. Dad's different, he's an extrovert and likes people. He's open about his life—the hard knocks he experienced to get where he is. They weren't so bad, actually. He got scholarships all the way."

"He's lonely," Carol said, startling herself. Yet her words

were true. He was warm and affectionate and didn't have a partner who reciprocated. In a way, Lola filled that role for him, the way they argued and cooked together, the way they managed family life. It was as if he had raised her to be the kind of woman he would have liked to be if he had been born female. Maybe that was why Lola defied some of his hopes and dreams for her—maybe she didn't want his vision, his mold plunked down on her. Maybe that was why she was angry inside, terse outside. And what about her grandmother? Did she worry that her grandmother's descent into a personal hell was related to her mother's antisocial behavior? Did she worry about her own future in the female line? Carol had so many questions now that she was briefly inside the Cohen family fold.

"Let's go to sleep now. It's been a long day. I'm glad you're here," Lola said, putting an end to further conversation, but for the first time mentioning appreciation for their odd friendship, something Carol also felt but for different reasons—Lola was a mentor for her.

A few summers later, when Carol was home from graduate school in New York and Lola was finishing law school in Cambridge, they went to Castle Hill for a concert on the mansion's lawn next to a long greensward that flowed like a river to the sea. Duke and Will came with them, Will finally catching up in age as a college sophomore. The car ride to Ipswich was full of lively talk, everyone excited to be together for a special cultural event. How different it was from those times when Carol had been alone with Lola and everything felt ultraserious, as if laughing and joking were frivolous. On the other hand, Carol knew she was frivolous in comparison to Lola. She still partied and drank too much. She did worry about her bad habits but hadn't yet turned her back on them. She had grown up with party-people parents, their cabinets filled with glassware for every kind of drink. Booze bottles lined the back of a kitchen counter—the bar. Now, after nearly a decade of use, she was aware of her dependency and assured herself she'd quit as soon as her stressful student life ended. But then there would be job hunting and full-time work, endless responsibilities. She knew there would always be the same stress in her life and she was only postponing the truth—the harder road to take.

Halfway to Castle Hill, Carol realized she had forgotten her need for wine to loosen up socially. Conversation was flowing naturally, animatedly, with Lola contributing stories, quips, and laughter. From the wheel, Carol kept glancing at her in the passenger seat, amazed to see her face lit up, her blue eyes dancing with high spirits. It was a transformation, a Lola she had never seen—the yearbook Lola—but her brothers knew this Lola and adored her.

The upbeat car ride set the mood for the concert that followed on the mansion's lawn with its view of the estate's long green slope to the sea, a sea that joined the horizon under miles of sky. They sat in white chairs on the lawn, transported by the quartet's music to the realm of the evening's golden light. Afterward, in a transcendent state, they milled around the hilltop, keeping close to one another, for the music had joined them in spirit. Voices and light laughter rose from other parts of the lawn—no one was in a hurry to leave the sublime setting and mood. Carol was feeling kinship with the Cohens, her insides humming. Her eyes met young Will's at close range. She saw the gray-violet pupils bright and curious, the lips curved in his usual half smile. He was short with broad shoulders and the body of a rugby player. His voice was softly husky, and in contrast to his brother and sister, who resembled their father, his features had been chiseled symmetrically, with high cheekbones, a square jaw, and deep-set eyes that his silky bangs shadowed alluringly. His face had beauty like a wooden carving, and Carol felt glad for him.

Lola wandered to the lawn's edge and looked out at its long cascade to the sea. While her brothers talked about music and past favorite concerts, Carol listened with only half an ear, for her attention was on Lola and her dreamy gaze on the distant sea. To Carol, she was a figure from poetry and paintings through the ages—a young woman in a soft white dress that fluttered lightly in the summer breeze, her heart yearning for true love—the man who would suddenly materialize and sweep her away to their blissful, ever-after life. That image brought Judy Collins's song to mind: "Will there never be a prince who rides along the sea and the mountains, scattering the sand and foam into amethyst fountains, riding up the hills from the beach in the long summer grass, holding the sun in his hands and shattering the isinglass." For just that moment, time stood still as the wistful music seemed to encompass Lola's solitary figure. Would the cosmos ever answer her? Carol wondered if a young person's inner yearning, inner sadness and aloneness, slowly aged into grief.

Lola turned at that moment and looked at Carol, as if sensing her eyes on her. The magical spell broke for both of them. But ever after, Carol felt Lola's soul—the tender soul that the egocentric world of achievement had forced her to bury. Carol had glimpsed the sweet, vulnerable, loving Lola who dreamed of a prince charming sweeping her up on a horse and riding away.

Another year went by. Carol stayed on in New York after finishing her master's degree. She got a job at the independent high school in Harlem where she had interned all year. The students came from disadvantaged homes and neighborhoods, and most were dropouts from the public schools. In its decade of operation, the school had sent more than half of its graduates on to college. Carol loved being part of the school's open-minded, motivated atmosphere. Teachers and students learned together. Her work was the one good thing in her life. The rest seemed a morass. She still pursued a decadent lifestyle with her housemates. The rare times when she retreated to her room and sat before her typewriter to write, nothing happened. Nor could she concentrate when reading for pleasure. Unless she was out reveling with her crowd, she felt lost, with no inkling of how to navigate herself to a better place. Every morning she tried to counter her lost self with a long jog through Central Park, all the while her teeth gritted in determination. School was her only wholesome place.

For a year, she had been engaged to Ian Quinn, an ambitious, conceited architect she had met her second year of graduate school. But as their June wedding date approached, she had backed out. He was too condescending for her to ever feel worthwhile. In their aftermath, she faced creating the rest of her life on her own without Ian in front of her like a shield. Somehow she had to find the way out of her rut, remake herself into a fully capable person, but her body and mind were inert. Her lifestyle with her housemates didn't help. Together, they partied, went out to bars, danced at clubs, and got high in order to feel alive through their senses. But what they were really feeling was their craving for love and fulfillment. They were riding the wilder side of the social revolution—an escape from the truth that their lives were headed nowhere if they continued this lifestyle. Carol knew this. She saw they were all floundering despite holding jobs. Like so many young adults set free to fulfill their dreams, there was no ready road, no open door, waiting for them.

When the school's summer program ended, Carol drove home for a week's vacation, imagining a long rest. As she stared through the car's windshield at the long highway between green trees, she was barely aware of driving, for thoughts crowded and clouded her mind. She felt disembodied, disconnected. Nothing about her hung together, and she couldn't even counsel herself in her usual pragmatic ways. She was out of effort, out of inner coherence, but where could she turn to for help, when no help could ever hope to reach the place she was stuck in.

As she parked in the driveway of her family's suburban home, Carol dreaded facing her parents, especially her mother. Her sisters were off pursuing their own lives, and it would be just the three of them at dinnertime. Her mother heard the car door shut and came out to the portico just as Carol arrived to its steps with her suitcase. She saw her mother's instant frown of judgment—something she always dreaded.

"You've gained weight," her mother said.

"Yeah, I've gotta lose it."

They hugged stiffly, Mrs. Edmund's disapproval blocking love.

Those first days home, Carol was careful to avoid her parents. It was too painful to see their looks of disappointment, disapproval, and their preoccupation with how she was ever going to get back on track—that is, back to good looks to attract a husband. She knew they talked about her in private and regretted her breakup with Ian—the ideal partner in their opinion. She could imagine their laments: If only she had married him, she'd now be the proud mistress of an Upper East Side apartment instead of a scourge on them—an unwed, unwanted, old-maid daughter.

Carol lay on her bed for hours those first days, her mind clogged with excruciating pain she could not dissolve. She felt trapped in a hellhole, its evil encasement suffocating her. And it was all her fault, she was a terrible person and would always be so. Nothing was going to change for her, nothing would ever fix it. This was how it was and would always be, and she had to stop the agony—but how? As the images of ways to stop the pain rose before her, she pulled a pillow over her face—no, she couldn't do any of those things—gun, water, pills, cliff—none of it possible. Then how would she get herself out of this unendurable place?

Just before her vacation ended, Lola phoned and invited her for dinner. "I heard through the grapevine you were home."

"You mean my mother's telephone line."

"Probably."

"Thanks, I'd love to come, tell me what to bring. And sorry I haven't called—it's been … super busy here."

"Come around seven. I work till five and have a long commute."

"Where are you working?"

"I'll tell you everything tonight."

Carol felt relief that she'd be seeing Lola. She longed to confess her sins, her state of nowhere land, and receive advice, direction, encouragement—Lola, her surrogate boss. All day as she watched the clock, she placed new hope in Lola. She went out for a long jog on the pretty, peaceful roads to kill time, and when her mother was out, she unlocked her father's wine cellar and took a bottle of cabernet that wasn't likely to be missed. Punctually at seven, she arrived at Lola's apartment on a tree-lined street in Porter Square. She rang the bell of the first-floor apartment in a large clapboard house with an old-fashioned porch. Lola greeted her in her formal way, eyes never meeting for long. She took the wine bottle and led them to the kitchen. She put the wine aside, disappointing Carol, for she wanted an immediate aperitif to loosen up. But she was also wary of showing her need.

Lola moved about the kitchen and Carol followed her with her eyes. Lola looked much the same as in the past—impeccably groomed in a summer dress, blond hair gleaming to her shoulders, handmade jewelry, and pump sandals giving her height and glamor. Her apartment mirrored her taste, with its hardwood floors, built-in cabinetry, and attractive furnishings—a lifestyle Carol envied.

"I made lentil soup."

"It smells good."

"I'm into vegetarian food." She picked up the wooden spoon on the stovetop and stirred the soup.

"You always liked cooking," Carol said.

"I still do. It relaxes me. My work's incredibly stressful."

"So tell me what you're doing."

"Legal aid for battered women. We serve a center in Roxbury. Some of the women are homeless with children, and a lot of them live in fear of being murdered. You wouldn't believe what these women have experienced in their lives, starting in childhood. I love my work, but it's also hard to take. Every day while I'm talking to the women, I'm thinking how these are real lives, real women's lives, and nothing's being done for them—everywhere, throughout the world—just band-aid efforts like ours. We need education, laws, integration, and protection programs that lead to safe futures, to futures period. But that's not going to happen, Carol, no one cares enough to change society for those in need—and that goes for mental health too. So many need help for their sanity, not revolving doors that perpetuate the problem. People just care about money—for themselves." Without glancing at Carol she added, "I see you've gained weight."

"Yeah, I have to do something about it."

"You're lucky you have good looks—you can almost get away with it."

Almost. Carol's eyes closed in shame, and her fantasies of unloading her angst to Lola vanished. They were too different. Lola was too strict, too harsh, too quick to judge and blame.

Carol's throat ached with longing for the wine, for a gulp of the red liquid that would momentarily dissolve her despair. But then, Lola would be watching her, frowning every time she lifted the wineglass to her lips. Suddenly, the medium-size hangover she had awoken with began to press against the inner walls of her skull.

"Is it because of your breakup? I heard about Ian from my mother," Lola said, stirring the soup.

"I don't know, it's probably related."

"Your mother told everyone he was any woman's dream."

"Yeah, my mother's dream—super good-looking with a job at the best architectural firm in New York."

"Jeez, what went wrong?"

"Everything. He was unacceptably condescending."

"Couldn't you work it out? Talk it over? All relationships need constant work."

"I tried talking to him, lots of times. I explained how I felt when he put me down, and that's when he'd get even nastier."

"Maybe you should have seen a couples therapist to wake him up."

"We saw one. But it didn't help. It was clear he wasn't going to change. He didn't believe he needed to."

"So you gave up."

"Yeah, the day he looked down his snotty nose at me and said, 'You have above-average intelligence, Carol, but I happen to have above-above-average intelligence.'"

Lola threw down the wooden spoon. "Good riddance! He didn't deserve you."

Carol felt a wave of gratitude. She hadn't expected such support. Ian and all of society had convinced her that he was superior, in the right.

"I'm glad it's over. I couldn't see myself as a bride anyway—putting on a frilly white dress and becoming a man's wife."

"Really? If I ever get married, I want to wear the most beautiful white dress."

"But it's a symbol of women's subordination to men—the pure virgin becoming a man's property—his chattel."

"I don't see it that way."

Carol fell silent. Lola, though a feminist, didn't see everything through the lens of gender inequality the way Carol did. And Carol's viewpoint had reached a pitch where she didn't know what to think or do about being "feminine." She didn't know what was "natural-born girl" in her versus what was born of chauvinism's dictate. After her breakup with Ian, she had begun stripping herself of any item associated with the world view of femininity, hoping to see her true self in the mirror and find out if the outer world—male-controlled—could accept her as her true self. She questioned whether earrings, makeup, and white wedding dresses were true expressions of a woman's biological femininity, or *man*dated ornaments to please and empower men and ensure their entitlement, egos, and control. Carol didn't know where to turn with her jumbled thoughts, she didn't know how to come out of the fog and know what was right for her as a woman. In the meantime, she wore unisex clothes—pants and shirts.

"Could we please open the wine, Lo?"

"Okay, if you insist. I was going to wait for dinner." She rummaged in a drawer for a corkscrew and handed it to Carol, whose hands tremblingly worked the cork out of the bottle. She poured herself a full glass and gratefully sipped the red ambrosia that sent instant relief through her system.

"What about your love life, anything going on?" she said to Lola.

"Nope. I dated an attorney for a few months, but it fizzled out."

"Sorry..."

"I'm not. You know when it's not right. You know by week five or six. It became clear he just wanted to see me at dinnertime, so that someone was feeding him."

Carol laughed. "That's awful."

Lola dished the soup into bowls. "It's actually pretty common. Men want to be taken care of so they're free for everything else. But, the pool's out there, Carol—and you'll meet someone soon."

"I really don't want to. I'm angry with men right now. They're all chauvinist pigs."

Lola grimaced and marched the steaming bowls to the

dining room table. "You could always afford to be a man-hater, Carol, but you'd better watch out and not let yourself go."

"Who cares?" Carol flashed back defensively. "I'm not just a sex object!"

For the first time that evening, Lola shot her one of her scathing looks. "When you're lucky enough to be born with good looks, you owe it to yourself to take care of them."

Her words struck Carol powerfully. For a few seconds she couldn't move while Lola's words reverberated in her head—"You owe it to yourself, you owe it to yourself!"

After the meal, they went to the living room. Lola told Carol to lie down on the couch. "I know how to make your headache feel better."

"How do you know I have a headache?"

"Because you keep rubbing your head."

Carol complied, feeling a bit uneasy about resting her head in Lola's lap. Was Lola a lesbian? She needed to make her boundaries clear.

"Relax," Lola ordered.

Carol relaxed, closing her eyes. She felt Lola's self-assured fingers applying just the right amount of pressure to key spots for headache relief—the hollows at the bridge of her nose, the back of her jaw. Minutes passed peacefully as Lola performed her therapy, palms now resting lightly on the sides of Carol's face, as if communicating a healing energy. At the end of the session, she instructed Carol to breathe slowly through one nostril at a time, while she controlled which nostril with the tip of her finger. Carol, already feeling better, thought how Lola was always learning new things that benefited herself and others. In the years of their on-again, off-again friendship, Lola had always shown her the pursuit of self-fulfillment and self-care, and Carol had persisted in being wasteful. As she lay like a patient under her friend's helping hands, she once again heard her words, "You owe it to yourself." They were a game changer, and she vowed to change her life, even if it took a long time. She had twenty-five years of unlearning to do, besides self-resurrection, for any transformation was going to depend on her alone.

The following June, on a Saturday morning, Carol's doorbell rang. She still shared an apartment with her partying housemates in Morningside Heights, though she had cleaned up her own lifestyle to some extent, staying clean from Sunday till Friday.

"Who's there?" she called through the old wood door.

"It's Will, Will Cohen."

Will Cohen. Lola's little brother. She opened the door to his fresh young face and artless smile.

"Will … what're you doing here?"

He shook his bangs from his eyes, his hair still long and silky. He was cute. "I'm here for the summer. Your mom gave me your address, but I lost your phone number."

"Come in," she smiled, feeling pleased to see an old family friend from home.

He came in. "I have an internship with a professor at Columbia."

"Ah, one of your dad's cronies," Carol joked.

He laughed. "You got it. What are you up to? Are you free? Do you want to get coffee or take a walk? It's beautiful out."

"Sure, I'd love to. I'll get my shoes, my bag. Where are you living?"

"In the West Village, I have a summer sublet from a professor who's on sabbatical."

"Another friend of your dad's."

"Actually, yes," he grinned. "Dad knows a lot of people."

"And isn't afraid of asking. I'll be right back," Carol said, her eyes quickly sweeping the living room for what Will was taking in—the shabby thrift store furniture, pop-culture posters, old plants on the radiator by the clouded windows, and a coffee table littered with Friday night's empties. Twenty people had been there.

Carol headed to the bathroom and quickly brushed her hair and teeth. She looked fine in the mirror. She had lost her excess weight from the year before, mainly from drinking less, but she hated herself for still wanting wine and battling its pull, for looking forward to Friday night and its release to wine. She hated herself not being able to shed the destructive habit.

She returned to Will smiling and hiding all her inner qualms and secrets about herself. They set out for their walk in Central Park, talking easily, convivially, as they strolled along, as if they were longtime friends or relatives who instantly connected. Will described his major, a new branch in history called "new social history."

"It focuses on the '60s and '70s social transformations,"

he said. "And I have minor in psych. I love psych—and this period is full of it—gender, relationships, sexuality. I'm studying race and popular causes. I've just finished writing a paper about 1969's campus unrest, and my father's helping me get it published. He knows people at the new social history journals. What about you, Carol—are you still writing?"

"Yeah, and papering my walls with rejections, as the saying goes. I could use your dad's influence."

"Don't feel too bad, rejections are normal—even my mother got them. Any chance I could read one of your stories? I'd love that."

"Sure, I'll give you one." But instant warning bells went off in her head. If she gave a story to Will, it was likely to travel on to Dr. Cohen's hands, at his own request. And she could just imagine him settling down in his armchair with keen anticipation of what she had *tried* to write, and then laughing heartily at her amateurish effort. No, she wouldn't be giving any of her stories to Will.

"How about we go to Union Square and check out the bookstores?" Will said. "If you're free, that is."

"I'm free, no plans, let's do it," Carol agreed. "I love bookstores."

"Me too."

They left the park and caught a train downtown. They stood in the middle cavity, facing each other, their hands holding a pole. Standing still like that in close proximity felt intimate. Their invisible body energies communicated. Their eyes had to meet while the train rattled along. Will was only an inch or two taller than Carol and had a nice body—

straight shoulders and strong limbs. He might end up stocky in mid-life but now, in his early twenties, he was lean and attractively proportioned. His company made Carol happy. He was positive and curious, warm and friendly, so much so that she didn't feel her usual barriers, the ones caused by her secrets about herself, her lack of self-belief and her drinking to escape it, which only worsened her problem. It was a vicious circle. She wondered about her ancestors, both the nearer and distant ones. Had genes through the millennia carried the same kind of pain that sought solace? And her predecessors' pain was far worse than anything she herself had ever experienced, having grown up in a sheltered, affluent milieu. Her thousands of years of ancestors had dealt with wars, hunger, torture, terror, and migration, and the women—her own female genes—had suffered rape and violence at the hands of men. She was the embodiment of all those other generations of wounded souls before her. But good things were also in her ancestral genes—overall family love, or at least cohesion—and moments of joy and lots of laughter. Creativity had come down the lines to her. So many of her near ancestors had been artists, able to express life's beauty and mystery despite their heavy smoking and drinking. The upshot was, the good and the bad lived in all of them, and life itself was composed of thousands of opposites. So, it was up to her to bring into balance her own life's opposing forces. They were totally out of whack, dependent on other people's approval instead of her own self-love, and she couldn't have self-love till she balanced the forces at war inside her.

"A penny for your thoughts," Will said.

She looked up and found his shadowy, perceptive eyes intent on her. "Just daydreaming," she smiled.

He smiled back, that sweet half-smile of his. A long look passed between them and in it was a definite man-woman intimacy. They were riding the subway together, a pair. Their hands were only an inch apart on the pole, their heads nearly as close. Their look into each other's eyes conveyed a natural and mutual attraction. It was so easy being together.

The lovely spell broke for Carol when Lola came to mind. Will was Lola's brother. Lola would be shocked and angry if Carol got involved with her brother. Carol was five years older and corrupt compared to Will's fresh, questing spirit. No, she could never face Lola—nor Dr. Cohen—if she got involved with him. It was out of the question.

The train squealed to a stop at their station, and as the crowd moved to exit, Will reached back and offered his hand to Carol to thread her through. The rest of the day sped by in pleasant, even tantalizing companionship. For more than an hour they roamed the used bookstore that claimed eighteen miles of books. Wandering between the towering aisles, they talked continuously, happy and at home in the environment of their shared passions—books, authors, stories, histories, and the arts. A few times, they sat down on the floor, shoulders pressed together, to pore over an old favorite, discussing what they loved about it. Being together flowed seamlessly, and with only looks and body language they had acknowledged romantic involvement. For the rest of the day, the titillating anticipation of new lovers and what lay ahead once they were alone added to their pleasure of being together.

At dinnertime, Will led them to a place he liked in the Village, a lively, crowded place that smelled of hamburger grease and stale beer. Perhaps it reminded him of his college hangouts in Cambridge, Carol thought. The decor had appeal—trendy with a high ceiling showing pipes and vents. Rough-hewn tables and chairs fit the rustic decor and plank floor. A busy waiter seated them at a table by the wall, and Will ordered a carafe of the house red wine. They looked at their greasy, tattered menus.

"You have to try their grilled potatoes," Will said, pointing to a picture of them on his menu. "They're known for them."

"I smell them." Carol said. Her taste in food was healthier, like Lola's, but she was happy to be here with Will. She took a first sip of the purple wine Will had poured for her. It tasted horribly sour and made her wince, but she quickly hid her reaction, especially as she welcomed the buzz the wine would bring. She sipped again and heard her gut protest loudly that the wine was rock gut stuff, and after the previous night's party could not be handled.

The noise was loud, making conversation hard because they had to shout. It was easier when their hamburgers and grilled potatoes arrived because they could eat and talk less. But the food was not going down well for Carol. She hadn't eaten a hamburger in years, and her already compromised ecosystem began to grind away in what felt like a desperate effort to digest the fatty beef and oil-soaked potatoes. She drank a gulp of wine, hoping it would sweep the food through her. But that was a fatal choice. Her stomach lurched in rebellion. She hastily excused herself to go to the ladies' room, where her guts erupted. For the rest of the meal, she feigned good humor and didn't touch another morsel or sip of the dangerous meal. Her stomach continued to grind away, as if fighting for its life, and cramping now and then as if in need of another purge. Her condition was all she could think about, and her anxiety only made it worse.

"You okay?" Will asked as they got up to leave.

"Fine," she smiled, fakely. Surely he could detect her lie with his acute sensitivity.

"You didn't like the food. It was really greasy, wasn't it? I feel bad for suggesting this place."

"Don't worry, it's got great atmosphere."

"Yeah, I think that's why I thought the potatoes were so good. But they weren't. The food was crummy and the wine was disgusting."

She smiled, he smiled back. They held hands leaving. They held hands from then on.

Outside, the night sky and cool air refreshed them and soothed their ears, no longer subjected to the din inside. They began walking hesitantly, for a destination needed to be voiced.

Will glanced at Carol. "Um … would you like to see my place? It's only a few blocks from here."

"Sure, let's see it."

It was decided. They were going to his place, where only one thing would happen. But it was still unknown how it would play out, and for the first time that day, both of them became quiet, a bit nervous about the physical connection that was so much more personal and revealing than any-thing they had yet experienced together. During the short walk to his townhouse on a picturesque, tree-lined street, they squeezed each other's hand every now and then to convey their connection.

They entered the dark house, and Will didn't bother turning on the lights. He paused to listen for a second. "No one's home," he said, and gave her hand a tug to lead her upstairs.

His room in the grouphouse was down a narrow hall. As soon as they crossed the threshold, he pulled them both down onto the twin bed with a happy laugh. Kissing began, their bodies pressed together—the contact and connection they had been waiting for most of the day. Their hands felt each other's bodies, and soon helped each other shed clothes so their legs could tangle up. Soon they were making love, and under normal circumstances, Carol would have been lost to that sensual realm, but her tummy had begun to churn and groan with Will's weight and movements on top of her. She felt alarm that she might lose her guts again.

Will's sensitive antennae picked up on her distraction, and he lifted his head above hers. "Am I hurting you?"

"No, sorry, it's just ... I have to go to the bathroom."

"Oh, it's just down the hall, on the left, do you want me to show you?"

"No, I can find it."

She fled naked down the hallway hoping his housemates hadn't come home. She reached her destination just in time. Everything in her rushed out with those horribly embarrassing human noises she felt sure Will could hear. She buried her face in her hands and wondered how she could ever face him—or herself—again.

Finally, she tiptoed out of the bathroom into the dark hallway, hoping to be invisible, hoping the passage of time had erased all remembrance of her episode.

But Will was right there in the hall, having heard the bathroom door carefully open. He, too, was naked, and she saw his beautiful jock body in the darkness, perfectly proportioned. She despaired at having gotten involved with him.

"Are you all right?" He came up close and touched her arm.

She flinched. She didn't deserve niceness. "Something didn't agree with me, those potatoes."

"And the wine, total crap. I'm so sorry, my fault for taking you there. Can I make you some herbal tea?"

So like his sister, a healer, a caretaker. "No, I'm just embarrassed."

She saw his deep-set eyes in the dark, his half-smile. "Don't be embarrassed about nature."

His voice, so kind, was off-limits for her. He was too good. "I'm so sorry," she said.

"Ssh, don't be. It was bad food." They went back to his room, sex obviously out of the question for the rest of the night.

"You need to rest, let everything settle." He coaxed her back to the bed and pulled the sheet over her. Then he sat down beside her and smoothed the cover over her shoulders.

How sweet he was. It made her feel worse, like she was a wasted woman having sex with an innocent young man who deserved true love, not a one-nighter with a wino. She ached to go home but had no energy or will to get up and embark on the long trip uptown, whether by taxi or the subway. She was too afraid of another emergency.

"I can sleep on the living room couch," he said.

"Don't be ridiculous, this is your room, your bed. I'll go home in a few minutes."

"Wait, I have a sleeping bag. I'll put it here next to the bed."

She lifted her left arm to half-hug him. "You're too good. Come on, we can lie here together." She moved over, and he, with a breath of gratitude, curled up next to her, his leg going over her thigh and his head resting in the crevice of her neck. Soon she heard his even breathing.

She never slept that night, but did the meditative breathing she had learned. At dawn's first dusky light, she quietly rose and dressed. She leaned down and kissed Will goodbye. He roused sleepily and asked, "Where are you going? How's your stomach? When can we see each other again? Do you have to go?"

She ruffled his silky hair and kissed his forehead. She thanked him for the lovely day and his kindness later on. Then she left and gratefully stepped out into the cool, slightly garbage-smelling Manhattan morning. To be alone, with just herself and the morning air felt so good, so free from all her worries and shame. She walked to Union Square and caught the subway home.

Around noon that day, Will called her, concerned for her health.

"I'm all better, thanks, and again, sorry for last night."

"And again, don't be sorry."

The line went quiet for a beat, then Will said, "Can I come by? I want to see you. We could take a walk or just hang out."

"No, I'm so sorry, I can't see you, Will."

"Why? It can't be because…"

"It's not fair to you, that's all."

"What? Because you're older? I really like you, Carol, and I can take care of myself."

"No, I just don't feel right about it."

He gave a hoarse laugh. "It's not such a big age difference, not for me. It's so obvious we enjoy the same things. I had a wonderful day with you. Unfortunately, you ate bad food and wine, but that wasn't your fault. It was my fault. I'm never going back there."

She didn't want to talk about that horrible experience that mortified her. "You need a real relationship, something beautiful, and I can't give you that. It's not about the bad food." It's about the bad me, she said to herself.

He was silent, pondering. Perhaps he had missed her point or just wanted to ignore it, for then he said, "Last night—it shouldn't influence you. I know I gave a bad performance—"

"What? I wasn't thinking that at all."

"You weren't? Really?"

"Yes, really. You were fine."

"Well, that's a relief to hear. Even if I wasn't. But thanks for pretending I was."

Carol shook her head in amazement. His word "performance" echoed in her ears—where had he learned to think about his lovemaking as a good or bad "performance"?

From his father? From his peers? From society? And that idea was what he worried about—his performance—not her disgrace. Oh, well, it didn't matter, she wasn't going to be in a relationship with him.

"I'm sorry, Will," she whispered firmly.

"Yeah, me too. Well, you have my number. We could still be friends. I like you, Carol."

She never saw him again. Her remorse for that night had one good outcome. It intensified her determination to make good on her life. She thought how uncanny it was that first Lola and now Will had sparked her intention to take on the arduous work of undoing—or healing—her past, including her ancestral DNA, the unwanted traits, and becoming herself.

In the weeks and months that followed, Carol made changes in her life. She moved into a small place of her own and began seeing a therapist to open up and reveal all her secrets. She joined a yoga studio and a women's writing group—the latter like a support group. The women shared everything—their writing, the books they loved, their relationships, and any problems that arose. It was a sisterhood, caring and regenerating.

By wintertime, Carol found herself dating again, this time with men whose looks weren't the first criteria. And she was taking pleasure in being a woman and feeling her femininity. Her curiosity returned and her enjoyment of people and group activities. In the new year, she attended a conference for overseas jobs and met Michael Blaine, another teacher. They immediately clicked, and from the start, Carol knew that Michael was different in the long-term way. Their combination felt right—as best friends, as lovers, as soulmates. They applied for jobs in Mexico City, got them, and married that summer before leaving the States. Lola came to the wedding and the party afterward at a venue in Boston. When the dancing got underway, she and Carol had a fun girls' dance together, full of smiles and warm, sisterly affection. They bumped hips playfully and twirled under each other's arms. It was the first time they had ever been that way with each other, and Carol felt it was Lola's send-off to her for her next chapter in life, one that had Lola's blessing.

A few years went by. When Carol and Michael came home in the summertime to visit their families, they hardly had time to see old friends. Their sisters and brothers had started families, and those reunions were more important. But Mrs. Edmund, ever the faithful letter writer, sent updates about family friends, including the Cohens. "Everyone's happy that Lola has finally met someone," she wrote. "He's a lawyer with political ambitions—planning to run for Congress—a true Democrat. Everyone likes him." Carol formed an image of Lola with her future husband—a young, energetic man with all the qualities and values Lola embraced for her own life. When the wedding invitation came to Mexico, Carol sent her regrets that included a loving note for her friend's future happiness.

Afterward, Mrs. Edmund sent a lengthy description of the wedding, with a critical assessment of Dr. Cohen's toast. "It was a bit unusual, in my opinion. He sounded like he was her former lover conceding the joy of his life to an inferior competitor. I couldn't help wondering what Lisa was thinking as she listened to all that. After all he's *her* husband, not Lola's." Carol remembered her Nantucket weekend with the Cohens and Dr. Cohen's unusually symbiotic relationship with Lola. She wasn't surprised by his speech, though it must have been somewhat uncomfortable for the guests and probably for Lola too. And maybe, knowing Dr. Cohen, it was really directed at Lola to ruffle her magical day and train the limelight on himself.

A year later came the news that the Cohens were getting divorced and that Lisa had moved into an apartment. "Lola is terribly upset, or so I'm told," Mrs. Edmund wrote.

Carol digested this news without writing to Lola—after all, Lola hadn't sent her the news herself, and they hadn't been in touch since her wedding invitation. Distance was growing. Mexico was too far away to keep in touch.

Mrs. Edmund's next letter shared that Dr. Cohen was now engaged to one of Lola's girlfriends from law school. "I heard that Lola's furious. It's a thirty-year age difference. She takes it as a betrayal, though I'm not sure why, since many men remarry much younger women."

In time, more news came in Mrs. Edmund's fine penmanship. "I haven't met Sol's new wife yet, and frankly, our social lives have taken different directions since the divorce. As for Lola, I'm told she's been trying to get pregnant for some time but without success. She's now working with a fertility clinic and taking pills. I hope they work for her—the family's breakup has been very hard for her, and having a baby, a family of her own, would surely help her. They say that stress prevents conception—this may be her problem. I'm glad your own life is less stressful, and that soon we'll be meeting your new son or daughter. I'm thrilled for you, Carol. Everything has turned out so nicely for your life. I keep hoping you and Michael will eventually look for jobs here, so we can see more of you. We all miss you so much."

Then came Mrs. Edmund's letter with the devastating news that Lola had taken her life. The shock to Carol was so strong that the baby inside kicked hard against her belly, as if demanding less constriction in the womb. Carol held her tummy comfortingly and moved to an armchair. Tears burned her eyes. Her mind refused to assimilate the news. How could this have happened? Why Lola? And how uncanny that their original trajectories in high school and young adulthood had suddenly switched places. Carol had somehow managed to crawl out of an obliterating dark, while Lola, always moving with intention, had somehow turned downward into the abyss. No, Carol couldn't imagine Lola suffering there, agonizing alone in a broken state, suffocating with mental pain too great to bear. And what of Will? And Dr. Cohen? Had one of Lola's motives been to punish him?—"So there! I'm going to make you suffer!" So many ingredients had led to this wretched moment, and now everything had toppled to rubble in their family, for Lola had been their center, their beloved.

Carol sat in a stupor, hands still resting on her round baby bump. Thoughts ricocheted in her mind. She and Lola had been friends but never intimate. Lola had always been tossing Carol a lifeline, helping her. Now Lola was dead and Carol hadn't been there to do the same for her. Would she even have noticed that Lola needed help? Probably not, given Lola's secrecy about her feelings. The deed was done. Lola was gone. Carol could only grieve, and her grief wondered at the irony that the woman who was dead by her own hand was the same one who had opened the first game-changing crack in Carol's own pain with her words, "You owe it to yourself."

Day at Wakan Lake

W HEN THEY ARRIVED late morning at Wakan Lake in the Blue Ridge foothills, Ethan and Meredith found a long line of cars waiting to pay an entrance fee at the gate. Ethan, behind the wheel, growled as he joined the line, "Piss off, we have to pay to get in." The state park was known for its massive granite rock overlooking the lake, and Meredith, gazing through the windshield, could already see numerous bodies dangling from ropes on the rock face.

"Piss off," Ethan repeated, inching the car forward. Meredith knew that his griping was nothing more than his personality, a kind of cynical humor. She herself was the breezy type, a good counterforce to his nerves—his beard-tugging and long-hair twirling. As they waited in line, she rested her right elbow on the open window and admired herself in the side-view mirror. She loved her lush auburn hair and liked to fluff its waves. For their day at the lake, she was dressed incongruously in a long, floral gown of clingy jersey material. It buttoned down the front, all the way from the V-neck to her ankles. From the knees down, she had left the buttons open to allow flashes of her legs. She felt sexy all over and wholly into herself, making it easy to ignore Ethan's irritation, which she knew was only a habitual quirk.

As Ethan drew up to the entrance booth, Meredith read out the various fees on a big green sign tacked to the front. "Imagine what it takes to run this place," she said. "What's $2.50 to us?" She reached into her canvas bag for the money. Ethan's slender hand with delicate dark hairs on the fingers took the bills. A young ranger was waiting to receive them. As Ethan handed over the money, his free hand fiddled with his beard. Beginning at age ten, when he had developed an ulcer, his hair had begun to gray, so that now, at nineteen, the black curls were threaded with gray, as was his beard. He was handsome, with a triangular face well-suited to the beard's lines. His nose was sharply chiseled and his hazel eyes were as round and beautiful as a baby's, the upper lids fringed with curly black lashes. The black eyebrows arched pertly.

The boyish ranger standing in the booth's doorway took the money. His felt hat, with its leather chin strap and shiny metallic seal in the middle, made him look like a Wild West sheriff. It was the start of the 1970s, when cops, or anyone in law enforcement uniform, provoked the young social revolutionaries to spit out: "Pig!" But Ethan, who had to say something to the ranger, merely griped in his usual way. "I can't understand why we have to cough up money to enjoy the outdoors we pay for in taxes. It's wrong. And it excludes the poor from getting out of the city and away from their burdens."

The ranger smiled hesitantly, not sure if Ethan's complaint

was just a weird way of joshing. "Got lots of folks saying the same thing," he answered in the pleasant, empty-headed American way Ethan detested. "But ya know, we gotta pay for all the maintenance around here—the cleanup, the trails, the campsites, the bathrooms—and we gotta make sure visitors obey the rules."

"You mean pay you guys to police innocent citizens," Ethan said.

"Yeah, I guess, if you want to put it that way. Here, want our map?"

"Yes," Meredith said, leaning across Ethan to take it, but her hand didn't quite reach the ranger's, so she said, "Take it, Ethan, it's free! And sir, could you recommend the best trail for hiking—one that gets away from the crowd?"

Ethan's hand snatched the map from the ranger while he simultaneously gunned the gas and let out the clutch, sending the car flying over potholes into the dirt parking lot. "Why did you say that, Merri? Now he's going to alert one of those patrols to keep an eye on us." He mimicked the ranger's voice speaking into a walkie-talkie. "Hey fellas, red alert! We got two hippies from the college comin' in, askin' where they can find privacy. Dame's a redhead and boyfriend's got a black beard—beatnik."

They burst out laughing and didn't stop till Ethan swung the car recklessly into a parking space and jammed on the brakes. They unloaded their gear, which consisted mostly of Ethan's camera equipment and drugs stashed in an expensive, cowhide shoulder bag. Meredith said, "Look," and pointed to a sign that said, "To Lake and Trails." They crossed the lot and followed a path through sparse woods that soon opened up at the lake, where a beach had been created with brown, grainy sand for all the day-trippers and campers. Voices chirped and mingled from all directions—from swimmers and canoers in the water, to dawdlers on the dock and frisbee players on the beach. The sedentary patrons sat at picnic tables gazing mindlessly.

Meredith stood for a moment, squinting at the climbers on the rock face that rose straight-up from the back side of the lake, its mica shards sparkling in the sun. Ethan saw her interest and let her know he wasn't impressed. "Bah, what show-offs—they think they're such hot stuff."

"Nowhere near your level," Meredith said ironically, turning to him with her smile that was as big and dazzling as her sunglasses. She had never seen Ethan climb a rock face during their relationship. He complained that he couldn't find any more East Coast mountains worthy of his skill. He wanted the two of them to transfer to a college in Colorado or California so he could get back to his passion.

Feeling like a model walking a fashion runway, Meredith sent one leg through the opening in her gown and set out on the dirt road that circled Wakan Lake. From behind her sunglasses, she scanned the scene for any appealing men that might have their eyes on her. But all she saw were kids and overweight mid-lifers. It dawned on her how she must appear to them—like a woman who had arrived at the park straight from an all-night blowout.

Not finding any male prospects on the scene, Meredith turned her gaze to Ethan, who trailed behind her, lugging his bulky camera bag. Smart and attractive as he was—the bearded intellectual majoring in philosophy—he wasn't long-term for her. He was just the person she was living with since winter term, the guy she felt ultra-comfortable with but could not imagine marrying for the rest of her life. Dream man had yet to materialize.

As they made their way around the lake, others passed them on their way back to the beach and gave them long stares. Who were these obvious outsiders? Where did they come from? Out-of-staters—Northerners—attending their proud Southern university? Yes, Meredith answered silently and just as proudly. New Yorkers, which is why we found each other our first week at your famous college that still has Confederate pride. But hey, it also has a great drama department, which is why I applied—back-up school. And here I am—spread the love!

Ethan, perpetually frowning, clutched his camera bag tighter to his side as if protecting it from the bumpkins or rednecks who looked so suspicious of him. He wore one of those collared summer shirts with a green alligator over the heart—the emblem of his world, his sphere, his class who read the *New Yorker*, played tennis indoors, and went to law or medical school after college. He was planning on law, if he didn't make it as a photographer.

Meredith knew how Ethan cultivated the abstracted philosopher look in his jeans and long hair and beard. He liked looking harried, preoccupied with problem solving— for he was now studying logic, a highbrow area of mathematics. Thinking kept him up all night, paging through books and scribbling notes. While Meredith slept, he chain-smoked—three packs a day—and ingested, snorted, or swallowed drugs—marijuana, speed, and quaaludes. He sipped scotch, the bottle on the floor by his armchair. And in the morning, he drank coffee, brewing several pots. In March, he had been hospitalized for pancreatitis, but the serious illness did not change his bad habits. Eating strawberry jam was another fetish of his and left the apartment's surfaces sticky. Sometimes, when Meredith came up close to give Ethan a kiss on the lips, she thought she smelled an amusement park.

Ethan usually crashed around four, a couple hours before Meredith got up for her summer job at the university library. Ethan wasn't working that summer, just taking two upper-level courses to prove his brilliance and graduate early. Meredith had to step over his books and paper mess on the living room floor. More books lay open over the arms of his chair. Their dining room table housed evidence of his substance consumption. Meredith didn't say too much about it, for she also smoked cigarettes, drank wine, shared joints with him, and, if prodded hard enough, swallowed one of his quaaludes, which he called sopors. They turned her loose and silly, but her tolerance was nothing like his, and his drug use scared her, made her want to break up with him as soon as she could figure out how to do it or better yet, meet the right man.

All of these images of their domestic life since winter, when they left the freshman dorms for an apartment, passed through Meredith's head as she turned off the lake's perimeter onto a trail that quickly entered lovely woods scented with pine, fern, and moss. She patted her satchel at her hip, anticipating the wine and cigarettes inside—the beef jerky for Ethan, his favorite snack, besides the unshelled sunflower seeds that he continuously cracked open between his teeth while reading.

Since leaving the parking lot, they had passed three large signs labeled "Rules." No alcoholic beverages or other drugs permitted in the park. The inclusion of "other drugs" made Ethan laugh sarcastically. "They've only added 'drugs' since our generation." He sounded proud, as if he personally was responsible for the addition of drugs to the sign. But Ethan did contribute to the counterculture. He was a vocal activist, one of the angry antiwar and freedom-of-speech demonstrators at their big campus protest in the fall that led to tear gassing. He had a draft card, after all—his life was at stake. But it wasn't just his political beliefs that drove him to protest. It was also his innate male genes, his manhood, his ego, what he could brag about later: Oh, yeah, I was there when they started gassing us—man, it was crazy.

Meredith had stayed in her dorm room during the protest. She tuned out the mayhem—violence terrified her. Fear of men's violence lived in her genes. Instead, she listened to Bob Dylan through her headset, album after album. But Ethan had been out there and returned to her room glowing and reborn with his scratches, bruises, and feverish tales.

"Hmm, looks like lots of kids are here," Meredith said, her brow furrowing behind her sunglasses. Kids would ruin their plans, which were to drink wine, get stoned, take photos of her semi or totally nude, and end up, hopefully, making love under open skies.

Ethan followed her gaze upward to a high ledge full of skinny, twelve- or thirteen-year-old boys in bathing suits. They pranced about, laughing as they prodded one another toward the ledge's edge. "This is how tragedies happen," Ethan said, as he blew out the last drag on his cigarette and flung the butt into the scrub.

"Hey! Go get that," Meredith said, with the southern drawl she liked to imitate since hearing it all year. And as a drama major, she had practiced great roles by Tennessee Williams.

Ethan grimaced but went to get the butt. His growl could be heard as his gray Wallabee shoe ground out the red-hot ember. He came back and gave Meredith a disgusted look. "I hope you're happy."

"But where's the butt? I brought a trash bag."

He ignored her and hoisted the camera bag over his shoulder. They walked on in silence, the trail gently ascending. Finally the lake was a distant memory, and the only sounds they could hear were those of little critters scuttering for hiding places in the underbrush. The trail narrowed and showed evidence of fewer hikers, for leaves and broken branches from autumn still mulched over the surface.

Suddenly, and at the same moment, Meredith and Ethan stopped. A possible location for their photo shoot had just caught their eye. An outcropping of rocks some fifty feet off the trail scattered ruggedly, suggesting a secret place behind for their illicit pursuits. They worked their way through the outer shield of rocks and found themselves in an enclosure with an opening to the sky like an oculus. The surrounding woods gave off a leafy fragrance, a natural aphrodisiac. They looked at each other and gave a happy laugh. Yes, this was it, they had found it—their own private paradise for the rest of the day. Just to be sure of their solitude, they stood still for a moment and listened with closed eyes for any sign of life besides whispering wildlife and the movement of birds. Eagerly they unpacked their essentials—cigarettes, wine, hash pipe, and Ethan's camera and lenses.

"Look at this rock, Ethan—perfect for posing."

"Go for it!"

She unbuttoned the rest of her long dress and mounted the smooth boulder. For a moment she splayed herself faceup on the rock, her dress falling off her body—no underwear. She sighed blissfully, feeling the warm sun caress her skin. She loved the rock, the rock was her lover, smooth and mighty under her. Ethan hurried to get his camera out of its case in order to capture her luxuriating moment on the sun-speckled boulder. Meredith heard the rapidly clicking shutter and gave a gurgle of laughter.

"Good," Ethan said. "Got it. Can't wait to see the contact sheet tonight." He had turned their bathroom into a dark-room, the small window covered with special blackout paper.

"Let's open the wine, Merri. And where are the cigarettes? Or better yet, let's take a toke. But first, I have to change the film. I just shot a whole roll of you."

He reached into his camera bag and tossed her a tin film canister, the one with nuggets of hash. She shook the canister against her ear—mmm, goodies inside. Then, while Ethan unloaded and reloaded film, Meredith selected a level rock to serve as their tabletop. She put out the wine, beef jerky, hash, and cigarette pack and then opened the wine.

At the sound of the cork popping, Ethan looked up. "I'll have some, and pass me that beef jerky, would you?"

Meredith handed him the bottle, and while he took a few swigs, she tore open the beef jerky's wrapper. It smelled disgusting. She pinched her nose as she handed it to him. He smiled, knowing how much she disliked it. Just to tease her, he ripped off a bite with the bared teeth of a wolf. Meredith gave him a tolerant smile and then turned her attention to the wine, drinking a few swallows from the bottle. It never tasted good when coming from the bottle—she preferred sipping from a shimmering stemmed glass.

Lighting a cigarette—the perfect accompaniment to wine—Meredith went back to the smooth boulder, where she practiced poses for the next round of photography. She liked that Ethan kept glancing up at her as he fooled with his camera and filters. His eyes winked appreciatively each time she changed position—one thigh held against her chest, the other leg dangling over the rock; a full-length sideways pose, propped on an elbow, rivers of red hair cascading over the upper shoulder and partially concealing a breast; and finally, her pièce de résistance, yoga's candle pose—legs straight up with her dress fanning out on the rock.

"Hold it! Hold it!" Ethan yelped, leaping off his perch and snapping shots faster than she had ever heard the shutter open and close—click-cluck, click-cluck, click-cluck. The camera was in a state of erotic ecstasy—it couldn't get enough of her. She laughed.

"Fantastic. Too much, Merri Ms.!" That was his pet name for her: Merri Ms.

Her back and legs slowly rolled down, one vertebra at time, as she had learned in yoga class. She picked up her still burning cigarette from a round dip in the rock—a perfect ashtray.

"Hey, light me one of those, will you?" Ethan said.

Languidly, Meredith slid off the rock, buttoned her navel button, and lit a cigarette for Ethan. He let it dangle between his lips like Bogie or Belmondo while he fiddled with the camera. She crushed out her own cigarette and put it in the trash bag. She swigged more wine and offered the bottle to Ethan. After his swigs, she corked it and tucked it back in her bag.

"Wait, aren't we going to drink it?"

"Yes, but it's incriminating evidence. Let me know when you want some."

"Hey, I brought some sopors, in case we want to do them," Ethan said in a hushed voice, as if her paranoia about surveillance were contagious.

"Okay, why not? Let's laugh our heads off."

Ethan hastily put aside his camera and rummaged in his bag for a tall prescription bottle, which he tossed to Meredith. "We'll need the wine to take them," he said. His gestalt therapist back in New York had prescribed them for his anxiety, but the only time Meredith had seen Ethan take them was when he wanted to get loopy. Taking the quaaludes scared her. They were big white pills that gave her a sickening feeling inside, like a poison infiltrating her gut and her brain. Yet, minutes after ingesting one, she got loose and silly and could ignore the queasiness. Overbrimming with love, she wanted to hug everyone. Her legs turned to jelly, her voice slurred, and she laughed and laughed. Nevertheless, her fear of the pills remained as soon as the euphoria wore off, so she didn't take them often. Moving in with Ethan that winter had awakened her skepticism of their relationship. When they lived separately in the dorms, she hadn't witnessed his round-the-clock ingestion of substances. In the spring, he had begun to sell pot. Students she didn't know came in the evening to buy the baggies of weed he stashed in the crevice of his armchair. Once a boy paid him, but because he got to chatting with Ethan, he forgot to take his baggie. Ethan knew it and let it happen. The baggie went back into the crevice to be sold another time. Meredith was outraged. That was wrong, unfair, stealing. Ethan didn't care, and when the boy came back later, Ethan said he didn't know where it was—the boy must have lost it on his walk home. Another reason Ethan was short-term for Meredith.

But today was for enjoyment. Meredith took the zinfandel from her bag and gulped down the fat, powdery pill that within seconds seized control of her central nervous system. Ethan popped a pill after her with a few chugs of wine. Meredith gave a surrendering giggle and once again splayed out on the big rock. The one button holding her dress together made a picture that Ethan quickly shot. Then he put away the camera and came to stand at her feet. High already, the sight of her lax toes transfixed him. "My God, Merri, your feet are sea creatures," he said. "They're fins, yes, fins, and no wonder—we've evolved from sea life—your fins are priceless relics!" A wondrous laugh choked in his throat, and his delicate artist's hands reverently caressed her feet, then slowly, tactilely moved up her legs, along her thighs as if the hands of a medium, hands at a séance, hands receiving a message. "Oh my God, your legs are exotic tropical fruits—papayas! So soft and ripe!" His hands scooped her round rear cheeks. "Such delight! Merri delight! Perfect cantaloupes."

Meredith laughed, arching with pleasure, but too clumsily so that her head banged the rock. "Ouch!" she cried out, half-rising to rub her scalp through her mane of hair.

"Poor baby," Ethan said, hurrying to add his hand to the thick waves. "Poor Merri Ms.!"

That set Meredith off. It was too hilarious, the whole scene—the two of them, derelicts on the prowl for promiscuous photography and its possible culmination in intercourse. Everything they felt—for they no longer could think linearly—was synchronous, so synchronous that Ethan was laughing too, laughing about the same thing even though neither of them could say what that thing was. They thrashed with hilarity on the rock, mere cells within the greater, over-arching, all-encompassing cellular, gaseous cosmos. This was the way Meredith loved Ethan most—when they laughed hilariously together.

The spasm ended when Ethan roused and staggered away for his camera. "We need a few more shots, Merri, and a cigarette." As if dangerously depleted of the body's essential ingredient for life, he lit up and drew the smoke into his lungs and his mind. He came back to the rock and offered Meredith a drag, which she accepted. They took another plug of the wine, and then Meredith moved unsteadily to stash the bottle in her bag.

"Ready for take two!" she said gaily, and with a flamboyant flick of her hand undid the middle button of her dress. She clambered ungracefully onto the smooth rock and stood up straight, at first wobbly but then steadying herself. She was high above Ethan, who gazed up at her as if at the goddess she wanted to be. She grinned at him and then struck a pose—the female figurehead on an ancient ship, her gaze fastened on the sea in order to give warning of Neptune's caprices.

Ethan scrambled around her on the rock, making sure the focal point in his pictures was her marvelous auburn bush. While he moved, tripped, fell, and squatted to snap pictures, his enthusiastic voice kept pace with his whizzing shutter. "Great, amazing, hold it right there, yes! Got it! Oh, and this one's good too, don't move, Merri, hold still—yep, got it! You're fantastic!" Euphoric laughter resounded. "No, no, no, don't sit down yet—I need one more shot. Could you put your right arm behind your shoulder, yes, perfect!"

Meredith's insides purred sensually as the camera clicked away. But her balance was weakening, and so was Ethan's. Suddenly, he tripped and fell headlong, his camera cracking against a rock.

Meredith dropped down on all fours and hung her head. "Time-out!" she said. Then her head jerked up in alarm. "Oh

God, I feel so queasy. I always forget how these things make me sick to my stomach." She carefully lay down on the rock and focused on her breath.

"We should have brought some pizza for you," Ethan said, examining his camera for damage. Seeing nothing but a dent in the frame, he dropped it casually on a bed of pine needles and came to comfort Meredith. "You need to coat your stomach, babe. Didn't you bring any food? None? How about some more wine?"

That set her off laughing again, a laugh he couldn't resist, and laughing himself, he crawled up on the rock and turned Meredith's body so they could lie sideways and laugh into each other's faces.

"You looked like a madman taking all those pictures," she said, gasping for breath.

"And you, you gave me this!" He laughed back, putting her hand on his erection.

"Ooh, I like that!"

They began kissing and feeling each other, he shedding his jeans. Their sensuality grew deeper and higher until it reached a dizzy oblivion. At last, at last, the climactic moment of their day at Wakan Lake had arrived—lovemaking outdoors, under the open sky, wholly enveloped in nature's soft breezes and fresh fragrances. The photography and the intoxicants were only the prelude, the foreplay, to this delicious, delirious moment. It was right then, when Ethan's erotic extremity was just entering Meredith's warm, exquisite realm that a branch outside their rocky enclosure cracked loudly.

"Oh, fuck," Meredith hissed in horror, pushing Ethan off her and pulling her dress together with shaking hands. She never buttoned faster in her life.

Ethan stumbled and fell in his rush to jam his legs back into his jeans.

Male voices could be heard coming through the rocks to the hideout. Their voices had the positive strength of foot soldiers singing the Caisson song: "Over hill, over dale, as we hit the dusty trail, and those Caissons go rolling along." Maybe they were even singing it. The derelicts were too shocked and confused to know what was going on. All they knew was that they had to defend themselves against the enemy, against law enforcement, now entering their secret lair. Rangers, two of them, uniformed, wearing those badged hats of authority with guns at their hips, came to a halt in front of them, the bigger dude folding his arms over his high-and-mighty chest.

"Well, well, well—what do we have here?" he said, pleased to have found some reprobates to discipline.

Feigning innocence, Meredith glanced at Ethan, whose eyes darted with fast thinking while his nerves buzzed tangibly in the air. The rangers swept the scene with their eyes, benign smiles on their pudgy faces. Ethan took that opportunity to dive for his hash canister on the tabletop rock, but with a sleight of hand made it look like he had moved to tie his shoe. Then, when the rangers' eyes fastened on Meredith for a longer assessment—yup, a mere pinup not requiring male or anyone's respect—Ethan slipped the canister into his camera bag. The deed done, he inched closer to Meredith, not to protect her from the rangers' contemptuous ogling, but to feel protected himself by her greater strength in such a situation. Women, even nineteen-year-old women, embodied the safety of mothers. And besides, she was a damn good actress.

The taller, meatier ranger, bursting out of his too-tight uniform, prepared for the interrogation, putting one foot on a low rock, one hand on his gun holster, and the other hand tapping his official hat, calling attention to its emblem.

Meredith smiled with total aplomb. "Howdy, fellas."

"Howdy," the big guy said.

Niceties over, the ranger again folded his arms over his chest and planted his legs firmly two feet apart. Adopting an ultra-serious look, he said, "We heard some reports. How about you folks tell us what you came to the park for, and what you're up to here in these rocks." His eyes swept over their bags.

"Nothing," Ethan and Meredith replied in unison.

"Oh really?" A slow smile curled the ranger's lips, as he reached for Meredith's bag and peered inside. "Looks to me like you've been doing some drinking. Didn't you see our signs as you came in—no alcohol, no drugs?"

"We must have missed them," Ethan said, and although his tone was arrogant, his face had paled.

The tall ranger shook his head with silent laughter that ended abruptly with a cruel stare. "Can't miss our signs, little buddy."

The shorter, stockier ranger pitched in—"People seen you two, seen everything. They reported you."

"What's in that bag of yours?" the big ranger asked Ethan.

"Camera equipment," Ethan said in an irate, bored tone.

"You like taking pictures?" The ranger stepped close to Ethan to impress his greater heft over the slight philosopher.

"Yes, I'm a photographer," Ethan answered, bearded chin rising. He liked giving the ranger this identity.

"Oh, so where do you work?"

"What do you mean where do I work?"

"I mean where's your office?"

"You mean do I have a studio? No, I don't need one. I specialize in outdoor photography. I don't do indoor por-traits."

"Mind if I look through your bag?"

Ethan froze. He didn't know what to say. It had been a mistake to slip the canister into the bag.

Meredith smiled and put on her fake southern accent, ever so soft and friendly. "Don't you fellas need a warrant to search personal property?"

The ranger ignored her. His hands rummaged in the bag. "What's this?" he said, holding up the canister with a sinister smile at Ethan.

"A film canister. I assume you've used them yourself."

"Nope, I got me one of those handy Instamatics. Doesn't sound like there's film in here," he said, shaking the little can next to his ear. "Now what could that be jumpin' around inside?"

His plump hand unscrewed the cap and he sniffed. "P.U.!" he said, cringing at the smell. "Looks like you've got illegal stuff in here." Slowly, grimly, he screwed the top back on the canister and pocketed it. He was very quiet now, very serious, letting it sink in that the delinquents were in deep trouble for possession of an illegal substance that could land them in jail. Or maybe ship Ethan off to Vietnam immediately, waiving medical clearance and training.

"What makes you folks think you can disregard the rules here that everybody else obeys, so that all of us can enjoy a good and safe time at the lake?"

The stockier ranger shifted his weight and nodded in agreement. His right hand took hold of his gun holster and gave it a shake.

Ethan and Meredith just stared, waited. They were caught and faced arrest for possession. They needed more information on where this interrogation was going before they tried to negotiate for themselves.

The big ranger surprised them by suddenly dropping his severe airs. His face changed expression as he turned and fastened his eyes on Meredith—greedy, oily eyes that sucked in her face and body. She moved her hand to the rock for support. He scared her. She felt vulnerable facing his swashbuckling aggression. What would he do next?

"I'd sure like to teach you a thing or two, young lady," he said, touching his balls. "How dare you contaminate our park with your whorism."

"Hey," Ethan objected, taking an automatic step forward.

Meredith was too stunned to react, and yet, she had been treated this same way by men since her first childhood memories—touched and spoken to sexually, inappropriately—so that part of herself believed she was only an object, made to be treated this way by men, made to be violated.

The ranger stepped closer to her and gave her shoulder a light push, but only so his hand could brush over her breast as it departed. "What do you have to say for yourself, missy?"

"We weren't trying to create a problem, sir. We're very sorry. We apologize."

"But the signs say no alcohol or drugs. And indecent exposure isn't allowed. You knew you were breaking the rules."

His hand rose and swept the air following the lines of her body in the slinky dress. He did it again, this time grazing her hip, fingers sliding to her rear and pausing there.

"Hey," Ethan said angrily, stepping up and thrusting his arm in front of Meredith.

The intervention worked. The ranger stepped back, dropping his eyes. And once again, his behavior changed when he lifted them and said to Meredith with childlike curiosity, "Are you a model or something?"

"Yes, I'm a model."

The ranger blinked—he had a real-life model right in front of him.

"Like you model for magazines?"

"Yes, I model for *Vogue* and *Cosmopolitan*—a whole bunch of magazines. Ethan works for them," Meredith said easily.

He digested the information and recovered a modicum of his male authority. "Well, this ain't the place for you to be modeling. There's lots of folks here, families, enjoying themselves, even when you don't see 'em. They're all around, and they don't know you're modeling. They think you've taken off your clothes for sinful reasons. I can't see why you and your friend thought it would be all right to come here to do your modeling."

Relief filled Meredith and Ethan hearing his words—they had been spotted and busted for nude photography and not copulation. Even the wine and hash were secondary.

The ranger's face broke into a red flush. "I mean, there are children crawlin' all over these hills. Kids saw you!" He took a deep breath to overcome his dismay that children had been exposed to immoral activities. "I want you folks to collect your stuff, and then me and my partner are going to escort you out of the park."

Meredith and Ethan blinked at each other as they hurried to gather their gear. They were free, they were not going to jail!

The hike down the mountain was accomplished in silence. Meredith walked behind the rangers with nothing to stare at but their khaki rumps, guns, and felt hats. Ethan trailed behind Meredith, shifting his camera bag from one shoulder to the other with his usual fidgetiness. As they came along the lake road, all eyes from the beach and water turned on them. Meredith held her head up high and amused herself imagining what each member of their little procession was thinking. The big guy who had harassed her led their pack, chest out, authority pulsing from his bulk and too-tight outfit. He was proud to be the park's law enforcement who had just caught some miscreants, but more than that, he was proud to be a man who had just had a close encounter with a magazine model, one he had even touched and could thoroughly ravish later that night in bed with his inflatable sex doll. Meredith laughed aloud, but the others were too lost in their own thoughts to notice. She turned her attention to imagining the younger, rookie ranger, who was beaming with pride for his first bust. After work, he'd go the bar with his buddies and brag about his success while downing beers. Then there was Ethan behind her, tugging the ends of his mustache, eyes on his Wallabee shoes, thrilled to be known as a photographer. It was better than being known as a philosopher. He was a photographer of semi-nude women— in this case, a fashion model—and had to be ejected from a southern state park for his activities. The notoriety was fabulous. It would pump him up for days. And Meredith? What was she imagining for herself as she strode past all the rubberneckers witnessing her banishment from the park? She grinned at them with her white teeth. She could barely refrain from waving goodbye like a celebrity. She held back only because she felt her mystique would be diminished if she waved. She imagined she was striding out of the park with her dress fully unbuttoned and fluttering behind her like a victory banner. Daring—she felt fearlessly daring. And all those people staring with open mouths could think what they wanted. All she cared about was her daring and its effect on them: awe.

In the parking lot, at their car, Meredith and Ethan said goodbye to the rangers. How funny it was that suddenly everything became gracious and friendly. Meredith and Ethan poured thanks on their perpetrators, because they were being set free. The rangers came close to apologizing for having to expel them. "Y'all take care now," the big ranger said.

Meredith reciprocated, waving affectionate fingers from her open car window. "Toodle-oo!"

Ethan let out the clutch in reverse and sent the car thumping hard over potholes. He shifted into first and screeched out of the exit gate. Now they were truly free. They looked at each other with incredulous smiles.

"That was really something, Merri. I can't believe it really happened," Ethan said.

"When I heard that branch crack, oh my God, my heart panicked."

"I can't believe they didn't arrest us."

"They probably have too many rule breakers to bother with."

"You were amazing, totally convincing—that accent!"

The big ranger filled her memory, his foul hands touching her body. "Yuck, that man was so gross!"

"Yeah, sorry for that. Hey, you're just an irresistible turn-on for men—that should make you happy."

She gave him a stupefied look. "Are you for real?"

"Sorry, I was just trying to cheer you up."

"You have no idea what it's like," she said, feeling her stomach turn—what it was like to be ogled by strange men, men sure of their entitlement to make sexual comments and innuendos whenever they pleased. Men who whistled and said lewd things from scaffolding or from their car windows. Old men, friends of the family, who hugged her goodbye, feeling her or patting her bottom. Younger men who forced sex on her, sneering that she owed them because they had taken her out for dinner.

Ethan looked worried and tugged his beard. "Merri?"

She reached into her bag and pulled out the wine bottle. She gave him her bright, fake, actress smile. "Wanna hit?"

Ethan exhaled with relief.

"What an adventure," she said and swigged. Then she laughed, her good mood returning.

He stepped on the gas with a surge of elated recklessness and laughed back. They glanced at each other, and laughed harder. A plug had been pulled and their hilarity could not be stopped and soared out of control. The day at Wakan Lake was just too funny to turn off. Tears streamed from Meredith's eyes—hilarity and grief mixed until they reached a point where they became one and the same. Ethan joined her, tears streaking down his face and landing in his beard where he tried to lick them. For a few minutes, they passed the bottle and gasped for air in their attack of hysterics. Finally a strange catharsis settled over them, and they rode toward home feeling emptied but at peace.

Taking Flight, the Hard Way

W HAT BEGAN AS A NEW ADVENTURE when Mary
Ferguson moved to Bristol City with Elliott Brown
soon spiraled downward. Weather was the first blight on
their bright horizon—always precipitating, always dismal
and gloomy. The city's industrial heyday was long over and
its Gilded Age buildings stood with an anachronistic, drab
weight. Mary—an eager and curious young woman—couldn't
imagine how people spent their entire lives and careers in
such a place, despite its respected university. Deeper issues
were at stake, the main one being her fiancé, Elliott Brown.
He was a newly minted PhD in mathematics setting out on
his first tenure-track position. He was twenty-seven to Mary's
twenty-two, and they had met their last semester before
matriculating from two of Boston's universities. Mary's older
sister, Judy, had introduced them, her husband being another
math nerd in Elliott's department. From the beginning, Mary
and Elliott had clashed. The problem was universal—the
man believing himself superior to the woman and letting her
know it. Mary naturally rebelled against Elliott's arrogance

and demanded equal respect, which Elliott refused. He let it be known with a curl to his quite beautiful lips that her thinking in the humanities was nothing compared to his genius in the realm of abstract theorems. And so, his job offer at Bristol University gave them the perfect opportunity to break up. But they didn't. They stuck together. For each, in a different way, it felt safer to face the unknown future with a companion as a buttress. Mary figured that Elliott needed her outgoing personality and domestic capability. He was embarking on the next stage of a successful man's life—the climb to professional acclaim—an identity that required a wife to make a home for him and produce heirs. Given his relative introversion, how would he find another suitable candidate if he broke up with Mary? She had been delivered to him on a silver platter by Judy and Pete. She fit his outward requirements—she was pretty, lively, and liked to cook. She enjoyed being a homemaker and even sewed some of her own clothes as a hobby. Her energy and enthusiasm pleased him, especially as his own nature was taciturn. It was a bonus that she liked sports, so that during their brief Boston courtship they had jogged after work and played volleyball on the weekends. She had grown up in the same educated circles as he, though a few rungs down because his grandfather had invented medical devices and his father had served as a State Department appointee during the Kennedy administration. Elliott's character made it hard for him to meet women, despite being handsome with ebony hair, arched brows, and a suave face like leading men of the 1940s. As a boy, he had convinced his family he wanted to be a priest, so they had sent him to a Jesuit boarding school where he received a fine education but also decided not to become a priest. Mary had introduced him to sex, which didn't excite him much, or perhaps it terrified him. But he tried to comply with his role in that department, though soon after they started living together, he let her know his true feelings because she snuggled up to him almost every night. "I think once a week is enough, Mary," he said.

"What?" she had answered with wide, incredulous eyes.

For her own part, Mary stuck to Elliott because she was graduating from college and didn't have a back-up plan once it became obvious they had friction. She had always assumed she would meet her future husband in college—that was the way society worked. If she and Elliott broke up, where should she go? What job was she trained for? Her only resume-worthy experience had been to do research for a professor's book. Should she apply to law school? It was too late. Those last weeks of college, sitting on her bed in anxious contemplation, she faced the truth that she had been raised to be a successful man's wife and support—sacrificial. At the same time, she had come of age during the vociferous feminist movement and was free to succeed in her own right, stand up against sacrificing and taking constant shit from men. Everywhere women were demonstrating for equal rights. They marched for an Equal Rights Amendment to the Constitution. They called for open marriages or no marriages at all, and they burned their bras at protests. Mary had gladly joined the movement but as it turned out, more with her intellect than her self-belief. When it came to leaving

Elliott, she realized she still embodied the conditioning of her upbringing—women's female inferiority, women's duty to sacrifice to men. Her inner self had not yet caught up to her outer liberated self. She did not feel at all prepared to step out into the world alone. So, she stayed with Elliott and hoped for improvement in their relationship. She wanted to make it work—he was the model mate she had been raised to find.

Moving, the new adventure, did improve their interaction. They worked together during the summer months on domestic plans and goals. They lived in the future's bubble of promise and hope. The university accepted Mary to its graduate history program, and in early September she and Elliott moved to northern New York and found a first-floor apartment in a 1920s duplex on an all-American street lined with maple trees that lent it some charm. Mary could walk to the main campus and library but had to take a shuttle bus to her history classes at the new campus miles away. Elliott's science campus was another new complex, and he drove there punctually at eight-thirty every morning. Except for the neighborhood surrounding the main campus, which was old and picturesque, Bristol's greater landscape was a wasteland with new housing developments that lacked any aesthetic. Shopping strips further ruined its appearance. They lined wide avenues with traffic lights at every intersection.

Despite the let-down of Bristol's environment, Mary and Elliott settled into their fall semesters, accepting the region's rain, mud, puddles, and gray, cheerless skies. Every night those first days, Mary made dinner with pleasure, her thoughts on their cozy first home together. As she cooked and then ate at the dining room table with Elliott, she anticipated his similar pleasure for the food made and served with love. But that never happened. Instead, when he finished eating, he pushed back his chair and sighed with manly resignation. "Well, back to that theorem." Putting his plate in the kitchen, he headed down the little hallway to his study, his head already far away in that mystifying maze of the numbers, letters, and symbols that he had held in place for dinner's duration. Mary stared after him, angry, resentful, and confused. Her feelings would soon burst into complaints.

Those first days, after cleaning up the dinner, she would pass by his small office on her way to the bedroom and see him slumped in his chair, forehead pressed in his hand as if his brain were in agony. He worked that way until bedtime, which came punctually at ten o'clock. It had been that way all summer in their Boston sublet, but now in a real home of their own, a future they were forging together, Mary had envisioned something else. But the truth was before her: he was not going to change.

As before, rage built in her. She wanted to throttle him. But it was as if he liked her exasperation and attempts to argue. For then he could strike back with put downs that augmented his own importance. And always he was the one to conclude a spat by ambling away nonchalantly to his loftier place where she wasn't necessary. He liked locking her out.

Mary never stopped rebelling against Elliott's treatment, even though she knew it only exacerbated their vicious circle of hurled darts. She also saw how being the rebellious one automatically placed her in the inferior position, for rebellion always happened against authority. And Elliott couldn't be anything but an intransigent authority, just like his father, for she knew he had rebelled mightily against his father, and as a senior in high school had moved out to live with his uncle, severing all parental ties until his college graduation.

Mary didn't mind taking care of the house, food shopping, or cooking until she fought with Elliott. Her complaints about the double standard and how he could contribute more, always resulted in the same reply from his smug face—"I'm not putting any demands on you."

In short, Mary became acutely aware that she was longing for an outside life with her man. She didn't want to stay home every night and do the same solitary work she had been doing all day in class or the library. She wanted a little night life with Elliott—a movie, a concert, a dinner out. Or, if they had to stay at home every night, why not one special, romantic evening on the living room rug with candles, wine, soft music, and affectionate conversation that led to lovemaking? But Elliott stuck to his weeknight regime. "I don't have time to play with you, Mary. I've told you before, we logicians burn out by our thirties. I have to prove this theorem before I can't." One time, when she pleaded with all her sweetness for a Thursday night out, he stood high above her and replied like a patient sage teaching a little girl a lesson: "To strive, to seek, to find, and not to yield." Another time, when she flung angry, double-standard accusations at him, he spat back with a familiar weapon, "I see our relationship as perfectly fair— you're spending my money."

Mary's domestic life with Elliott descended into deeper trouble as the semester progressed. She hated herself for smoking more when she had worked so hard to curb the habit. And she was drinking coffee throughout the day and then wine at night for stress relief. She felt as if she were sucking in surrogate soothers to fill the empty place inside her, the place where a loving and supportive relationship should have been but wasn't. And what was she to do? How could she untangle herself when she was in this deep, when both families were already preparing for a June wedding? She kept putting off dealing with reality and instead concentrated on her academic and outer-world life. On the main campus near home, she spent time in the library, cafeteria, and other haunts to study. She shuttled to the history department for her classes and to check her mailbox, but she never stayed long. The new complex was devoid of personality. Hideous contemporary buildings had been plunked down on barren land. Dorms mixed in with offices and classrooms as if to be avant-garde in conception. But the sprawling complex was empty and eerily lit, its atmosphere unpleasant. Its low-ceilinged, carpeted spaces with concrete walls and vinyl furniture smelled synthetic.

The place held one perk—Joseph Grumman. He was teaching his favorite subject in American history—the New Deal. Mary was in his class and spellbound by the old and ailing curmudgeon. He had survived a stroke and mouth cancer and now moved with a cane and spoke with a foamy drawl and lax tongue. He regularly sprayed artificial saliva into his mouth, but more, it seemed to Mary, to punctuate his admonishments to his four students than to hydrate his mouth. They met twice a week, and Grumman began each class by bitterly denouncing the three men and Mary who sat stiffly around his underattended seminar table. He was old school and unpopular. He griped and lectured. "Your generation never learned to read or write. In my day, only the best, the very brightest, the ones headed for important careers were admitted to graduate school. I'll bet there isn't one among you who can tell me why the Greenback Party opposed the Specie Resumption Act of 1875." He glared at each young face around the table, not one of them meeting his eyes. "And I'll bet you know nothing about the scandalous election that took place the following year." Again, silence, so his drawl rose louder. "In my day, you had to recite the American presidents backwards and forwards, and then go on to the vice presidents. You had to know their tenure of office and their cabinets. Why, if you didn't know every shred of important legislation passed during their administrations, you were out, out I said! What do any of you hippies know about President Roosevelt's New Deal? If you really think you're going to be historians, then you have to burn the candles all night!"

Old Grumman, as he was known to students behind his back, stimulated Mary, and she did her work for his class. She wanted to show him she could think and produce, be a decent historian if life led her that way. But she quickly found that her real motivation for attending his class was to listen to his storytelling. It always began as soon as he finished denouncing the students for their despicable qualifications for graduate degrees.

During the two-hour class, Grumman's rolling drawl would impart fascinating stories about America's past. No one said a word. Everyone listened, spellbound, as the old man's mind traveled from one association to another, bringing the Roosevelt years to a live stage where the characters talked—for he quoted them. He described with awe the era's pivotal events, some of which had happened before his own eyes. Seamlessly, he hopped from decade to decade, forward and backward in time, occasionally making a leap of centuries to show a precedent for later political or economic developments, his mind effortlessly linking historical material. It was as if he entered a trance where history converged from thousands of tributaries to flow seamlessly from his mouth. His captivated listeners absorbed everything he said. Toward the end of his lesson, the spell broke when he asked if any of them could add to the events he had just illuminated. Mary and the others stared down at their notes, faces flushing.

"You're nothing but a bunch of ignoramuses!" Grumman said. "Universities don't care anymore—they'll take anyone's money. It's a disgrace. We used to have values, we used to accept only those who demonstrated high aptitude and dedication." He squirted his bottled saliva into his mouth.

Grumman was the highlight of Mary's first semester in Bristol, so she didn't hesitate signing up for his second semester course on historiography. And as much as he let her know she was part of the generation he found despicable, he also showed a slight indulgence toward her, and not only because she was the only one who had returned to study with him, but also because she had written her term paper with sincere effort and had earned his rare A. His approval helped to make up for her low self-image around Elliott. At home, she had held out her term paper with Grumman's scrawled compliment at the top, hoping for a pat on the back. But Elliott had looked down his nose at her and said, "Good for you, Mary," and then walked away. She knew she had set herself up for that response but still burned inside that he could be so callous. He was with her because he wanted her for his life, but all he was doing was destroying that possibility.

The second term began in January, accompanied by Bristol's gray skies and constant rain, sleet, or snow. Once again, Grumman's class was Mary's weekly highlight, especially given the dark afternoons and gloomy weather. In the second week of classes, as Mary packed up her notes after Old Grumman's lecture, Kevin Garrity came around the seminar table and said in a deep voice that he purposefully exaggerated, "Uh, excuse me, Ms. Ferguson, do you happen to know who ran against Abraham Lincoln in the 1864 election? You don't happen to be an ignoramus, do you?" He stuck out his hand with a big smile and added, "And, by the way, in case you weren't listening during introductions, I'm Kevin Garrity. I've been sitting across the table from you for two weeks now without, I might add, the least success in catching your eye. And so," he drew up his chest, "rather than risk a complete breakdown in foreign relations, I thought I'd practice a little good neighborliness."

Mary smiled at his clever use of Grumman's historical

terms and his deadpan delivery of them. She liked how his heavy eyebrows bobbed up and down on particular words, while his green eyes behind horn-rimmed glasses twinkled humorously into hers. Not waiting for her to answer, he stepped back as if surprised and added, "What? You've never heard of Abraham Lincoln? Who were your parents anyway, to ignore your education and let those peacenik hippies get control of you?"

Old Grumman was just shuffling out of the room, cane in one hand and stuffed briefcase in the other. But he turned his ear to hear Kevin's parody, which Kevin, with a sly glance at his professor, had intended. Mary liked his dare-devil confidence in imitating the old geezer who continued to denounce his students at the start of every class. Kevin wasn't going to accept that image of himself. And because he had just read his short essay to the class—at Grumman's request— he was pumped up. As he read, Mary had felt envious, as though no longer the only star in Grumman's class. Kevin's language flowed with all kinds of impressive vocabulary that he wove gymnastically into eloquence. Her only consolation was they belonged to different departments—his education. He was working for a PhD.

Kevin drove her home that day, nice and slowly in the slick weather but also to prolong their time together. He was a fiery personality and full of laughter. He asked her one hundred questions about herself, interspersing his interrogation with jokes and word plays so that she didn't notice how he had culled her life story from her in twenty minutes—including her unhappy relationship with Elliott.

When he parked in front of her house, he smiled with warm sympathy, his green eyes conveying understanding for what she was about to encounter behind the front door—conflict. Mary hurried to give him a bright smile—no self-sorriness. She felt uncomfortable for having divulged so much of herself. How had he so skillfully drawn all of that out of her? Was she that lonely?

"Hey, I didn't find out anything about you," she said.

"I planned it that way. Now you'll have to have coffee with me tomorrow—your turn to grill." He grinned—a great grin—hands resting casually on the wheel. She grinned back, taking in his attractive face—the smile with perfect teeth, the solid chin, the fresh shadow of masculine whiskers. His wavy brown hair fell past his ears, and it had been impossible not to notice his body—the taut thighs and muscular chest like a wrestler's. As she got out of the car, she poked her head back in with an afterthought. "What sports do you play?"

"Hoops. But mainly bouncing off the walls." He grinned at her.

"Ha—I already knew *that* about you."

"Damn! But I bet you didn't know I also jump rope in the basement when I need to work off that excess steam."

"I noticed the steam."

"Yikes—odorless, I hope! And what about you? What are your sports?"

"Just jogging, tennis sometimes."

"Good, we can play—if Bristol ever dries out. And where did you say we're meeting tomorrow? Was it the cafeteria at ten?"

She laughed. "Yah, that works for me."

He smiled, intentionally showing his liking for her, his brows bobbing.

She closed the car door and watched him pull away, his jalopy rattling. She stood there for a moment longer, feeling a welcome tingling inside, a happy anticipation for seeing Kevin again. She could hear them laughing over coffee as they roasted Grumman and shared with each other their lives and dreams. What was she getting into? They were obviously attracted and brazenly going forward despite Elliott. Mary turned and headed to the front door, switching her thoughts to her relationship and how she found no personal fulfillment in it, no reciprocal love, no respect or validation. She switched from feeling elation to depression.

Kevin quickly became a stimulating perk in Mary's second semester. Elaine Mayer was another. She was a PhD candidate in women's history. She had a bright, perky face, sharp blue eyes behind wire-rimmed glasses, and a jolly but firm way of talking. Her thesis on women's suffrage had just been accepted by a university press, and she was now waiting for news on her first job applications. Mary looked up to her. She was a few years older and full of advice. Best of all, she introduced Mary to the women's history department, located in an old house across from the main campus. There, Mary met young teaching assistants and professors, hardworking scholars determined to impact women's place in both the historical record and the current times. Mary signed up for a labor history course taught by Ann Laughlin, whose book on the horrific conditions experienced by young girls in nineteenth-century textile factories had won a prize. During class time, other women dropped by to announce upcoming lectures, films, or conferences. The department was active, with frequent get-togethers in someone's apartment to share the latest articles, books, or research on women. Mary felt empowered and inspired by these women and their momentum. Through their goal-driven intensity, she had found a place and a cause for herself. By the third week of the semester, she had an idea for an independent study and went to Ann's office to ask for sponsorship.

It was early morning, before classes, Ann was busy at her desk in a dusty room cluttered with books and papers, many on the floor. Her outer appearance matched her environment. She had little concern for what clothes she threw on for the day and may have forgotten to comb her hair. Work consumed her, it was a cloud of tension around her, and she made it clear Mary was interrupting her.

"I have a quick request," Mary said, sitting down across from Ann. "Would you be willing to be my faculty sponsor for an independent study? I want to interview women who've started college after marriage, children, and divorce. I want to see if the patriarchy kept them from fulfilling their own purpose until their forties."

"But we know it did," Ann said.

"Yes, but I want their stories—the spectrum of their experiences. I want to investigate how the double standard affects women's psychology, like do women automatically lose self-respect if they live with a man—automatically become subordinate?"

Ann stared at her, and Mary blushed. It was obvious from what she had just said that she wanted to hear from other women in order to substantiate her own experience with Elliott.

"Are you in a relationship?" Ann asked bluntly.

"Yeah, it's an influence, but our conditioned gender psychology, or behavior, exists and I want to explore it."

"Look, I can't sponsor you, Mary. My area's labor, not psychology and relationships. You'll have to ask someone else."

"But this is about labor, one branch of it—women fulfilling their own purpose in life instead of sacrificing it to a man's. I want to demonstrate it in life-story form, which hasn't been done yet. I've checked. It's something I'm dying to do."

Ann's lips pressed with impatience. She picked up her pen and held it over her papers, indicating she had work to do. "It's oral history, Mary, maybe you should recast it that way and find the right sponsor. It's not my thing and I don't have time."

"But I wouldn't take up your time. I know how important your work is. All I need is a signature for the department's paperwork. I don't need meetings and you don't have to read my paper."

Ann sighed grimly. "If I sponsor you, Mary, I can't get involved at all. I'm swamped. I have my lectures and my new book with a deadline I've already missed. I can only eyeball your paper to see that you've completed it. And the grade will have to be pass-fail."

Relief filled Mary. She had the green light to go! "Thank you so much, Ann! And I promise not to disturb you."

Ann got up—time for Mary to leave. Mary hurried to the door, repeating her thanks.

Ann called out after her, "I'm only doing this because women have always been prevented from pursuing their passions, and I hope the project helps you in your own life. Good luck."

"Oh, thank you so much!" Mary repeated with a grateful smile. She felt the power of sisterhood.

Mary filled the next weeks conducting interviews with a dozen women who volunteered for her study. She found relevant articles in the library and ordered review copies of new books pertinent to her topic. The interviews and readings were her favorite pursuit that term—besides Kevin. The two of them met nearly every day, in the cafeteria or the pub across the street from campus. It didn't take long to start hanging out in his dorm room, where they could snuggle and laugh playfully on his bed, though never quite making love. Between get-togethers, they left each other love notes or poetry tacked to his dorm door—their "tree hollow" of secret lovers in bygone days. Indeed, they were trysting and secrecy was a powerful stimulant, but only at first. As the winter moved into spring, their initial exuberance faded. Mary's duplicity put a blight on the relationship. Even though they said, "I love you," Mary was always leaving Kevin to return home to Elliott. She was living two lives with two lovers and it couldn't last. The situation was slowly devouring her. And drinking frequently at the pub with Kevin only exacerbated her bad mood. Nothing was fun anymore. She was flaring up at both men, as if the downward slide of her life were their fault. Only occasionally, when she felt like crying in despair, was she willing to face that it was her own guilt, her own choices, that were ruining her life.

Kevin reacted differently to her anger than Elliott, who always slashed back with his swift sword. In contrast, Kevin wilted, her wounding words penetrating him to the quick, but without loss of love for her. Tentatively, he would reach out to touch her arm and say in the most compassionate voice, "What's wrong, sweetie, tell me—is it Elliott again?"

She couldn't bark back at such loving kindness. And it infuriated her. He was so nice and she so awful. Moodily, she would answer with the gripe still in her voice, "I don't know—I'm all mixed up." Her thoughts, though, were whirling with clarity—How can you like me? I'm a woman who can't be trusted. You've witnessed it, so how can you *really* like me? And how can I trust your liking of me when I can't stand what you're seeing in me—Mary the two-timer.

But they carried on that way as spring continued to unfold with crocuses, daffodils, cherry blossoms, and dogwood. The warmer days even produced interludes of sunshine, a rarity for gray Bristol. Spring uplifted everyone's spirits, but not Mary's. She worked at home where she could smoke, raid the fridge, and brew fresh coffee. Her interviews and research now filled a couple of cartons—too much material to cart to the library. The kitchen table became her desk.

Early in April, as she sat paging through new books that had arrived, someone knocked on the kitchen's vestibule door. It was Elaine, still wearing her winter overcoat and scarf.

"Hey, I hope I'm not barging in at a bad time. You look busy."

"No, come in, it's good timing—new books just arrived." Mary said, clearing a path through her papers and books on the floor.

"Great, let's have a look," Elaine said, hanging her coat over the back of the kitchen chair that faced Mary's.

"Coffee? I just made a pot."

"Sure, that would be nice, thanks."

Mary poured coffee, and for a few minutes Elaine paged through the new books while they talked. Then she pushed them aside.

"I ran into Ann this morning and asked how her class was going. She mentioned your independent study and I realized I haven't heard in a while how it's going."

"It's going great—I love it. I've finished the interviews, and I'm trying to decide how to organize them, or the material." Mary picked up her binder from the floor and passed it to Elaine. "These are the transcripts, with my list of questions at the front. "

Elaine ran an eye over the pages as she turned them. "I can see you've done a lot of work."

"I've learned a lot—it's an important topic."

"I agree, and I'm sure the conclusions you're planning to draw are true. But you know, for scholarship, they won't be worth anything."

"Why?"

"Because even if you're right, you can't make hypotheses without examining a complete cross-section of women—

the way Hite did in her report—and that's an enormous undertaking. It would take years and big grants."

Mary sighed. "I don't care if it turns out to be just for me. And I'll still try to publish it."

Elaine nodded. "Good. And even if you do it for yourself, that's good enough—and we both know why!"

Mary reached for her cigarette pack, but then, in consideration of Elaine, pulled back her hand.

"Right. I want to hear how these women felt angry and trapped in their marriages because of their husbands' sexism. And I want to see if unmarried women who achieve their professional goals just like men are no longer attractive to men," Mary said.

"That second part will be hard to prove, and besides it's a separate study. At any rate, I wish you luck writing up your research, and I look forward to reading the article when it's ready."

They fell silent for a moment and sipped their coffee. Then, Mary, with some trepidation, revealed one of her recent upsets to Elaine. "You know, Grumman didn't recommend me as a good candidate for the PhD on a form the department sent out. He checked the 'no' box. I don't even want a PhD, but what if I did one day, like some of the women I'm interviewing who go back to school in their forties? I don't want that box checked in my records."

Elaine huffed. "Grumman's an old windbag who has consistently voted against tenuring our female faculty."

"I went to see him about it."

"Good! And what did he say, the old sourpuss? I bet he

sputtered and then wimped out—he's the type who's actually intimidated by strong women."

Mary stared for a moment, never having thought of Grumman that way. "That's amazing," she said, "that's exactly what happened. He fumbled around and then said, 'But why would you want to study for the PhD, Mary? You're pretty.'"

Elaine snorted. "Yeah, let us men do the hard stuff, and you pretty women serve us at home."

"At least he unchecked the box."

"Well that's good—you won the battle, and rightly so!" She paused and squinted through her glasses at Mary. "I want to know what's happening with you and Kevin."

"What's there to tell?"

"Well, are you in love with him?"

Mary grabbed her cigarette pack and this time lit up. "Yeah, and everything's a total mess!"

"I'll bet," Elaine said flatly. "And what are you going to do about it? You know you can't have both. You have to choose."

Mary squirmed uncomfortably. Elaine was forcing her to face her problem, but it was so hard to talk about it, and even harder to admit that she would ultimately choose Elliott over Kevin, even though Kevin was a far better friend to her—playful, energetic, talkative, affectionate, and loyal. She felt he really loved her. And they shared interests—literature, history, and writing. Why choose Elliott over Kevin? Why?

Elaine answered for her. "You want Elliott for security, and besides…," her tone soured a bit, "he's handsome."

With a jerk of her chin, Mary agreed. She could hide

behind Elliott's indomitable shoulder. To the outside world he looked and acted important—besides being handsome. She couldn't yet claim her own life and identity that way. And Kevin, for all his aptitude, social skills, and care for the world, was diffident in the face of her force. No, she couldn't say to Elaine that from the beginning of her affair with Kevin, she knew she would never spend her life with him.

"Well, that's enough on that topic for the moment," Elaine said, reaching for her coat on the back of her chair. "I've got to go now—office hours. Thanks for the coffee and chat—always fun to be with you. And before I forget, I'm hosting a brunch on Sunday—I hope you'll come. Men are invited too." She smiled and gave Mary a quick hug, affirming friendship and support.

Late in the day, Mary headed to campus to meet Kevin, whose days were filled with tutoring programs he had organized in the city's underserved neighborhoods. The days were now longer and Mary enjoyed the short walk to campus, checking neighbor's yards for the latest spring blooms. She also checked the trees, most of them still bare, but a few, like the crabapples, showing tight red clusters at their twig tips—soon to flower profusely. Here and there the willow trees' long branches in their first yellowish color swayed like grass skirts. In one yard, a magnolia had burst with white, star-like petals that looked like a baker's confection. It was amazing how every change in spring budding happened overnight. But luxurious green—green lawns, green trees in every shade—had yet to come, if Bristol's climate allowed it. This was Mary's first Bristol spring and likely her last. She smiled wryly, wondering how it would all unfold. And not with spring's usual cheer.

When she crossed Main Street in front of campus, she could see Kevin getting out of his car in the parking lot. Her heart leapt a little for the sight of a friend, a buddy, a confidant. He wore a flannel shirt like a jacket, rumpled jeans, and scruffy sneakers, the laces untied. His wavy hair had gone wild during his long day on the road checking up on his programs. Mary gave a skip to her step and waved. "Kevin!" she called out.

He started with surprise and dropped his knapsack in order to open his arms for her. "Ms. Contrary!" he sang out in his deep voice. Then he surprised her by diving down to grab her around the knees with a quick wrestler's move, collapsing her into his arms. "Gotcha!" he growled, his green eyes gleaming into hers like a tiger's. "And just where do you think you've been all my life?" He pulled her up and pecked her face with kisses and exaggerated rapture.

Mary laughed. "I'm so happy to see you!" And she felt a genuine return to their first exuberant days.

He crushed her against his chest. "Don't you know it's a sin to hide yourself from me? It's been torture all day! But now, I've got you and I'm going to abduct you to my cave!"

She loved how his eyebrows bobbed up and down in rhythm to his fast and furious speech. And his compact body was just as fiery. It always had excess energy to burn that he poured into his academic work or his jump-roping in the dorm's basement. He never released it by making love, and she imagined he believed this ultimate chastity saved him—and them—from sin. He had been raised in a devout Catholic household.

He released her, grabbed his backpack, and took her arm in a possessive grip as they walked away. "Coffee, beer, wine, dinner, or how about me? Can you spare a little time for a love-struck Irishman?"

"Always!" she laughed.

A few minutes later, seated on bar stools at the corner pub, they ordered wine. They liked sitting at the bar because they could snuggle up close and kiss between their silly chit-chat. But that night, they stayed too long and Mary drank too much on an empty stomach. She felt off balance walking home and wondered if passersby had noticed her uneven gait. She focused hard on walking a straight line and composing herself. The night was clear with stars, the air cold, but without winter's bite. It felt so good on her face and breathing it in helped restore her equilibrium. Her senses prickled deliciously with Kevin and her longing for the moment when they would fulfill their desire.

Nighttime's tingling spell broke when Mary reached the house and woke up to the reality of Elliott waiting inside for her. She sat down on the cold kitchen-door steps and smoked a cigarette, her whole being imploding to a leaden state. Slowly, she switched worlds from Kevin to Elliott, and finally, with dread, she rose and went inside.

As she came into the kitchen, she could see Elliott on the living room couch reading. He sighed, closed his book, got up, and came forward, lifting his hands as if for a hug, but then dropping them as if becoming aware of his gesture—his natural affectionate instinct. She felt sorry for him—he had a tender spot like everyone else—a human need for love and touching. But it had been raised out of him and replaced with conceit and spite.

She turned away and opened the fridge. "I'm so hungry!" She didn't want him coming too close to her because she smelled of wine and cigarettes. She crouched down to look for bread and cheese to make a sandwich.

Elliott was now standing near her, and she could feel the tension that always rose between them. She put her food on the counter and took off her jacket. Ignoring Elliott, she concentrated on making her sandwich.

"Where were you—jeez, it's past nine," Elliott said.

"I was with Kevin, working," she answered.

"You certainly see a lot of him."

"Do you mind?"

He hesitated and then answered in his sparring mode, "Why should I mind? I should be thanking the guy for babysitting you—takes the burden off me."

Mary caught her breath. "That is so nasty."

"Well, if the two of you always have so much work to do together, how come you aren't carrying any books?"

Her anger flashed. "You never give me any credit! You know nothing about my work. At least Kevin and Elaine like to hear about it."

"Yeah, well, I've noticed how gung-ho you are about interviewing those women who have nothing good to say about men."

"It's not like that at all! They're good, sincere people reflecting on their lives and how they couldn't be their true selves in their relationships."

"Because of men, always blaming men."

"Because their husbands insisted on being rulers and enforced that paradigm through intimidation and disrespect—in half the cases through violence."

"Yeah, well I just don't buy it, Mary, not as the general rule. From what I've seen, if a woman has drive enough to become a professional, there's no one stopping her. Your premise is just a typical feminist platitude."

Mary's jaw dropped and she stared at him.

He backed off a bit, changing his tone to sound more conversational. "Why, take your sister for example. Judy's intelligent, pretty, scathing in her opinions of men, and happily married to an intelligent—I might add unusually intelligent—man."

"There you go—putting Pete above Judy in your assessment of their intelligences. Assessing intelligences period."

"I'm only being honest, Mary. Pete happens to have been born with a one-in-a-million mind—even I'm jealous of him, though I wouldn't go telling him that. And I'm not saying any of this to be sexist, it just happens to be the truth."

Mary deliberately threw her sandwich into the trash can. "I give up on you. All humans are equal and worthy of the same respect. Pete absorbs information, while other people have gifts he doesn't have. No one is better than anyone else."

Elliott's brown eyes gleamed, primed for the fight. "Well, you can give up on me, Mary, but I still think your claim that men cower in the face of intelligent women is too much to expect your audience to swallow."

"I'm not counting on an audience. I'm hearing from women about their experiences in relationships that limit their freedom to be themselves. I'm learning, caring."

"Oh, really? Well, the way I see it, you're living with a man, you're an achievement-oriented woman—if we stretch the definition a bit—and I'm not holding you back."

Mary heard a loud crack in her head. He had succeeded in shattering her with his "if we stretch the definition a bit." She picked up her jacket and left. Blindly, incoherently, she walked toward campus, her limbs shaking uncontrollably. She felt a wall in front of her, a cage around her. She couldn't go on living with Elliott. She was free to leave and pursue her own life but the mere thought of it made her blank out. She could see no beginning for herself—where to start, how to do it. She wanted to close her eyes on everything, blot everything out.

She barged in on Kevin, seated at his desk, giving him only a second's warning with her urgent knock and entry.

"Mary!"

"I can't go on living with him!" she cried out.

He got up, his mouth a perfect O, and his eyes wide, afraid. "What happened?" he said.

"He's just so hateful! Insulting! I can't take it anymore. I have to leave, get away from him, but I also have to finish my work—the semester's almost over!"

His arms lifted and dropped as his eyes scanned his own quarters—a dorm. He was helpless to offer a safe haven.

And they both knew she was in no position to finance an apartment on her own. Kevin was immobile, not a joke or gurgle of laughter emitting from his lips. She saw he was scared. She saw for the first time that their untenable relationship actually fit his current life, for he faced several more years as a poor student working toward his PhD.

"Maybe he'll get that job he wants at Columbia and go away," Mary said, calming a bit, and sounding dreary.

"But what about you? You'd stay on to finish your master's, wouldn't you?"

Mary shrugged. Yes, she wanted the degree, but she didn't want Kevin to think she would have to lean on him if she stayed in Bristol. She sat down on his bed, her hands falling between her knees. It was so hard to think, to know what to do.

Kevin's green eyes flickered with worry as he sat down beside her and put a comforting arm around her shoulder. Yet it didn't feel genuine. She knew he was thinking about his own predicament. Carrying on their affair worked for him while he managed on student loans and grad housing. And maybe he sensed the truth, yes, surely he knew it, given his perspicacity—she would never live with him, she had many more mountains to climb. Still, he surprised her by fumbling for words that fit the moment. "Don't worry, sweetie, we … we could always get an apartment."

She quickly shook her head and smiled kindly at him. "I'm not asking that. You're all set up for your PhD. I'll figure out my own mess. But thanks for letting me purge. I was so upset."

She stood up and he quickly followed her, taking her hand. Their eyes met and she wondered if the same thoughts ran through his mind—that their love had always been unreal, ungrounded because she lived with Elliott. They had been complacent about that premise, and for different reasons—she had been his diversion from the tedious grind of school work, and he had been her escape from Elliott. And now, they had reached a culminating moment where their lives—their three lives—would diverge into separate directions. Yet, she still needed Kevin—he was her closest friend—and he still needed her for the same reason. They put their arms around each other and hugged for a long moment. Then he rocked her gently and said lamely against her head, "We'll manage somehow."

And that was how they left it—that they'd find a solution for staying together.

After that night, with six weeks left in the semester, Mary lost her direction and ability to think, organize, and execute plans. A terrible fuzz clouded her mind. She couldn't write up her study of the women. None of her research cohered for her. She felt despair when she woke up in the morning and couldn't muster any motivation. She no longer had feelings for Elliott or Kevin, but interacted by rote, often irritably. She drank at the pub with Kevin for an hour of falsely uplifted spirits, but ultimately drinking only worsened her mood.

One night, when she returned tipsy from the bar, Elliott was already in bed. When she crawled in, her body sensually craving from the wine, she nestled up against him and, to her surprise, he responded. She gave him her all and he returned her caresses but then stopped at the critical moment to say, "Shouldn't we take precaution?"

"It's okay, it's the last day of my period—safe."

But the next month, her period didn't come. She was pregnant. She never considered keeping the baby. In her current loveless state, the meaning of pregnancy didn't involve a baby. Pregnancy was a microscopic foreign body inside her that had to be removed as soon as possible.

When Elliott came home from work the day of her positive test, she was waiting for him at the kitchen table. She gave him the news. "And I made an appointment for an abortion."

Elliott was stunned and dropped his briefcase on the table. "An abortion," he echoed.

"Yeah, Planned Parenthood game me a name."

Elliott opened the fridge and looked for something to eat. He emerged with an apple and a can of soda. He said nothing more, though he stood there not looking at her.

"Is that all?" Mary said. "Aren't you going to say anything?" She wanted comfort for what she was going through.

"Yeah," he said, lips becoming churlish, "I have something to say. I wouldn't want a baby that had been conceived in a drunken state—all those damaged chromosomes. On the other hand, it's good to know I can at least conceive a baby."

Mary's mouth dropped. Hatred ripped through her and she rushed out of the room to get away from him.

In the library the next afternoon, she shared the news with Elaine and her plan for the abortion.

"I'll come with you," Elaine said, firmly.

Mary started in surprise—neither Elliott nor Kevin had suggested coming with her when she gave them the news. Kevin had listened sympathetically that morning and had even offered whatever help she might need, but his body language had been distant, frightened, afraid for himself, even though he knew he wasn't the father. Tears of gratitude welled up in Mary's eyes for Elaine's support and also for women throughout the world for being the rock foundation of life, of selfless help during difficult times.

When Mary got home after her meeting with Elaine, all the feelings she had been suppressing for so many weeks snapped, and an animal cry rose out of her gut. She curled up on the couch and let herself cry.

It was a bleak spring day when Mary entered Dr. Gleason's office, accompanied by Elaine. Abortion was legal but still something shady and unsavory. It seemed fitting that the waiting room was dark with vinyl chairs and a frumpy nurse who also handled the reception desk. Mary checked in and moments later was ushered into the procedure room. Elaine said firmly to her back, "I'll be waiting here."

The procedure room was fairly large and smelled musty, as if the walls and linoleum floor had endured a century of flooding. The surgical table stood in the middle of the room. A lamp hung over it and trays with gleaming instruments lay ready on each side. Mary stiffened in fear. The place looked and felt sinister, but maybe it was the reality of abortion that affected the atmosphere. The grouchy, late middle-aged nurse told Mary to undress and lie on the table with the sheet over her. Then she left.

Mary did as she was told and then waited, shivering a bit for the unknown experience that lay ahead. Dr. Gleason entered the room. He didn't look like any of the doctors she had known in her life, doctors with serious faces, erudition, and white lab coats with neckties showing at their collars. Dr. Gleason wore plaid polyester pants and a muddy green pullover that went well with his orange skin and balding, crusty scalp that produced a few threads of red hair. In late middle age, his body had lost shape, leaving him with a flabby bottom that jiggled when he walked around the table. On the outside, he was grotesque, and with the plaid pants, red hair, and orange complexion, he reminded Mary of a circus clown.

Mary tensed and held her breath when Dr. Gleason's strange energy came alongside her and his pocked face grinned down at her with yellow teeth that reminded her of a werewolf's. "Hi there, kitten, and what naughty things have you been up to that bring you here?"

His speckled hand swiftly took up a syringe from the tray on his side and without pause, he injected a barbiturate into Mary's arm, all the while joking with small talk, as if they were flirting at a party. The drug hit her brain within seconds, producing a woozy high that brought her right into his joking orbit, which underneath she could feel was all wrong but she couldn't control. When he came to her head again and looked down with his clowning mask off for a fleeting second, she saw ice-cold hatred in his face. But the fatuous grin came right back as he flipped the sheet to her waist, causing her to freeze in startlement, her breasts so suddenly exposed, her modesty compromised, powerless in his command.

He began poking, pinching, and fondling her breasts, talking nonstop and sociably, as if to make his touches appear as a normal breast check, but they weren't. "We like to show you young women how to check for lumps," he said with his immutable grin. "It can save you a lot of time, trouble, and heartache later on." He gave her left nipple an emphatic twist, his voice carrying on without interruption, but his tawny snake eyes glinting with sadistic pleasure. "One kind of lump forms right behind the nipple," was his excuse. Then he pressed down, forming a cave in her soft flesh. "But you're in the clear, honey, at least for now. Keep an eye on 'em."

He prowled around the table, talking facetiously about women, sex, and boyfriends. Deep down, Mary felt anxious, untrusting, and vulnerable. But her upbringing automatically made her cooperate with him, in fact, made her try to please him to be approved. On the outside, with the help of the barbiturate, she participated in his banter and made him laugh with her quips. But as soon as he paused at her side and put his flaking hands on her hip, she stopped, for his threat could not be ignored.

"Do you like sex, Mary?"

It was not a normal question and again she froze, his danger upon her. Slowly, he drew the sheet down past her knees and let it drop by her feet with cold indifference.

She trembled with fear. A recurring nightmare flashed

in her mind. In it, she lay powerless on an operating table where masked men in long white coats bore down on her with needles that would end her life.

She looked at Dr. Gleason and saw him as a dumpy charlatan shamelessly studying her body with a gloating expression on his face. He hated women and he had found a way to have power over them. Then, without warning, with a swift aggressor's movement, he inserted two fingers into her vagina, while she yelped in surprise and protest.

"I have to examine you first, sweetie, right? Keep your cool, just relax, think of something funny—me, for instance." He shot his clown's grin at her. "And I can always make things easier with another shot, if you like."

"No!"

"Hmm, you've got a tipped uterus. That makes intercourse painful, am I right?" His fingers went up and down to demonstrate "pain" each time they rammed her. "Now turn on your side, darling," he said without removing his fingers.

"I don't need to, I get the point."

"Just do as I say, I want to show you something important." He nudged her with his free hand, so she turned, and then he started ramming her again. "See? Any pain now?"

She didn't answer. She kept her eyes shut tight to him and the world, while the same thought, the same prayer, repeated in her mind: Please God, let this be done, please God, get me out of here.

"So, just remember, have intercourse on your side from now on and you'll be all set for life." He removed his fingers, grimaced at them, and then washed them in the sink. He came back to her and stared down coolly at her face, as if considering his next torture.

"Tell me, Mary, do you douche at least once a week?"

"No."

"Really? Why not?"

"My doctor said it's not necessary, that the bacteria's natural and the body takes care of itself."

"That's baloney! You women listen to any old myth! Your doctor's a lady, right? One those newfangled advocates of 'our bodies, ourselves.'" He grabbed a shiny steel speculum from the tray, keeping his other hand firmly on her hip, just to let her know who was in charge, as he prepared to enter her again.

"Wait'll you get a *load* of this—if you'll excuse my pun," he said, grinning, and quickly slid the cold instrument into her. He moved it all around as if she were a glass jar he could scrape as carelessly as he pleased. Then he withdrew the instrument and brought its milky discharge up to her face.

"See that, sweetheart? That's only a fraction of all the gunk that's up there inside you. Do you like oral sex, Mary? Huh? Do you like your boyfriend? Huh? Do you have any respect for him? I think you do. So in all fairness to him, are you going to continue subjecting his face to this gross stuff?" He pushed the speculum right under her nose, as if she were a dog who had pooped in the wrong place and the angry master was now rubbing its nose in it. "This is filthy!" he said.

Mary, even in her drugged state, could still think. She hadn't ever been told such things about her female parts and how men could be so revolted by them. A brand-new mortification spread over her, and she had no feminist weapon ready with which to counterattack. She had only her timeless, traditional female responses—in this case, hanging her head in shame and half-believing him.

He proceeded with the abortion, his lobster claws at work while he attempted to distract her with his insipid chatter. Then he was gone, and she was left alone. She lay there inert. The deed was done. Yes, she was glad, relieved, but now she felt dead, without any life stirring in her veins. She needed to get home and curl up in bed, forget everything, obliterate the memory of this horrible experience and of her whole life.

Dr. Gleason returned, his cheery mood restored. "Hey, babe, how're you doing? It was like eating peppermint candy, right?" He squeezed her upper arm as if to test her degree of recovery.

"I've just looked at your chart—weight's perfect. Don't gain an ounce, you hear? Men only like slim bodies. So … let's talk about birth control. What're you going to do about it, sweetheart?"

"I have a diaphragm."

He shook his head. His fingertips dug into her arm. "You ladies come here as if abortion were a form of birth control."

"What—" Mary started to say, but he cut her off.

"There are girls out there right now who've been here two, three times. I mean, I like you, in fact, your looks improve the appearance of this place, but let's be realistic, Mary, if you want to see me again, you don't have to get pregnant to do it. Just give me a call, you have my number." He coughed into his hand, then continued, "Diaphragms are a pain in the neck and unreliable—as you yourself now know. This is the perfect time to insert an IUD."

"No," Mary said. "I don't want one."

He grimaced. "It's the ideal method of birth control if you want an active sex life."

She shook her head adamantly.

"That's awfully selfish of you, Mary. You're not thinking of your boyfriend—do you really want to force him into a mouthful of that disgusting jelly? Be considerate of him for a change."

"No, I had one, and I got rid of it. I don't want another."

With a huff of exasperation, Dr. Gleason strutted out of the room, his flabby rear jiggling in the plaid pants. How Mary hated him. How she wanted to get out of there. Maybe she could just get up and leave. Yes, she would do that.

Just as she started to rise, the unpleasant nurse came in and snapped at her, "Why are you refusing to let the good doctor give you an IUD? Haven't you been enough trouble already—sleeping around and getting pregnant? You owe it to this kind doctor who's helped you out of a serious predicament to abide by his wishes to insert an IUD."

Her lecture only stoked Mary's resistance, and it was easier to fight a woman than a man. "No, I don't want one, so forget it."

The nurse huffed off of the room, slamming the door.

Mary rose, clutching the sheet close to her as she hurried toward the chair where she had left her clothes. As if expecting her attempt to escape, Dr. Gleason returned, feigning noisy cheerfulness. "Hey, hold your horses. We're not quite done, sweetheart. You've been a good girl and we'll get you out of here in just another minute." He patted the table. "Hop back up, I have to make sure everything's safe for you to leave."

"Like what? I feel fine."

"Gotta make sure there's no bleeding or complications. You don't want an infection, do you?"

She hesitated. She didn't want complications. Reluctantly she got back on the table, hardly breathing, all her barriers up.

His scaly hands moved around the instruments on the tray and then held up a shiny needle to the light and squinted at it, but more for her benefit—to instill fear about his next move and her powerlessness to avoid it—her nightmare. "Just one last little shot, honey, to prevent infection," he said blithely, but with a diabolical gleam in his eyes that he wanted her to see.

Seconds later, Mary was high on the same drug as before. Exhilaration and delicious sensations tingled all through her. Fear and suspicion were swept away. The ugly, moldering room swayed and tilted. The hard bed felt like a boat at sea tipping precariously on waves. She laughed and gripped its sides to keep from falling off. She heard her own ludicrous chatter and Dr. Gleason playing along with it. But he had much more important things to think about, to execute.

He moved to her feet, looked at her. "How about I insert that IUD now?" He smiled like the kindly doctor.

"Oh, all right," Mary said with a laugh. "Who cares!"

He sprang into action as if to accomplish the deed before

she realized her mistake and kicked him away. It was done in seconds. Exhaling in satisfaction, he gave her a victorious grin. She cowered, she had allowed his victory over another hateful woman. He brushed his hands as if to rid them of her contamination, but she knew the gesture was just one more insult to her. He headed for the door, but then stopped as if remembering to say goodbye—but his way—"Be good, now...." He snapped his fingers, as if trying to recall her name. "Well, whatever your name is—sorry it's slipped my mind—I see so many of you." He was gone, gloating that he had rubbed in her total insignificance, her loathsome existence, her nonexistence.

Traumatized and physically unstable, Mary dressed and went to the waiting room. Elaine put down her book and looked at her. "Gee, are you okay?" she said rising and putting a hand on Mary's arm.

"Let's get out of here," Mary whispered—the only voice she could muster.

Safe in the car, Mary sat unmoving, unable to speak the entire ride home. Her throat ached as if a hangman's rope had tightened around it. Her mind couldn't function. She felt she was sinking into a black hole of oblivion, and all she wanted was to fall on her bed and blot out the world. At the same time, she was grateful for Elaine, Elaine who had come with her to the appointment, Elaine whose competent hands now held the steering wheel taking her home. Their mutual silence was fine, for it was the silence of understanding, of women's innate strength and empathy in times of grief or calamity.

Finally Mary was home. She went straight to her bed, got under the covers, and nestled into the comforting pillow. She lay there motionlessly, her mind blank. It didn't take long for warm tears to rise in her eyes and run down her face into the crevice of her neck and shoulder, where the wetness grew cold. There was no wailing, just a silent bleeding of tears that came from deep inside, where fragile walls of protection, of lifelong self-defense, had broken down.

That evening Elliott came home from work in a state of excitement. Mary was drinking a cup of tea at the kitchen table, her untouched books and papers surrounding her. She had showered and put on clean clothes in an effort to rid herself of Dr. Gleason's toxicity. But that had been her outer self, and she couldn't wash off her inner state, which contrasted so noticeably to Elliott's rare gaiety and smiling happiness.

"Jeez, Mary, you aren't going to believe what just happened! Columbia called and offered me that job!"

A tiny spark lit in the fog of Mary's mind—they could leave Bristol! She could start over in New York—that is, if she stayed with him. She smiled wanly to show she was happy for him, maybe even for them.

"Just imagine!" he went on, circling the kitchen restlessly and clasping and unclasping his long, sculpted hands. "It's a dream job, my future, and we can get out of here." Then he stopped and gave her a doleful look, like a puppy dog with a tilted head. "I hope you're coming with me, Mary," he said as if asking.

She smiled again. She wanted to say yes in his moment of happiness, but no words came.

Suddenly his face changed, his excitement vanishing, guilt replacing it. He put an apologetic hand on her shoulder. "Jeez, Mary, I totally forgot—what with the job offer and the prospect of getting out of here … damn, how are you? How did it go today?"

She managed to say, "Fine, I'm fine." There was no point trying to share her experience. He had never tuned into her feelings, and this time the feelings went so deep. And she was right, for he gladly accepted her answer and suggested they go out for dinner to celebrate his job and the end to her problem. Yes, "her problem," he had said, and she had to agree—it had been hers, he had not involved himself.

The last weeks of the term whizzed by. It came as rote for Mary to write answers to Old Grumman's take-home exam, though she still had a few details to check in the library about the Wounded Knee Massacre's inaccurate news coverage in 1890. Her main preoccupation was how to articulate conclusions about her interviews with the women. The transcripts lay on the dining room table, along with her research on marriage, professional women, and so-called "female psychology." Now, when it was time to write what she had learned, she couldn't start, she couldn't see how to put it all together, analyze it, make arguments to support her original hypotheses. She kept thinking of Elaine, who had warned her about not having a scientific framework from which to state supported conclusions. Days kept passing as Mary sat at the dining room table or in the library, her pen poised over her legal pad, her mind repeating the same question, as if the question alone had the power to loosen the words, the connecting ideas she needed in order to begin: What do you want to say? What do you want to say?

Well ... she wanted to say what Elliott called her "feminist platitudes." She wanted to corroborate her own situation through the other women's stories and somehow gain the courage to "unstuck herself" the way they had. She was resisting the possible truth that the interviews were merely personal stories and not the concrete psychological data she had imagined herself collecting and proudly presenting to the world as proof of its patriarchy. How could she write conclusions that didn't exist in the mounds of research spread out on the dining room table?

Finally, with time running out she cobbled together a paper lacking any verve, any evidence of the heartfelt hours she had put into its research. But she had to release the work, not only for course credit, but also because Ann, Elaine, Kevin, and Elliott were waiting to see it. She had talked of nothing else all semester.

Ann soon left Mary a message to come by her office before her first class—a time she was always at her desk. Mary went the next morning and found Ann eating a Danish pastry, the flakes falling on her papers.

"Have a seat," Ann said through a mouthful, waving sticky fingers at the chair facing her. "Sorry to be eating—I have class in five minutes."

"No problem," Mary said, trying to smile, but her face

felt stiff. It was fear of being judged for her mediocre performance. Carefully she sat down on top of papers and magazines already occupying the chair. She folded her hands in her lap to quiet them.

Ann squinted at her in perplexity. "I'm kind of stumped about your paper, or your project. Like I said before, it's not my area—I don't even know what area it represents. It's like psychology but without the science. I'm into the Knights of Labor. I'm writing a theory of feminist Marxism. So, I can't respond to this, but I can give you a pass for the course. I know how hard you worked on it—I can see you really struggled with the topic."

Mary longed to disappear. She felt so exposed and ashamed, especially knowing the others, the far more important others, also had her paper and were probably blushing for her.

Ann saw her distress and quickly filled the gap. "Didn't Elaine tell me you're engaged?"

"Yeah, but it's actually up in the air." Tears were in her voice, and she swallowed hard for composure.

"Well, if you decide to continue with this project, maybe you could get a grant to really do it." She looked at her watch. "I've gotta split—class." She stood up, pulled down the hem of her faded blouse, and brushed off pastry crumbs. Then, she picked up her crumpled lecture and gave Mary a last baffled stare. "Hey, look, just because I didn't relate to your study doesn't mean it isn't perfectly valuable to someone else." She attempted a smile but couldn't quite manage it, and fled, relieved to be done with Mary.

That evening, Elliott came home from work, her paper in his hand. He dropped it on the kitchen table, where Mary was working on Grumman's take-home exam. She braced herself for his coming comments.

"Well, I read your paper."

She didn't answer and her eyes glazed as she looked at him.

"Well…," he said again, sitting down in the other chair. "Shall I be nice, or tell you what I really think?"

"Obviously what you really think."

"In that case, it was much more interesting to hear you talk about it."

Mary's fingers trembled as she slid the paper over to her side and then down to her lap, out of sight. "So, what didn't you like?"

"Well hell, Mary, I don't know, it just seems you haven't done your topic justice. And then, well Christ, haven't you ever read a grammar book?"

That ended the conversation. Mary would hear no more.

The next day, Elaine was much kinder, gentler, in her assessment. She came by the house and joined Mary for a coffee at the kitchen table. "You put some interesting ideas into your report," she said in her firm way. "But what I want to know is why you completely omitted some of the important issues we talked about—like why it might be necessary for high-achieving women to go it alone in life—forego husband and children in order to fulfill their purpose? And you never brought up whether marriage inevitably results in self-sacrifice and psychological or physical abuse for a woman. You left that out." She took a breath. "Anyway, I wish it had been longer, and you should know how to spell 'develop.'"

"I know how to spell 'develop.'"

"Good, then the extra 'e' was just a typo—in three places. Anyhow, you undertook an enormous subject and needed more time and resources than you had at your disposal."

Kevin was the last critic for Mary to face, and the hardest for her ego. They had not seen or phoned each other in several days, and she knew it was because of her paper. How could he, the gentle, loving soul, face her with his honest opinion, and how could she face him feeling like a failure? Finally, she trudged the few blocks to his dorm. It was a rare sunny afternoon and should have lifted her spirits, but she was too full of dread and unhappiness with herself to feel nature's golden touch—or even notice it.

She knocked on Kevin's door, calling at the same time, "It's me."

His deep voice answered right away, "Mary! Come in!"

Both of them blushed when their eyes met. He didn't pretend to be light and witty but immediately lifted her manuscript from his desk and gave it to her.

"I wanted to call you, but I had a paper due. Here—thanks for sharing yours with me." He turned back to his desk and busied himself with gathering up photocopied articles, which he then dumped in his closet, on top of laundry, sports equipment, and piles of books. He turned back to her, looking anguished.

"I feel so guilty for keeping you from your work this

semester. I've been terribly irresponsible, and I'm sorry." He picked up a paperback from his desk and held it out to her. "Look—I was reading this book last night and it reminded me of you and your love for writing. Willis has all kinds of practical advice for us that I'm already putting to use. Borrow it—I think you'll like it."

Mary took the book and looked at its glossy gray cover: *Writing Clear English*. Horror filled her. She wished she had never come to see him. She wished she had never been born. His smelly room—like a men's locker room—now turned her stomach. He instantly grabbed the book back from her. "Never mind, I didn't mean it the way you're thinking. We both know you're a superb writer—even Old Grumman praised you—you a mere woman!" He jested with a hopeful smile, but Mary was unreachable.

"At any rate, Mary, Willis has great advice for us, that's all I meant—like how to avoid prepositional phrases—'important women' instead of 'women of importance.'"

He realized immediately his mistake and rushed to hug her, but she pushed him away and headed for the door.

"Promise you're coming back," he half-whimpered.

She barely glanced at him, hating him because she hated herself.

"Mary!"

"See you around," she said bitterly and strode out, aware she was punishing him for her own defeat.

Blindly, without any forethought, she made her way to the one place that all her life had provided solace and refuge: the library. Like an automaton, she scrolled through microfiche for newspaper coverage of Wounded Knee—all the false news that had made excuses for the government's killings. She needed to finish her last short essay on Grumman's take-home exam.

While her eyes scanned headlines, her mind tried to rationalize the failure of her paper. She consoled herself that by the time she was ready to write her conclusions, she no longer dared to make assumptions. By then, it seemed that for every male-initiated threat to a woman's quality life, there were exceptions that suggested there were no hard-and-fast rules about male and female behaviors. It seemed that women's psychology wasn't really a class unto itself. Instead, each individual, regardless of gender, developed behavior according to his or her own life experiences within a family and a culture, in addition to genetic behavioral inheritance, all of which could be modified or transformed by anyone who sought change. And yet, there still existed the fundamental patriarchy—the world over—and that was what she had wanted to demonstrate through the women's stories.

Mary kept scanning for two words: "Wounded Knee." But two other words brought her to a halt: "Woman's Lot." It was the bolded title to a three-stanza poem by a woman. It cleverly denounced the double standard, politely asking why men should be indulged adulterous amusement, when women were banished and punished for the same behavior. Mary printed the poem, noting that her heart was beating excitedly as if coming back to life. If this poem existed in 1890, then there had to be more poems by more women in other newspapers and periodicals that printed feminist sentiments. She wanted to find them—America's presuffrage, feminist verses. She could start over the summer, a few weeks away. It could become her master's thesis, even if she left Bristol and lived in New York with Elliott, or someplace else on her own.

During those last days in Bristol, Elliott was in a good mood, alive with a sustained energy that Mary had never seen in him. After work, when they made dinner in the kitchen, he now put his arm around her waist and swung her into a swing-dance twirl while humming happily and saying, "Hell, Mary, we both hate Bristol and now we're getting out!"

Mary packed up her belongings and took charge of selling the secondhand furniture they had bought. Elliott believed she was going to New York with him, and Kevin believed she was staying behind in Bristol. Mary lied to both men, not out of meanness or a heartless soul but out of paralysis to face them with the truth—that she didn't want to spend her life with either of them. Part of her inertia was fear of being labeled an "evil woman," the horrible creature men had never been able trust from the beginning of time, or at least since Adam and Eve. And she still had no idea how she was going to make her own life. Would it turn out that she was one of the women from her interviews who had to live alone in order to fulfill her purpose?

Her lie only got worse her last days in Bristol, when she couldn't give Kevin any definite plans about her future— where she would live for instance, how she would support herself. Imminently, he was going to find out she was leaving with Elliott, even though remaining with Elliott would be of short duration until she severed ties. As it stood, they planned to stay at his parents' house outside Boston until their move to New York, which in the end would not include her.

On her last night in Bristol, Mary headed to campus to finally tell Kevin she was leaving. But surely he already knew it, and their awkwardness together as they set off for the field behind the campus confirmed such feelings. It was a beautiful May night with a clear sky and full moon glazing the field's fresh grass with silver light. They lay down on their backs, held hands, and stared at the deep, mysterious sky with its glittering stars and glowing moon. But the magnificence of the universe could barely be appreciated, for weighty things, rotten earthly things to do with humans, held them captive.

Kevin dared to broach the topic first with a stammered whisper, "Did you tell him?"

She squeezed his hand, a desperate squeeze that answered before any words came out. "Every time I try, he misunderstands—and then I chicken out."

"But he's leaving tomorrow."

Mary sat up and rubbed her face in her hands. "Yeah … it's just not going the way I wanted. I'm really sorry, I think I have to go too."

"You think…?"

"I mean, at this point it's easier to split up with him in Boston, away from here. And I can start my research there— there's a women's history library in Cambridge."

Kevin tugged her back down and buried his head against hers. "I just have this ominous feeling," he said.

Mary didn't answer. She held him and felt awful. She

sealed her lips to keep from saying, "I'll be back, don't worry." That was her instinct, to comfort him, to promise something she knew she wouldn't uphold. And he didn't ask her to promise that. He knew the truth.

"We'll write each other," she said.

His head came up. "Every day." Then, in an effort to revive some of his old playfulness he said, "As soon as you leave, I'm switching majors to 'Mary Ferguson.' It's going to be a lifelong project that results in a twenty-volume work that Grumman introduces."

They laughed, but without their early freedom. They had a history now, one that felt heavy and unhappy.

When Mary headed home later that night, she crossed the campus parking lot to Main Street. At the curb, she looked back at Kevin who stood on the other side of the lot under a street lamp watching her. The cone of light illuminating him was like the spotlight on an actor's last tragic scene in a play. She waved and hurried on, eager to free herself of her guilt. But she couldn't escape it, for she still needed to call him from Boston with her decision to go it alone.

There remained only Elliott with whom to sever ties, but his protective indifference would make it easier than parting with Kevin—Kevin who showed his feelings, who allowed himself to feel.

And after Elliott? What then? What was her plan? How would she survive?

She didn't know yet. It would take time, stepping stones to know. The only thing she could imagine at that moment was sitting at a library table—the one in Cambridge with a feminist archive. She would spend hours there, poring over disintegrating brown pages of nineteenth-century American newspapers and magazines, her eyes looking for verses by protesting women. She wondered if the male editors of some of the publications had been in agreement with the women's outcries for equality, or if they had printed the poems with an indulgent chuckle for the women attempting to be as respected, as valuable as men. Digging into "Woman's Lot" was all Mary knew about her future.

Wonderfulioso

I T WAS THEIR LAST MORNING of sightseeing in Florence. Fran wasn't ready to leave. She heard the noises of Friday morning through the open second-floor window—the grinding and gusting of delivery trucks and garbage collectors, the clatter of vendors and merchants setting up, and the strange, whisking sound of street sweepers with twig brooms. Steve was in the bathroom. He didn't seem to mind that the toilet choked with every effort to flush, or the wildly spraying, handheld shower head that flooded the tiled floor. There was no curtain, no porcelain threshold protecting the shower. He had studied in Bologna and was accustomed to the culture of Italian bathrooms.

Fran reached down for her clothes on the bed and began to dress. She had gotten no further than her bra and slip when a sharp rap sounded on the door. She knew at once it was Jane, her white-haired, owl-eyed, intense mother-in-law. Fran knew Jane was standing there, impatient to state her desires for the day. They were touring northern Italy together, now that Steve had his first assignment as vice consul in the foreign service. Jane's husband, Hubert, just followed whatever the others were doing.

Fran opened the door a crack, concealing her barely clad body behind the door. Jane instantly barked out her message. "Good morning, Fran, there are just two things I want to do this morning before we leave Florence. I want to find a leather shop to buy gloves for Jim, and I want to track down some of that pretty Florentine stationery. Do you agree?"

Fran gave a short nod. It was a gesture she had developed after days of touring together. Hubert was all right. He was much older than Jane, physically slow like a big lumbering bear, and content to trail after them. He reminded Fran of an elderly, docile pet. She humored herself imagining Jane training him to follow her commands so that he no longer needed a leash. This image came to Fran because Steve had told her that his mother used to put her sons on leashes when she walked them down the lane to the beach—five frisky boys tugging in all directions while frazzled Jane tried to maintain control of the litter.

Fran was a bride of nine months, and her only knowledge of marriage was the usual vision fed to the world in novels and movies—"happy ever after." She had often heard that children eventually turn into their parents—daughters into their mothers and sons into their fathers—but of course she couldn't imagine that for herself, just as she couldn't imagine ever dying. But now, traveling with her in-laws, she wondered if her high energy and Steve's spaced-out manner could actually evolve into Jane and Hubert. A horrifying thought!

Having agreed to Jane's wishes, Fran closed the door. Steve came out of the bathroom, fluffing his black hair with a towel. Fran stared at him. What beautiful skin he had, smooth and soft, and that brown patch at his pelvis with its dangling phallus—her insides lit up. She forgot about his possible evolution into his father—who was terribly overweight—this young man drying his body thrilled her.

"Who was that?" Steve asked.

"Your mother."

"What did she want?"

"To remind me she has souvenir shopping to do before we leave Florence—gloves for your brother, stationery for her."

"I can tell you don't like her."

"I do like her, but she never stops talking. She's like one of those little yappy dogs—yap, yap, yap—the kind you want to strangle." Fran laughed and dropped backwards onto the bed, legs dangling over the edge—voluptuous in mood, sexy in just her underwear. She fastened a seductive gaze on Steve, but he only rummaged in his suitcase for clean clothes. Her hands spread over her tummy, eyes closing and thoughts drifting to what it would feel like to be filled with his child.

"You have to remember traveling to Italy was always my mother's dream," Steve said, putting on his shirt and starting to button it. "She studied foreign affairs in graduate school and dreamed of a job like mine, even though she knew women in her day could only hope to serve as secretaries. She longed to travel."

"But she married and had children instead. Sealed her fate to women's lot. I definitely want her to have a good time here. We just planned too much, too many places. And we still have Venice to go. That means three hours in the back seat with her—for me, that is," Fran said.

"Try to remember this is our vacation too—your first chance to see more of Italy, something you've been dying to do."

"You sound like your mother: preachy," Fran said, rolling off the bed and resuming her dress. Did she really know her husband? She had definitely fallen in love with his beauty first, his manly five-o'clock shadow that sprouted needles when he kissed her and got aroused. And she liked his education and career, his New York background. She was a teacher and had found a job teaching English at their post. She's wasn't much older than her university students and had become friends with some of them.

"I'm just glad my career is giving my mother and father a chance to travel."

"I'm glad too."

Fran wondered if Jane and Hubert hadn't traveled because raising five sons through college had made it financially impossible. Or was it Hubert's feet? In childhood, surgeons kept cutting into his defective toes until he lost several of them. No, it wasn't Hubert's feet—he managed to hobble along as they moved from one church to another or through museums. The issue was money, letting go of it, contributing a share to the hotel and restaurant bills, the entrance fees to cultural heritage, and even the smaller refreshments at Italy's ubiquitous bars. And the problem wasn't handling foreign currency, for Steve and Fran could easily help with that. When bills came at check-out or the end of a meal, the white-haired folks froze and looked alarmed and said nothing. They made no move to reach for their wallets and offer to contribute a share. Fran had grown up with her parents covering such family get-together expenses, and the reversal of roles bothered her.

And so it was, at the hotel's front desk that morning—Jane and Hubert stepped back as soon as the clerk laid *il conto,* the bill, on the counter. Fran watched their white hair bristle on their scalps. She saw their bodies retract into their long trench coats, as if trying to become invisible. If they just waited long enough, they'd be relieved of any responsibility, for Steve would react first.

The scene played out just as Fran had imagined it, for it was their fifth check-out. Once again, Steve stood there with the hotel bill in hand, attempting to share the column of figures with his shrunken parents. Jane's walking shoes kept inching back, her eyes wildly seeking escape. Hubert stood like a tree trunk with a dazed expression, his brown eyes darting from side to side as if oblivious to Steve's presence. All in all, Fran thought, the two of them looked positively deranged. She let Steve handle the situation. These were his parents, but his junior officer income could hardly cover their combined touring.

With a defeated sigh and droop to his shoulders, Steve turned back to the desk clerk and paid the bill. Fran noted that Jane now pressed against the wall as if facing a firing squad. She had pulled two withered lira notes from her raincoat pocket and twitched them in the direction of Steve.

Now that the bill was paid, she croaked out, "I don't suppose these would be of any use?"

Steve gave her an exasperated roll of his eyes and said, "That'll buy your next cappuccinos."

A few minutes later, they were winding through the streets of enticing windows for Jane's gloves and stationery—just the right ones, pricewise, that is. Finally, Jane approved a leather shop with "sale" signs in the window. Steve, fluent in Italian, explained to the elegantly dressed, stern-faced woman behind the counter what his mother wanted. Nervously, Jane bent her white head over the pair of soft leather gloves that the shopkeeper gingerly placed in her hands, as if to emphasize the preciousness of their Italian craftsmanship that Jane might damage.

"How much?" Jane said, like a growl, twitching the gloves and not looking up at anyone.

"About twenty dollars," Steve said.

"Twenty dollars seems awfully expensive, don't you think?"

"They'll cost forty in Venice," Fran said impatiently.

"It just seems like so much for a little old piece of leather."

But under pressure, her resistance slowly caved and she agreed to buy them. From her quilted shoulder bag, she withdrew a small black change purse, the kind Fran had seen local nuns using. She opened the brass snap at the top and stared at the lira inside. "I suppose she wants some of these," she said.

"Yes," Steve sighed, "twenty-five thousand lira, about twenty dollars."

"I can never get used to all those zeros. Are you sure I'm

not buying a house? Why are they so expensive? I really wanted to bring home gloves for Jim. He needs them. But they only cost four dollars at the drugstore."

The shop owner couldn't restrain a huff of contempt—Americans cared more about money than quality and one's appearance! They cared more about money than giving a special gift to a beloved son! Americans and money!

Steve's patience wore out. With a disgusted grunt he reached into his back pocket for his wallet.

Jane sprang into action, her owl eyes beaming. "No, no, no! Here, you find it for me, but don't give her too much."

The purchase proceeded with Steve counting out the lira notes.

"Are you sure you're not giving her too much?" Jane chirped with an effort to sound cheery. But when the change purse emptied, alarm filled her face. "How many of those things did you give her, Steve!"

Steve ignored her. A minute later, the shop owner proudly and delicately handed Jane a most beautifully wrapped package with a gold, twirled ribbon and an embossed label testifying to the shop's Florentine origin. Jane managed to say thank you as she gazed at the package. They all gazed. No one in America made gift wrapping look like a work of art.

"What else did you say you needed?" Steve said.

"Stationery. But obviously I'll have to give that up. Jim's gloves just consumed all my pocket money." Then, abandoning her grumpy tone, she added gaily, "I'll just have to come back to Italy! And by then, I hope you'll be a better bargainer, Steve—or the ambassador!"

In late morning—a beautiful spring day with trees blooming across the hilly Tuscan landscape decorated with stands of cypress—they drove toward Venice. In the little Fiat's back seat, Fran was happy for their various packages that now formed a little wall between Jane and herself. Fran didn't want to talk or prompt Jane to talk by saying anything. Just in case the packages weren't enough protection, Fran opened her guidebook and put her nose in it, defying anyone to intrude.

Jane got the message and turned for a last, loving look at Florence's pink, octagonal dome, higher than the city in the growing distance. "Oh, goodbye, ancient, beautiful Florence! We really adore you and don't want to leave you and wish we could stay forever. You are truly remarkable!"

Turning to Fran with a smile intended to open up mutual reminiscences of Florence, Jane received no encouragement. Reluctantly she opened her own guidebook, but the first sentence made her gasp with excitement. "Have you been to Ravenna, Fran? Have you seen the mosaics?"

"Not yet."

"Well, you'd better get there before you leave Italy. It would be a shame to miss such a golden opportunity when it's available to you. I really hope you and Steve are making the most of your time here."

Fran refrained from snapping back: We work, and besides, travel costs a lot and you're spending our travel money!

Jane lunged forward between the front seats and shook her finger at a plastic espresso cup wobbling on the dashboard. "Hubert! Give me that little wobbling cup. It's about to fall and much too precious to throw out. I'm going to save it."

"What?" Hubert yelled, for he was quite deaf and often answered as loudly as he wished others would speak to him.

"Give me that!" Jane shouted back, shaking her hand impatiently.

"What the hell do you want, Jane!" Hubert yelled again.

"That thing, Hubert, that thingy!" she blasted, unable to produce the word "cup."

Several kilometers of silence followed, Jane having heard herself. But she soon returned to them, in a light, bubbly voice. "Look! They even have irises growing along the highway. And I think that must be oleander. Isn't that oleander, everyone?"

Nobody answered. They didn't know.

"Yes, that must be oleander. Oh, what a wonderful country this is! Look over there! What's that big thing on top of the hill? Don't you think it's just so clever of the Italians to put up so many campaniles right next to each other? I would be perfectly happy with just one. Oh, goodbye dear Apennines! I don't know when I'll be seeing you again, but I really love you! And now that Steve and Fran are here, I'm sure to be back. Oh, Look! Those must be fig trees. Imagine such gigantic leaves. No wonder painters use them to hide private parts. Oh my, have you ever seen so many poppies—a whole Monet field of them! How can something so perfectly beautiful contain something so deadly? Here comes another tunnel. And one of those *galleria* signs. Lights up, Steve-o, remember to turn on your lights. I can't understand why *galleria* means tunnel. What's the relationship? You two must know, having studied Italian." Her white head stretched over the packages toward Fran. "Of course you, Fran, you're so smart and knowledgeable about everything Italiano, I'm sure you can explain the relationship to poor old dumbbell me!"

"I don't know," Fran said.

"It comes from Latin for a covered passageway," Steve said.

"Thank you, Steve. At least someone here knows a thing or two."

A brief pause followed. But not for long.

"Look at that little row of cypresses up there on top of that velvety green hill—how simply Tuscan. Don't you look, Steve, we'll describe everything to you. And I'd say the Italians have used their artistic supremacy to the limit by placing umbrella pines just so in every landscape the eye encounters. I can never see enough of them. I love their green bushy treetops. Don't you all agree?

She inhaled the landscape, then resumed. "Please tell me when we cross the Po—I want to be sure I don't miss it. And look! There are your cherries! Oh, how simply *delightfulioso* to be in Italy! Don't you think it was just so ingenious of the Italians to dream up all these cherry blossoms just for our visit? Now you won't have to miss Washington in springtime, Steve-o. There I go again, the eternal optimist!"

Fran couldn't help the burble of laughter in her throat. Did Jane really see herself as an optimist? She was more like a pressure cooker with the toggle squealing to blow off.

"Now, Fran, now that you've become so proficient in everything Italiano—you've been to Firenze, Bologna, Verona, Siena, and Venezia—which would you say is your *favoritissimo atmosfero Italiano?*"

Fran deflated. She felt like the target of a teacher who had singled her out just to bring her down. She knew in advance that no matter which city she picked, Jane would contest it: But why? And why not this one or that one?

"They're all nice, and all the *cittadine* between the big ones. How could I ever choose?" Fran answered.

"Oh, but Fran, don't you have to agree that Florence is really the crème de la crème? That Uffizi Gallery has to have the monopoly on world art."

"What about the Louvre?" Steve called back over his shoulder.

Jane's fingers twitched in her lap, as she considered whether to argue or not. She decided not and returned her gaze to the dreamy landscape.

"Ah, and there are your olives. See, Fran, how they have a silver shimmer? That's how you can recognize them. Don't you look, Steve, we'll describe them to you. Oh, I just love the Italians! Look at their sycamores! They've pruned them to give us the tunnel effect. I just can't believe we're really here! And I wonder what that is? Why do you suppose they've cut back those dwarf trees into nubbly knots like that? Does everyone you know make their own wine? How did they build those churches with such extraordinary domes? Do you know how Brunelleschi did it? I'd like to know. Are those marble quarries over there? Is that where Michelangelo got his marble?"

"No, his came from Carrara," Steve said.

"What I'd really like to know is, does any marble come from your part of Italy? And, where do they get their copper? Do the Italians grow all their own food? Well, of course they do, what a dumb question—Italy is Europe's garden. But where do they grow artichokes? And what do artichokes look like when they're growing? I hope we get to see some, but then I wouldn't know they were artichokes unless I could see them on their stems. Oh, I just love everything here! It's all so *wonderfulioso* and exciting, and I'm going to pack it all up in my suitcase and take it home with me! There I go again, the eternal optimist!"

All that night it rained, a soft pattering rain that lulled Fran to sleep and gave her gentle dreams in spite of the exasperating car ride to Venice that day. She awoke with a smile—she was in Venice, in a small hotel—a *pensione*—on the peaceful Giudecca side. An instant image of the opposite shore's mazelike passageways sandwiched between moldering buildings and crossing miniature bridges made her throw her legs over the side of the bed with a surge of anticipation. They would be outdoors exploring all day.

Steve's first posting was close to Venice—a short train ride away—and Fran had visited several times on her free days. She came without a specific plan though she carried a fat guidebook that identified every bridge and hidden church treasure. She had rung priests' doorbells in order to see churches with wood-beamed ceilings. Though she loved the city's main sights, especially standing in San Marco's square and gazing upon its magnificence as if for the last time, it was the inner, hidden Venice she loved most. Forget the map, wandering was enough, winding through passageways and coming upon artisanal workshops or sudden courtyards with ancient wells and upper-story windows bright with plants and hanging laundry. Deep in the byways, she loved seeing the little boats rocking against their moorings, parked by their peeling front doors awash in water and black brine. Someone lived there, upstairs, and their mysterious lives filled Fran's imagination. She wondered what it would be like to live in Venice and be part of its secret, damp walls and esoteric life. Books had given her glimpses—Brodsky's *Watermark*, Hemingway's *Across the River and into the Trees*, Mann's *Death in Venice*—but feeling it for herself, knowing its intrinsic essence, would take dwelling there.

The night's rainfall ended by morning, and sunshine spread across a purified sky. The air glistened as if freshly dewed and the decomposing lagoon shimmered with its antique splendor. They had plans to visit Murano, the island where glassblowers worked in front of red-hot, thundering furnaces. Already, over breakfast, Jane was reading aloud from her guidebook and disrupting Fran's magical aura of the place.

"Oh, listen to this, everyone," Jane's voice rippled out. "Jan Morris says, 'If a glassmaker took his knowledge out of Murano, and set himself up in business elsewhere in the world, inexorable and pitiless were the agents of State sent to find him, wherever he was, and kill him.' But apparently the law wasn't strictly enforced."

Fran knew she had a serious case of mother-in-law and wrestled with herself not to succumb to the stereotyped relationship, and more, not to blame Steve for his mother. And how did she herself factor into the equation? How did she provoke or exacerbate Jane's behavior? Surely her impatience and overt grimaces contributed to Jane's loquacity, her innuendos, and her constant "you shoulds." If Fran were able—and she wasn't—to behave lovingly to Jane, would Jane ease up in her annoying behavior? Was everything Fran's fault, or at least partly? She preferred to dismiss the possibility and blame Jane for her own exasperation.

As they set out for Murano, catching the appropriate vessel, Fran quickly moved to the opposite side of the deck from her companions, ostensibly for a better view of the Grand Canal. She closed her eyes for a moment to transition from Jane's voice in her ears to the wondrous impact of the palaces that lined the waterfront when she opened them up again. There they were—the fabulous marble facades with mosaics and frescoes rising up from the green water like a chain of mysterious, dripping sea life curling through the waterway. These palaces were different from the drab, dank buildings soaking in the inner canals. But like them, Fran longed to know who lived behind those lofty *piano nobile* windows. She imagined descendants of ancient families, aristocrats who didn't mix with the rest of local society. What was their private life like surrounded by soaring, frescoed ceilings, cold echoing chambers, secret doors, massive, brocaded, and musty furniture—and what about the privies? Were there updates?

She turned her gaze to the canal and the dilapidated tugboats and barges crisscrossing its choppy waves to deposit or take on goods. Gondolas bobbed gracefully over the water, steered by muscular, hardened, silent oarsmen. The mood was languorous, despite the noise of vaporettos chugging from pier to pier, to drop off and pick up passengers.

As their transport approached the pink lacework of the Ducal Palace with Saint Mark's domes and spires behind it, Jane swung into action, her unruly white hair blowing in the gusts of wind caused by the boat's motion. "What's that? What're all those towers? Why's that building pink? And look, way up there—is that the famous clock? And what year did the campanile collapse? Come on, Steve, you must know that."

"1902."

"Thank you. And are we going straight to Murano, or should we visit Saint Mark's first? Isn't St. Mark's more important?"

Just then a water taxi sped by, spewing black exhaust over their deck. Jane leaned out and called after it, "Stupido! You want to save your lovely city from extinction, and look what you do to it!"

Suddenly Steve caught Fran from behind and pressed her against the rail. "Ha ha, how would you like to go for a swim in Venice's biggest cesspool?"

"Yuck. It really does smell like a latrine, but I don't notice it anymore. It's part of Venice—which I love!"

A tandem of black gondolas glided past.

"What are those?" Jane snapped, joining them at the rail.

"Gondolas," Steve answered blandly.

"That's what I thought." She gave Fran one of her piercing owl looks as if to say: I'm here, you can't avoid me. Her short, white sideburns sprang out from her temples like hooks. Fran imagined Jane had to tape the wings down each night to make them behave the next day. But the wind had freed them.

"Oh, oh, oh!" Jane squealed, clapping her hands under her chin like a delighted child. "Look at that! Take a picture of that, Fran! Oh, darn, you missed it!" She looked up at Steve with a petulant face. "I brought all that film along so you could take pictures of our trip."

Fran hurriedly snapped a picture.

"What was that?" Jane demanded. "Was it important? What was that, Steve?"

She didn't wait for an answer but turned to Fran with a stern expression. "You know, Fran, you really should learn to take pictures so somebody's in them. I just know Hubert and I will get home and find we have all these pictures of things but no one in them." She stopped. She seemed to hear herself—her tone, her force. She made an effort to soften up. "We really brought all that film along so we could have pictures of you two newlyweds, just starting out on an amazing life adventure. We think you're just so marvelous, and we miss you all the time."

"Leave her alone," Steve hissed under his breath.

Jane half nodded and drifted back to Hubert seated on a bench.

Fran was finding it hard to regain composure after the

photography attack. She wondered how Steve had survived growing up with a dictating mother. She was a litany of dos, don'ts, shoulds, and musts, leaving no room for spontaneity or laughter.

"Straighten up, Steve, and you'll be happier in old age," she now advised with a friendly smile from across the boat.

Automatically Steve straightened.

Fran wondered what sermon Jane had delivered when Steve told her he wanted to get married. Who is she? What's her background? Who are her parents? What's her father's profession? You'll want someone who will take care of you, support your work and career. Will you last until death do you part? Are you sure she's the right choice? Shouldn't you wait?

When they arrived at Murano, its tranquility immediately enveloped them. The island's soft, muffled atmosphere caressed their faces, slowed the pace of their minds to match the pace of the sleepy fishing village resting under a timeless sky. Here, simple lives passed from birth to death not needing the greater lagoon or world beyond it.

The foursome headed inland from the quay with its line of little boats tied to haphazard wooden poles. On the main street, they found colorful, squat buildings stretching along a central canal. Steve ushered them into one of the glass factories before Jane could question which one was best to visit. No one greeted them or interacted with them inside. They were free to stand at a protective railing and watch the black-armed, perspiring glassblower at work in front of his blazing oven. Over the course of several minutes, a ball of molten glass on the end of his long blowpipe contorted, changed shape, grew colors, and ended up a beautiful object. The wonder of it, the trance of witnessing the master glassblower create art, shattered when Jane's voice chirped loudly, "Isn't he just so marvelous to make that little ball of gobbledygook turn into something so indescribably *wonderfulioso*!"

Fran stiffened at the intrusion and especially at the word *wonderfulioso*. Jane was starting to repeat it with every observation. And it ruined the natural absorption of Venice's ineffable qualities. The trip with Jane was showing Fran how much she herself preferred silence—hours in the Italian-American library or afternoons roaming trails above the Adriatic. She was not a talker, nor was Steve, though he did talk in bed at night, as if pulling the plug on his day's mind. He talked in a soft flow that came to Fran like a lullaby so that she usually dozed off. Perhaps their quiet, vulnerable, natures had brought them together like invisible magnetic fields.

Soon it was lunchtime, metal shutters grinding down over shops and streets becoming deserted—not that they were heavily populated before the one o'clock shutdown for lunch and siesta. Steve began reading aloud weathered menus tacked to humble doorways. He suggested a trattoria with the cheapest prices—the Antica Pergola. The dour proprietor in worn clothing led them (the tiresome Americani) through his small establishment to a table outside in a simple, peaceful courtyard. He dropped worn menus on the table and left.

They took seats under a little pergola fragrant with wisteria tendrils dripping over them. Blotchy yellow buildings with laundry hanging on the balconies, surrounded them. Red geraniums poked through the rusted iron railings, adding splashes of color. Curtains, pillows, even a bumpy mattress hung down to air. Windows and doors were wide open, and occasionally a neighbor called out to another from one of the balconies. Cats were around, slinky, unafraid, content with their stray lives. For a moment, all was perfect in the homey courtyard with sunlight flickering gently through the wisteria onto their table.

Then the famous perky croak rent the air. "Look at all those roses! Wisteria would have been quite enough, thank you, but these Italians won't stop. They have to make sure I'm truly bewitched, so I never leave! Well, I can assure you, they've cast their spell and it has worked. I think Italy's simply *glorioso,* and I'm not going to think about having to go home in just three days!"

I'll think of it for you, Fran said to herself with her eyes drilling into her mother-in-law. Immediately she felt guilty for such antagonism and tried to soften up inside. She wanted to sympathize with Jane, commiserate with how hard it was—for anyone—to say farewell to Italy. Besides, Jane was Steve's mother and Fran wanted a good relationship with her. She focused on the lunch soon to arrive—pasta—and this made her smile with pleasure and patience. The proprietor returned with water, wine, and a basket of bread. He took their order.

As soon as he shuffled off, Hubert reached into the bread basket, and fumbled to tear off a piece of the homemade loaf. He looked furtive, afraid of being caught for theft. Fran felt sad watching him. Was this her future old age, Steve like Hubert, herself like Jane? How could she and Steve avoid such oddity? How could they stay young, free, alive, and laughing, snuggling forever?

"Stop eating the bread, Hubert," Jane said.

Hubert snatched back his hands as if rapped by a schoolmarm's ruler. But no sooner had Jane looked away than the gleam returned to Hubert's eyes and his trembling fingers made another dive into the basket.

"You'll spoil your lunch with all that bread," Jane advised with a sideways glance. "And I ordered you such a nice Veneziano fish."

"As long as it didn't come from one of these canals," he retorted with a crackle of laughter.

Jane ignored him and changed the subject. "I'm just so excited to be in Venice. Did you hear that rain last night? Does it rain here often, Steve? I knew it was raining just to give us this *bellissimo* sunshine today! Those Italian weathermen really know how to plan for us! I think we should send them a telegram of thanks. Where do you think they are? Would it be easy to get their address?"

No one answered her. It was meaningless prattle, automatic. Fran wondered if women in Jane's day and from her cultured class had been raised to always keep the conversation going, always appear charming, no matter what emitted from their bright smiling faces and lips.

"I hope you don't butter your bread like that at your diplomatic dinners," Jane said to Steve.

"Like what?"

"A whole piece at once. Don't you know you should only butter one bite at a time?"

Steve picked up his knife and deliberately respread the butter on his bread. It was the closest act of defiance Fran had seen him make to his mother.

"Ooh," Jane cooed, changing subjects again, "there goes one of those sweet little Italian kitty cats, always looking for food."

"What?" Hubert yelled.

"Oh, just a little old cat, the Italian kind."

"What kind's that?"

"You know, can't you see him there? A regular old alley cat!"

"Was he big enough to catch that rat we saw coming in?" Hubert said, chuckling so that his girth jiggled.

"Read us the guidebook, Steve. I want to know all about Saint Mark's. What did Mark Twain call it—a vast and warty bug? Isn't that what he called the church, Steve? And I want to know why Venice was so against Genoa, and how it got its nickname, the Serene Republic. Go ahead, Steve, I want a *colorfulioso* description of all the Venetian merchants and nobles. Ssh, everyone, listen to Steve. Go ahead, Steve, read."

In midafternoon, they waited on the empty wharf for a boat to come and take them back to the main lagoon. It was siesta time, with far less service. Waiting in the sunlight, a warm tedium penetrated Fran's skin to her inner sensibility. The entire island rested in listlessness. Not a ripple of intellectual energy could be felt, nor was it asked for or needed. Mindless waves lapped the long quay where dozens of dinghies knocked shoulders like unambitious brothers. Steve moved closer and draped his arm around her. They didn't speak but their thoughts were the same—it was just the right hour to laze in bed, the hour after lunch when sensuality filled the body and shutters closed on reality until four o'clock. But they were far from their hotel.

Hubert sat on a bench, his weight spilling out, his brown eyes glittering the way they always did. Jane was the only one alert and impatient, her owl-like eyes shifting this way and that to spot a boat. Finally a lone fisherman chugged softly by, his weathered face skyward, lost in a daydream or just permanently vacant.

"Is that our boat?" Jane barked out.

"No," Steve answered without turning, "that's something else."

"What about that one? Where's that boat going? Can't we just ask if we can get on it?"

"No, we can't."

"Why not? Why are we waiting here? I feel like I'll never be back to Venice, and instead of doing all the looking I can, we're just standing here doing nothing."

Steve rumbled but didn't answer. He was fine with the peaceful interlude and closeness of Fran's body.

Jane stood her ground, quilted bag clamped tight to her

side. "I'm sorry, but until you're ambassador to Rome, Steve, I don't think I can afford to just stand here. I should be moving, looking, taking in as much as I can. Can't we just walk?"

"Off the island? Be my guest." After a beat, he added, "A boat'll be here soon."

That night they went to the opera, Verdi's *Troubadour*. The music and voices transported all of them to a faraway realm. Fran forgot about Jane, and Jane forgot about herself. Rippling, heartrending feelings poured out of the tenor's depths, carrying all the passion, beauty, trauma, and tragedy of the human race from its first consciousness. In the final scene, he sang from a dungeon, dark and filled with cobwebs. Dead, decayed bodies hung from hooks or lay across rafters. Skeletons stretched on racks and skulls littered the floor. Everyone watching felt the moment, the pain. Their beloved troubadour was face to face with his imminent execution. Fran's eyes blurred. For her, the scene conveyed the experience of millennia, the cruelty embedded in humanity. All week she had stood before paintings depicting torture and human suffering—beheadings, crucifixions, slaughter, murder of children—real or mythical chapters in human history. She felt a chill for all the barbarity that belonged even to her through ancestry, and yet, at the same time, couldn't be truly imagined, for such horror could only be lived, experienced. The tenor's voice captured and embodied humanity's collective grief that reached the audience. It was a relief when the curtain fell and thunderous applause erupted—gratitude for the concrete sharing not only of grief, but also of the miracle, beauty, and joy of the human voice, of human singing and music.

The foursome spoke little on their short walk to the nearest vaporetto stop. It was late, almost midnight, and the usual tourist traffic in the heart of Venice was gone, the stone pathways empty. Fran noticed Jane's silence and reflective expression. She was musical and sang in her church choir. Opera had been one of her youthful passions, lost when marriage and raising children in New York's suburbs took her away from the city and an active cultural life. *Il Trovatore* had been a splendid treat for her, and Fran felt glad. It had been a treat for all of them, something they had intrinsically shared that brought them closer together.

They waited on the floating, roofed dock for a boat. The spring night had become chilly, and Steve snuggled up to Fran for warmth. Hubert sat on a gently rocking bench studying the program, which formed a V between his knees in baggy khakis. The canal was beautiful by night. Street lamps, dock lights, and chandeliers behind palace windows lit up the crescent shoreline. From the opening in the rail, where they would board the boat when it came, Fran and Steve looked down at the cold, slapping water. It swayed choppily like a hungry sea creature. "I don't trust myself," Fran said with a laugh, moving away from the unprotected opening. "It makes me dizzy, as if it the water has a magnetic pull."

"Funny what the brain does," Steve commented, following her and putting his arm around her.

Jane suddenly woke from her reverie and moved to their vacated spot. "Look, I see a boat coming. Do you think it's ours, Steve?"

"Too soon to tell."

On the *riva*, two teenage girls suddenly appeared chasing their younger, naughty brother. He leapt onto the dock, making it rock strongly enough that Hubert held onto his bench. The boy laughed gleefully as he dodged a swipe from one of his sisters.

"You dirty rat!" his sister screamed. "You can't spit on me like that!"

"Well, if you hadn't stood right in front of me, you wouldn't have gotten hit," he laughed.

"Get over here, Timmy, and mind yourself!" the other sister said.

But the boy continued to prance about the dock, daring them to catch him.

"I think you'd better stop that right now!" Jane ordered him.

The boy halted at her elbow and looked up at her face, as if to gauge her authority.

"Where're you from with that accent of yours?" Jane said, changing her tone to a friendlier note.

"Australia," he said.

"I thought so. I'm from New York. Do you know where New York is?"

"I've been there."

"Oh. Well, are you in Venice for vacation?"

"No, my father works here. We've been here all year. We're having a really good time."

"So I see," Jane said. "Don't you have school tomorrow?"

As if caught for delinquency, the boy darted out of the shelter.

"No school on Saturday," one of his sisters called back as she took off after her brother.

"Good riddance," Jane muttered. Then she perked up seeing the lights of a boat chugging toward them. "Look, a boat's coming. I have this really good feeling it's ours. Cross your fingers, everybody. Hubert, are you crossing your fingers?" She placed her right shoe on the gateway's yellow stripe in readiness to board the boat. She would be first.

Suddenly the boy returned, scooting and yelping into the shelter, his sisters flailing their arms after him. Jane never had a chance—she was knocked off the dock and into the foul water with such speed that the rest of them nearly jumped in after her in reflex. But the sight of the icy, putrid water and Jane gasping and spluttering the spume and crud checked their impulse.

Steve was yelling for help and telling her to swim to him at the gate. At the same moment, a rugged man appeared from nowhere, thrust Steve aside, and tossed a white life preserver to Jane. In gruff Italian with arm motions translating, he shouted orders to her. When Jane reached the side of the dock, he pulled her up and then, gently, humanely drew her into the shelter, his arm going comfortingly about her. She stank. Dark strings of slime clung to her drenched clothes. She gave a pitiful splutter but then let out her usual bark. "How much hepatitis do you think I just swallowed? I'm going to strangle that boy, if his sisters haven't done it already! Obviously it's a hit and run, but I know you'll let the Australian consulate know about it tomorrow, Steve."

Suddenly Hubert erupted with a crackle of laughter.

"What's so funny?" Jane snapped.

Hubert laughed again, his funny bone tickled.

The man who had saved Jane told them to get into his boat, an exclusive water taxi parked next to the dock. He would take them home, gratis of course—the Italian way.

Wrapped in Steve's and Hubert's raincoats, Jane made her way down the dock to the man's boat. She sat in the middle seat with the others in front of and in back of her. The driver opened the throttle and they swerved out into the choppy canal, just as the vaporetto they would have taken coasted into the dock. A lone, older man who had missed all the action boarded the vessel.

Jane shivered under her two coats. They all shivered. The wind gusted against their faces and muffled Steve's and Fran's voices as they kept asking Jane, "How are you doing?"

She was busying herself, getting her last looks of the Grand Canal by night. Her head turned right and left, her owl eyes memorizing the magical, twinkling lights bathed in the night sky's depth of pulsating stars. It was Venice, a place of incomparable mystery and subtlety, unfathomable layers of history, humanity, and art. It was its own cosmos. Her gaze settled on an anonymous palace, its ground-floor doors swishing with tidal water. A few lamps glowed seductively behind soft orange curtains on the second "noble" floor.

"What's that?" Jane barked out, louder than the wind, louder than the boat's motor. "What're all those windows?"

Acknowledgments

A heartfelt thanks to the talented editors who helped me strengthen these stories: Anne McPeak, Tess Renault, and Annalisa Hansford. Thanks also to my friends and colleagues who read early drafts. Any book designed by Jeremy Eberts is something to treasure forever. I'm grateful for his artistic eye and creativity that have added elegance to this collection. Gratitude also goes to my loving and supportive family, the Dickersin-Brays, with a special shout out to Joseph Spilsbury, who has been a trusted and insightful reader of all my writing.

www.ingramcontent.com/pod-product-compliance
Lightning Source LLC
Chambersburg PA
CBHW021218260626
47172CB00002B/489